Erased
From
Memory

Diana O'Hehir

BERKLEY PRIME CRIME, NEW YORK

THE BERKLEY PUBLISHING GROUP
Published by the Penguin Group
Penguin Group (USA) Inc.
375 Hudson Street, New York, New York 10014, USA
Penguin Group (Canada), 90 Eglinton Avenue East, Suite 700, Toronto, Ontario M4P 2Y3, Canada
(a division of Pearson Penguin Canada Inc.)
Penguin Books Ltd., 80 Strand, London WC2R 0RL, England
Penguin Group Ireland, 25 St. Stephen's Green, Dublin 2, Ireland (a division of Penguin Books Ltd.)
Penguin Group (Australia), 250 Camberwell Road, Camberwell, Victoria 3124, Australia
(a division of Pearson Australia Group Pty. Ltd.)
Penguin Books India Pvt. Ltd., 11 Community Centre, Panchsheel Park, New Delhi—110 017, India
Penguin Group (NZ), Cnr. Airborne and Rosedale Roads, Albany, Auckland 1310, New Zealand
(a division of Pearson New Zealand Ltd.)
Penguin Books (South Africa) (Pty.) Ltd., 24 Sturdee Avenue, Rosebank, Johannesburg 2196,
South Africa

Penguin Books Ltd., Registered Offices: 80 Strand, London WC2R 0RL, England

This book is an original publication of The Berkley Publishing Group.

This is a work of fiction. Names, characters, places, and incidents either are the product of the author's imagination or are used fictitiously, and any resemblance to actual persons, living or dead, business establishments, events, or locales is entirely coincidental. The publisher does not have any control over and does not assume any responsibility for author or third-party websites or their content.

First edition: December 2006

Library of Congress Cataloging-in-Publication Data

O'Hehir, Diana, 1929-
    Erased from memory / Diana O'Hehir. — 1st ed.
      p. cm.
    ISBN 0-425-21216-5
    1. Egyptologists—California—Fiction. 2. Fathers and daughters—Fiction. 3. Women detectives—Fiction. 4. Senile dementia—Patients—Fiction. I. Title.

    PS3565.H4E73 2006
    813'.54—dc22

                          2006020590

PRINTED IN THE UNITED STATES OF AMERICA

10 9 8 7 6 5 4 3 2 1

Once again
For Mel, with love

In writing this book, I have consulted a number of helpful texts on archaeology and Egyptology, including ones by E. Wallis Budge, R. O. Faulkner, Miriam Lichtheim, Bridget McDermott, R. E. Parkinson, and Miriam Stead.

Any mistakes in this text are my own doing, not theirs.

🦉 Chapter 1

My father has been accused of murder.

At least, I think he has.

The scene is extremely confused.

It involves a man outstretched on a floor in the attitude of those chalk outlines the traffic police draw at accident scenes—head back, arms extended, legs splayed. This man wears a tan cashmere sweater, blue jeans, a Rolex watch. I think he's looking at the ceiling, but his face is hidden by my father, who kneels over him. And my father himself is half hidden by a spiky-haired woman wearing a striped T-shirt and blue warm-up pants; she clutches Daddy's back and screams, "Help! Stop him! Help!"

"Murder!" she screams, turning a streaked, contorted little face at me. I have just arrived in the room, panting, dropping my notebook, pencils, a book about Queen Hatshepshut, a tin museum pass.

Because all of this is happening in a museum. In the Egypt Regained Museum. In a room named after my father, the Edward Day Room. This is the resting place of his great discovery, Coffin Lid #267, the artifact about which he wrote his books. My father has Alzheimer's now, but he didn't used to. He used to be mildly famous in archaeology circles.

He is a gentle, sweet man who is not murderous. I know he isn't murdering anyone now. I try to pile into the scrimmage on the floor.

The final note of confusion is supplied by the museum guard, a hefty lady in a tan uniform.

She drags everybody aside, yelling, "Cudditout!" and bends her face to the prone man's face; she thrusts a finger in his mouth; after a minute she begins the breath-of-life procedure. I hold on to my dad and watch her bottom move up and down.

"Don't cry, dear," I say into his hair. "It's getting better."

He subsides enough that I can look around us and try to understand the situation.

I can't see the collapsed guy's face, but his body looks completely finished. Boneless and flattened. For the first time I think that maybe he's really dead. I haven't been taking this hysterical accuser seriously.

"Okay, honey," I say into the back of my dad's head. And I quote a piece of Egyptian poetry, "Don't be sad; the road is ending."

Egyptian archaeology is still the most important force in my father's life.

The spiky-haired accuser is standing up now. She has square glasses in front of brown eyes and a necklace of those blue clay beads they try to sell you in the Valley of the Kings. Her eyes lock into mine. "He was," she says. "I saw."

My father lifts his head from my shoulder and stares at her. "Why, hello," he says, "Rita."

She tilts her chin; light flashes off her glasses. "You thought you could get away with it."

Daddy stares at her for a minute more and offers an opinion: "He was trying to eat life."

Twenty minutes later, chairs have been lined up against the walls of Egypt Regained's Great Hall, and a row of people is sitting on them. The spiky-haired accuser camps opposite us, slumped. She is small and her feet don't quite touch the floor.

Beside me, my father has recovered and is unsuitably cheerful. The museum staff is handing out sodas; he attempts to drink his directly from the bottle; he finds this amusing.

I have tried unsuccessfully to get him out of here. "He's old," I've said, "very old; he's sick; he has Alzheimer's disease; the sheriff knows where we are; he can talk to us later."

The guard grunts, "No way, ma'am."

The spiky-haired woman, glasses flashing, offers to perform a citizen's arrest.

"Nine-one-one is comin' in," the guard says. "A rescue squad, a doctor. An' the sheriff. I sent for them. They'll all be here. Because that gentleman is dead. I had a aunt that died an' I know dead when I see it."

I don't say so but I agree. I worked in the animal lab at school and later I witnessed some fatal events at Daddy's retirement home; I know about death, too.

The director of the museum, a man named Egon Rothskellar, arrives at this point. Under normal circumstances Egon is jumpy and fluttery; now he is close to incoherent. "Oh, good heavens. Oh, I cannot imagine." He tries to embrace my father, but can't figure out which cheek to kiss first. He approaches the furious, static Rita and tells her, "Dr. Claus, Dr. Claus." She stares at him so stonily that he mutters a few incomprehensible conciliatory noises and backs away into the hall toward a door labeled ADMINISTRATION.

I ask the guard if I can take my father to the bathroom.

She says, "Sure, but somebody goes with you," and she delegates a scared-looking blond youth in a turban who accompanies us as far as the door of the men's room.

I go right on into the men's room. The hell with sexual restrictions.

This restroom is made of marble and brass and has Egyptian-type fixtures, including a fountain serving as a urinal. I face my dad. "You knew that woman?"

"What woman, dear?"

"You called her Rita."

He sighs. "Names. Lots of names."

Most of the time he doesn't remember names at all. "And who was the man? The one on the floor? Is that somebody that . . . Somebody from Egypt?"

Daddy stares at me intently. "The son of Isis is injured."

"How do you know him? Or her?"

"Know her? Did I say that?" He reaches for a soap dispenser that looks like an Egyptian canopic jar. "Why do you suppose they put metal on this?"

"Daddy, come on. Phase in. Please. What was happening there?" I debate telling him we'll camp in this restroom until he comes up with an explanation.

He squirts soap onto his hand. "This jar was supposed to have intestines in it. Part of the burial process. Interesting."

* * *

Back in the Great Hall we sit for a while and then we sit for a while longer.

Conversation is restricted. Our group consists of my father, me, Daddy's accuser, and three female visitors who got caught in this event. We stare at each other.

And finally the sheriff arrives, bumping across the marble, trailed by a following of one doctor with a black bag and two deputies with collapsible platforms and tool kits.

Director Rothskellar returns to bob up and down and make hand motions. "Sheriff. Yes. Oh, my goodness. Can't understand."

This sheriff stares at him and says, "Where?"

This sheriff is someone I know. He's been in office only two months but has already become my enemy, having arrested me for speeding. He said I was doing eighty; I said sixty. His name is Sheriff Munro; he is small and wiry and perhaps handsome, if you like the quick suspicious type with eyes too close together. The old sheriff, who left to go live in Alaska, had dandruff and brains, and didn't care how fast I drove. He and I were friends; I miss him.

Sheriff Munro scans the room and fixes on me. "Don't try to leave." After that he includes everyone. "Don't anyone leave." And he and his entourage go off toward the Edward Day Room, shutting a pair of nine-foot-high folding cedar doors behind them.

The Edward Day Room is a small exhibit room, which normally contains nothing except a display case with Daddy's coffin lid and some explanatory literature. No sprawled bodies.

We in the big room shift and wiggle and listen to muffled sounds from next door. A thump (something has hit the floor?), a mechanical squeal (maybe the stretcher is being dragged). I picture events from television programs. The body is probed, turned over, listened to. Its jacket is removed, shirt removed. Belt undone, shoes, socks. Maybe they cut the rest of the clothes off. Oh, nuts.

"Are you all right, Daddy?"

"Why, fine, dear."

Maybe they're zipping the body up in a black plastic bag.

"I think I knew her," my father says.

"Rita," I prompt.

"Danielle. There was a Danielle."

A while later the sheriff has led my father and me into one of the small museum offices. We aren't the first people to be pulled in. Both the bristle-haired accuser and the security guard got it first.

The sheriff addresses me; he says he doesn't care whether my father has Alzheimer's or not; he is going to interview him. "You sit here and he will sit there." He indicates a chair several feet away from me. "He can answer questions; I've seen him do it."

Daddy takes a small white handkerchief out of his breast pocket and dabs at his mouth. "You need me to sit there?" He does so. "This chair, you know, is not a real Egyptian chair, only an inaccurate copy; the real one would not have had—"

"Dr. Day, listen." Sheriff Munro clears his throat and tries to pitch his voice low; he's not totally successful. "What was your relationship with the victim?"

"The victim?" Daddy looks troubled. "It would probably have had animal feet."

"Huh?"

"But not always. Are you on your way to Egypt, young man?"

The sheriff has tilted forward. He fusses with the pages of a green-bound notebook. His firmly ironed tan pants stick out as if they're made of metal. "Please pay attention. The guy . . . man. On the floor. Lying on the floor. You *knew* him."

"Were you one of my students, then?" Daddy sounds pleased at this idea.

"You are pretending. Faking incompre . . . faking not understanding."

"Tired, yes. A little tired."

Sheriff Munro turns to me. "Impeding justice. Obstructing an investigation." He squints. His little, too-close-together eyes waver and get unfocussed. "I have a reliable witness. She saw him. He was assaulting that man."

I try to be mild. "I think he was trying to help."

"Help? He had him by the throat."

"No, no. He was loosening his collar . . ."

"He had his hands *around* his neck. This witness is highly reliable. She's sure what she saw." He turns back to my father. "You got to pay attention. I can arrest you. Insanity's not an excuse."

Daddy reaches toward me. "We can leave now, I think."

"You're accused of *a serious crime*." The sheriff offers this flatly. Maybe I'm just imagining a coating of pleasure on the statement.

Daddy sits poised, arm out.

"You understand me," Sheriff Munro pursues. "Dr. Day, listen. The man. The one that you . . . The one on the floor."

"There is no million years."

"You knew him."

"The cavern is opened for those in the abyss." My father

offers this neutrally, his only sign of disturbance a tremor in
his outstretched hand.

The sheriff compresses his lips. He leans forward and his
pants creak. "I can put you in jail. Do you understand?"

Daddy sighs. "That's difficult, isn't it? Understanding.
There have been arguments about the nature of understanding. When I was at the university—"

"You're not at the university now." The sheriff is half off
his chair. He reaches out and snaps his fingers in front of my
father's face, the way you do to get an animal to behave. "Are
you listening? Are you letting it get through? *Jail*. That'll
stop this garbage. Jeezchrist, what's the matter with you?
Jail. That'll give you something to quote poetry about."

I later tell a newspaper reporter that my father didn't strike
Sheriff Munro. He was simply showing him a kind of Egyptian exercise.

The reporter accepts this.

"Look at him," I say. "He's famous. Learned. A well-known
archaeologist. And gentle. He *couldn't* strike anybody."

The *Chronicle* reporter regards my gentle, quiet father,
who is picking his way through a bag of peppermint Jelly
Bellies. He agrees. Obviously I speak truth.

Which I do not. My father did strike Sheriff Munro. He
raised his arm above his head and brought it down fast and
tapped him with the side of his stiffened hand. He said, "I
cleanse this area of evil influences."

I don't think it was the hand-tap that Sheriff Munro re-
acted to so violently. That couldn't have hurt much. It must
have been what my father said.

"Cleanse? Evil influences?" Sheriff Munro yelps. "Old

man, what in hell is the matter with you? What the fuck do you mean?"

Some people go all rigid when you recite at them like an incantation. I guess the sheriff is one of those people.

"I mean what I mean," Daddy expounds.

That's it for the sheriff, who pulls out his cell phone. "Jerry," he tells somebody on the receiving end, "get back here and get into it, this old idiot has gone completely off his fucking rocker," and then he clicks off the phone and grabs one of Daddy's wrists and wrenches it behind his back.

Right then is when I lose it.

I have enough sense not to grab hold of the sheriff, much as I feel like it.

But I do try to free my father's arms, and that's a no-go. Jerry arrives with a sidekick and they get into the action. They are strong guys, one big one and one small one, each with muscles and biceps and a tan uniform; the big one pries me loose from my dad; the other helps Sheriff M. get both Daddy's hands high up and backward behind his shoulder blades; after that they screw his wrists together with a plastic handcuff.

I begin squawking and jabbering. "Let go of him, you bastards. Let him loose. Undo his hands. You're hurting him. I'll call Elder Abuse. I'll call the ACLU. I'll call my lawyer. I'll call the newspapers. I'll get you demoted."

Meanwhile I'm trying to wrench myself free.

"Dad, Dad, don't let them take you. Go limp. Flop down. Sag on the floor."

Of course, he has no idea what I'm talking about. "That hurts a little," I think he's saying.

"He's sick; he has a heart condition"—as far as I know this isn't true—"he needs medication; I'll sue." The goon holds me tighter each time I speak.

My father somehow manages to look brave, shoulders back, turning his head inquiringly, like a little bird.

Eventually I resort to Rape Defense.

The main move in Rape Defense, in which I took a one-day Santa Cruz course, is the knee in the groin. I apply this move now, up and hard, and the goon precipitately lets go of me to bend over saying, "Jesus Christ, you fucking bitch," and grab his testicles.

While I stand free in time to watch my poor dad be hustled away, stumbling slightly, murmuring something indistinct.

٦ Chapter 2

My father and I have a complicated history.

He's not now the concerned, responsible father that some women dream about. But then, he never was.

"My dear," he would say, looking at me in puzzlement when I had some early grief—a lost pet, a classroom argument. "*Why*, my dear." He would stare, puzzled; he would frown for a while. And then do the best he could. His idea of how to take an eight-year-old's mind off her troubles was to teach her some Egyptian archaeology. "This is the way they did the face," he'd say, showing me a photograph of a mummy. "With a plaster mask. They painted it to look like the dead person." He surveyed the photo, a gray, smeared encyclopedia reproduction. "Sometimes a little better than the dead person, wouldn't you think?"

After all, Daddy was old to be the parent of a third-grade child; he had been sixty when I was born. He seemed fairly baffled that I existed at all, but he also gave me the feeling that he liked me. In fact, despite his confusion about how it had all happened, that he loved me.

My mother didn't make me feel loved. She was the opposite of my father. Almost completely. Reserved where he was responsive. Organized where he was scattered. Ambitious where he was indifferent. So unlike him that I often wondered how they had gotten together. Except for the fact that they were both archaeologists, they had little in common. My mother was programmed, calm, and, the archaeology journals said, brilliant. She was also very handsome, which didn't interest her at all. *Removed* was the word for her.

Not that she was neglectful of me, exactly.

She would lower her book, watch me analytically, and suggest some noninterventionist remedy. The library? A long walk? Thinking about it further?

I had clean dresses and adequate meals. When Mother was away, there was a capable child-care person, a nice lady, I am told. I don't remember her.

Actually, Mother was away an awful lot. She was off at conferences in London, Paris, Rome, Helsinki, where she debated the dates and authenticities of the markings on the Phrygian brass pots that were her specialty. She was off at archaeological digs in Turkey, working carefully with a small spade and whisk broom to uncover more pots. When I was ten years old, she simply remained in Turkey. There was a productive site and a colleague named Dr. Hakim Kasapligl. I think she is still there, in Turkey, digging up her pots, although perhaps Dr. Kasapligl has been dismissed.

So for most of my life my household consisted of me and my father. Daddy tried to take care of me and I tried to take care of him. "You are so capable, Carla. I do admire that quality." And if I didn't deflect him, he would go on to talk about Hatshepshut, the Egyptian queen who was indeed capable, so much so that she combined the offices of king and queen. "I do appreciate your helping me, darling," and he'd reach out to squeeze my wrist.

We went to Egypt together a lot. That was something else he thought of to do with an adolescent girl. We went to Cairo and Thebes and Luxor and to the Valley of the Kings. He would be down at the bottom of a hole sending up shovelfuls of rocks or baskets of dirt or slings containing pottery figures along with occasional other finds—stone carvings, beads, bits of clay tablet. I would collect these, list them in a notebook, put them in a box. Until he found the coffin lid, which changed his future and his reputation, Daddy never discovered anything exciting.

The coffin lid was important not because it was a coffin lid—there are a great many of those in Egypt—but because it had on it some hieroglyphs that were repetitions of the ones on the tomb wall, and by comparing the two versions, Daddy was able to settle several major disputes in Egyptian scholarly circles.

After our first time in Egypt, Daddy took our next-door neighbor's son along on our explorations. This was a boy named Rob, who was three years older than I. I was frantically in love with Rob. It's hard not to be in love with someone you have been to Egypt with, and sat under the stars there with, and discovered archaeological firsts with. Later we lived together in Santa Cruz and still later we loused things up between us pretty thoroughly. But we still see each other all the time and have a mutual reliance system in crises.

It's Rob whom I am trying to summon now by punching angrily at my cell phone.

Rob is a doctor and works in a hospital twenty miles from here. I can hear the hospital intercom intoning, "One—four, one—four." That's Rob's number; he chose it because it was our campsite number at the tourist camp in Thebes.

"Carla?" he says now. "Hey. How. What gives?"

When I have partly explained, he cuts right to the jugular with "My God, my God, your dad, in jail? What're you doing, who've you called . . ."

I don't say I haven't called anybody because what I've done is to commit mayhem on a sheriff's deputy. But Rob deduces some of what my silence means. He says, "Honey, oh Jesus, ohmigawd, I'll be right over; I'll meet you at your dad's place; hold on there, chin up, okay?"

One of the big troubles between me and Rob was that each of us thinks of him/herself as the caretaking one.

Now I am waiting for Rob in Daddy's apartment in Green Beach Manor. My father, of course, is not here. He is off at wherever Sheriff Munro has taken him.

Daddy has lived in this elegant retirement colony for a year. Green Beach Manor has everything—romantic Victorian architecture, assiduous staff, fairly decent food, seacoast climate, a capable director who is a friend of mine. I know all about the Manor, all its ins and outs; I live here, too. I am the assistant director. I didn't intend to do that, become the assistant director of a retirement colony; it just happened. It keeps me close to my dad; it gives me housing and a salary. And it makes me feel that I'm wasting my life. I want a different job; I'm ready for something new.

I'm twenty-six years old. I want an occupation that will Make a Difference.

And my father, who is eighty-six, also has aspirations. He wants to feel needed. He does not feel needed here at the

Manor, but he feels that way at the museum. And so we visit Egypt Regained at least twice a month, where he looks at his coffin lid while Director Egon Rothskellar, who likes superlatives, says "Wonderful" at him. The museum is Daddy's lodestar of the ideal place where he is truly needed.

Rob bursts into the apartment now in a gust of warm air from the hall; his trench coat flares out behind him. He grabs me by the shoulders and kisses me. He says, "You've been crying."

"That was half an hour ago."

"Tell me everything, how in hell did this happen?" And then when I'm halfway into my chaotic story, he stops me with, "Oh, God, I forgot. I brought Susie, she's on her way in; she stopped to make a phone call."

Susie is Rob's mother, Daddy's and my former next-door neighbor. She is also my oldest friend, my best friend, my surrogate mother. She's the one who got me through my difficult childhood.

She's loving and overwhelming and I don't want her around now.

A minute later she billows through the door in a surge of purple wool, trailing an embroidered cape. "My psychic is going to do an intention for Ed, that will help enormously; this psychic is totally powerful. And I've brought this"— extending a bunch of fibers—"a bayberry smudge; we'll burn it to expel the harmful influences. Darling Carla, I am so sorry, how is it possible, Edward is such a complete human being."

Susie is a sexy old hippie who likes tie-dye dresses and macramé jewelry. She says she wants to continue the image of the sixties. Tie-dye is fashionable again this year, but I don't tell Susie that.

"Mom, we need more than a roseberry smudge." Rob sounds cross, which is the way he usually sounds around her. She corrects him, "Bayberry," and then kisses me, enveloping me in purple fabric.

"Love will find a way; love will get Ed out of jail, although going to jail is a sign of your personhood; many of my friends have done it." And she subsides onto Daddy's couch.

Rob sits on a chair and looks at his knee. He gets a notebook out of his pocket and asks, crossly, as if he's addressing somebody feeble-minded, will I please try for a *sequential* account of what happened. But right away he's sorry. "Oh, hell, Carl; jeez, I'm out of line," and after that he's good about listening. It's only when I'm almost finished that he starts firing inquiries like, "Where is he now? You don't know? Well, what did they say?" and tries to look patient.

I don't tell him, "Hey, Rob, that was my *dad* it was happening to." He knows I'm not usually like this.

He makes more notes. "We need a lawyer."

He adds that he has a good friend who is a lawyer, but this friend lives in Madison, Wisconsin.

I remember that the Manor has two lawyers. But they're the stocks, bonds, investments, bequests kind of lawyers. "They wouldn't get anybody out of jail."

"Well, *I* know a lawyer." This is from Susie, who has been crossing and uncrossing her knees on the couch. She smiles her sunny Susie smile. "I know a very good lawyer. She would be fine for getting somebody out of jail. She does it all the time.

"And I just called her. She's on her way over here.

"She was my lawyer for the grocery store," she adds.

Susie owns a natural foods grocery store in Berkeley. These days the Berkeley landscape is littered with organic stores, but when Susie started up her store it was the only one. She got sued frequently. She needed a lawyer. People love to sue natural foods stores because, what with organic fertilizers and no pesticides, the products get multiple worms and dirt, which customers don't want; they just want the ORGANIC label.

"She was wonderful," Susie says. "She saved me a bunch of times."

I stare at Susie, who still surprises me pretty often. In my childhood I alternated between loving her passionately and being cross at her for being so scattered. It was usually when I was most cross that she came up with one of her interesting and helpful solutions. But I'm not so sure I want to trust her with choosing our lawyer.

"Her name is Cherie Ghent," Susie says. "She is really, really good."

Cherie Ghent shows up half an hour later. The three of us have been speculating about various questions: Where is my father? What's he charged with? How long can they hold him? How do we get him out? That'll take money; where do we get money? Susie says she has money, which is a lie; Rob claims he has money, also a lie. We are deep into this discussion when Cherie Ghent arrives.

Cherie doesn't inspire confidence. I look at her and reject her hands down. I have a preconception about the ideal lawyer. That ideal lawyer is a tall woman who wears a pantsuit and glasses on a chain and has wider shoulders than usual. She commands respect.

Cherie is the opposite of all this. She's a small enameled person with blond lacquered hair, turquoise eyes, and a curvy figure in an exquisite gray suit, size two. She looks as if she has been wrapped in bubble wrap and sent direct from the top floor of Saks Fifth Avenue. "How do ya do," she inquires in a deep, strong Southern accent. "I'm Cherie." Yipes.

"Your daddy is eighty-six years? I am so sorry. Eighty-six. And to meet up with arrant cruelty. Did you know, there is a survey"—she pronounces it "suhvey"—"a U.C. survey; it shows that rural police forces"—"po-lice," she says—"are more corrupt, more prejudiced, hidebound, narrow, easily bribed . . ." She moves manicured hands in an inclusive gesture.

Susie watches proprietarily. "She's a pistol," she informs us. "Lawyer for every demonstration. She did a peace march across Central America and got arrested in Costa Rica."

I try to imagine Cherie, with her trim gray suit and lacquered nails, in a Central American jail.

"Of course, I believe," she says, "that most police are corrupt. There is another survey, from the London School of Economics, that compares the police forces of four European countries . . ." Cherie plunks her briefcase on the floor and sits down.

"Now," she says, "less jus' get to work. Less jus' figure it out, because, you know what? I am very good at this sort of thing."

She smiles a dazzling smile, gets out a binder, and starts quizzing me on the details. "We got to be specific," she warns. She makes lots of notes. She likes numbers. She likes facts. She produces a computer and a pocket dictionary and a pocket crisscross directory. She makes phone calls.

"Your dad is in Innocente Prison," she announces finally, emerging from a long e-mail exchange. "You all here in Del Oro County, you're too poor to have your own prison, you got a contract with Innocente." She doesn't give us time to exclaim about Innocente Prison, which is a famous dropping-off point where they used to send war protesters and now incarcerate Latino farm workers. She says, "We'll get him outta there. Count on it. I'll grab those bastards by the balls.

"Let's us get on over there."

⚓ Chapter 3

Innocente Prison is out in the California hinterland.

It's in a world of undulating golden-gray fields punctuated by expanses of cultivated green stuff, rows and rows of it, sometimes with large, proud identifying labels: ARTICHOKE, LETTUCE, GARLIC—CALIFORNIA AGRICULTURE AT WORK FOR YOU. Off in the distance are plywood houses for the workers who tend this stuff, and here in the foreground are the workers themselves, lines of workers bent double along the rows, brown people in brown clothing, followed by vast Rube Goldberg machines with many triple-jointed arms.

We churn through dusty towns with names like Esperanza and Purissima, towns heavy with signs for Coca-Cola, Pepsi, and Marlboro cigarettes. The Marlboro cowboy broods reflectively over tin roofs. "They smoke a helluva lot around here," Cherie says.

She drives capably, mostly with only one manicured hand on the steering wheel. Her car is a handsome white Mustang convertible with leather upholstery and bright spoke wheels. Rob reacts enthusiastically, "Wow! A 'sixty-six!" and leans forward to appraise the lighted turquoise dashboard. He and Cherie launch into a half-hour's review of the car's history: Cherie bought it from a friend who bought it from a garage dealer; he bought it from the original owner. "Just three previous owners and I paid only five thousand," to which Rob says, "Hey, a steal, but the wheels are new? The paint job's new?"

And so on and so forth while Susie and I in the back seat lament the venality of a penal system that could jail my father for . . . "Carla dear, what *is* he jailed for?"

I haven't wanted to think about this. I've been squeezing it into the background. "I don't know, Sue. It was a mess. Somebody died." There it is; what I don't want to think about. *Somebody died.*

Susie says, "Awful, that place is so death-oriented." She means the museum, of course. "But you can count on Cherie; Cherie will get him off."

"Cherie," I interrupt the automobile discussion in the seat ahead, "does this jail have a hospital?"

"It's a prison, darling. And yes."

She doesn't ask why I want to know. I guess she understands. I'm picturing my dad, incarcerated, restrained. Medicated. Overmedicated. "I mean, a big one."

"Yeah; it's big." She turns around in the seat, keeps on driving perfectly straight, gives me a wide, lipsticked smile. "Don't worry, darling, he is *not* goin' to end up there."

Oh, yeah, I think.

Susie supplies an anecdote about Cherie and somebody

accused of growing pot in the chancellor's garden. Susie's stories tend to meander.

Suddenly our miles of sand-colored grass are interrupted by a razor-wire fence with a gate and a guard. Cherie offers him a plastic card; we get waved onward. In the hazed distance, buildings begin appearing, the same color as the fields, low except for four towers with light flashing back from their windows. We slow down; Cherie sticks her chin out at the prospect. She says, "Mordor."

Innocente Prison was a tradition around Berkeley. By the time I got to high school, the arrests had slowed down and none of us got sent to Innocente, but we knew that that was where you could end up. The Guerrilla Girls tried hard to get there.

Closer to the prison is more razor wire and a new guard with a red label pasted to his helmet. He bends to peer in the car window. "Hey, for God's sake. Hey. Is that Cherie?"

Cherie agrees, "Uh-huh."

"Well, baby, hi. Long time no see. Where in hell ya been?"

Cherie inches the car forward. "You miss me, huh, Ron?"

"Hey, sweetie, bet yer sweet ass. Damn right. Got a new kinda clientele these days."

Cherie turns her face; she seems to be giving him a mean stare. "New clientele. Latinos and old men, Ron, right? Incarcerate the helpless, right? No more pretty college protesters. Brand new *demographic*." She emphasizes the word, makes it sound dirty.

Ron shakes his head as if he's caught a mosquito. He gestures. "Park your car over there."

*   *   *

At the barrier to the prison entrance we negotiate three sets of sensors. Susie surrenders her silver jewelry; Rob is told he can't come in; he's wearing a blue denim shirt. Cherie says, "Oh, shit, I forgot.

"The prisoners wear blue denim," she explains. "Jesus, am I dumb."

I tell Rob just to take his shirt off; he has a T-shirt underneath, doesn't he?

He looks at me. "Are you scared?" I agree, "Yes."

Cherie disappears into a steel-barred booth, where I can hear her arguing about something. Not about Rob's shirt. About what they will do with my father, who left his victim dead in the middle of a museum floor. My father the murderer. "No, I don't," I hear Cherie say. And, "No, we don't." And, "Well, just make that telephone call then. That's your job." And later, "Well, I am going in there to see him and it is all going to be real simple."

She's in the booth a long time.

She sits straight in her chair and looks forceful. I alternate feeling scared and feeling hopeful. Rob draws cartoon pictures of the guard on the back of his prescription pad. "I can't believe this crap," we hear Cherie say loudly; she turns and mouths "Crap, crap" at us from behind the row of steel bars.

The official she's with keeps his back and his bald spot to us and writes.

And finally Cherie emerges. She looks smug and is clutching a wad of papers. "Come on, kids, we are going on in. Follow along, all you ducks."

*　*　*

The holding room at Innocente greets us with noise—music of all kinds: Latin, country, hip-hop, overlaid with multi-lingual announcements, outcries, arguments against a background of TV car sounds, explosions, all this resonating across a vast wooden space with a metal-strutted arched roof. I dimly remember that there's a World War II aircraft hangar in this building's past. Men in all stages of sleeping, sitting, lying are propped on the floor, against each other, against the wall. Somebody may be playing a guitar somewhere. Somebody invokes Jesus.

The guard who's leading us in yells, "You that old gent's family?"

Susie, Rob, and I agree. Yes. Family. Rob puts his arm around my waist.

The guard gestures. "Over there."

And yes, over there. It's my father.

He looks all right. In fact, he looks pretty good. He has one of the few chairs in the place. It's a metal chair left over from the aircraft hangar days; Daddy sits on it, knees together, body half bent forward in a concentrating posture, head cocked intently; he's saying something to a small crowd of people grouped on the floor around him. It looks as if he's telling a story. He gestures and they nod. He lifts an arm; they also lift arms. A story circle. They had story circles in Egypt; they happened late at night in the coffeehouses. I never got to see those, of course; no ladies admitted, but I knew what they looked like. Sometimes the workers at a dig would group together like that at lunchtime.

"Old gentleman," the guard mouths at us. He leads us on a circuitous path through the room. Rob clutches my hand and squeezes.

Daddy has reached the crunch-line of his story. His voice

wavers at us through the other din. "So when they finished chipping the hole in the door . . . you've seen pictures of that?"

A couple of heads in his class bob.

"And a light was held up to the hole . . ." He's telling them the tale of the discovery of Tutankhamen's tomb. He looks up and sees us. He holds his arms wide. I think he says, "Some other members of my party."

"I guess he was a famous old guy, huh?" the guard asks in my ear.

Daddy scrambles to his feet and one of the floor sitters grabs his chair.

Cherie doesn't bother to be introduced. She fights her way through to him and kisses him on the cheek. She says, "Let's get outta here, Crocodile Dundee."

Daddy smiles at her. He seems to think Crocodile Dundee is a perfectly good name.

Outside, Cherie looks at us and says, "Damndest thing I ever heard of."

I start out with, "Well, I thought it was pretty bad, arresting him," and I'm warming up for a speech about my eighty-six-year-old handicapped father, but Cherie puts her had on my arm.

"Honey-pie, you don't know. You don't understand; I don't understand; they don't even have a clue; damndest case; I just can't believe . . . Crocodile, you been sayin' Egyptian spells at 'em?"

"No."

Rob says, "What're you talking about; what's up?"

Cherie switches gears and becomes professionally reassuring. "Everything's fine. Jus' fine. They're not charging Edward here with any crime. What'd he do? He insulted the sheriff. That sheriff is an insecure creep. He doesn't want the story circulating about how he was insulted. And your dad didn't exactly resist arrest. Too many people saw; he didn't resist arrest."

She adds, "I guess that rich guy—the museum owner one—put some pressure on, too."

"But . . ." I say. I don't really want to ask outright: *There was this man on the floor. I thought he was dead. I thought that my father . . . well, that my father . . .* "Somebody died," I say.

"Listen, honey"—Cherie is forceful—"there aren't any charges. Not any at all. And that man—he's a museum trustee; his name is Marcus Broussard—he wasn't dead."

"And, well, this is the part that's so fucking weird—you're not gonna believe it—they brought this Marcus Broussard to the hospital, stretched flat on a gurney, in a coma, half the time breathing, half not, cold as a fish; they turn their backs, and guess what—he *disappears.*"

I stare at Cherie, probably with my mouth open, but Rob interprets: "Somebody stole the body." He and I saw a lot of old movie videos when we lived together in Santa Cruz.

Late afternoon sun slams down on the four of us where we are stopped in the middle of the gravel walk, halfway up to the parking lot. Faint chaotic musical noise travels from the prison. Cherie's admirer, the guard on the upper road, starts sauntering our way.

Cherie says, "Nobody stole the body. He wasn't a *body*. He wasn't dead. He'd had some kind of attack. An *episode*, is what they call it. He was comatose, but not, what they say is, expired. They dumped him and this gurney in a private room and went off to get their machines—they're real upset about this; they keep trying to explain it—and when they came back, he was gone. But they say they're sure. He wasn't dead."

My father hasn't seemed to be listening at all to this conversation. His attention has been occupied with attempting to scrape a blob of prison detritus off the sleeve of his tweed jacket. He looks up now and says, "Not dead? Oh, yes. Of course he was dead."

"Crocodile, darlin'," says Cherie, "that man was alive. They're taking oaths on it."

"No," my father says firmly. "He's dead. He was trying to eat life, but that won't work. Maybe works for today, maybe for tomorrow, but that's all. After that he's dead."

He smiles at Cherie, his little boy smile, as if he's sharing a secret. "It's a mug's game, my dear, trying to eat life."

✝ Chapter 4

Egon Rothskellar, the director of Egypt Regained, is waiting for us at the gate of Innocente Prison.

Egon waits in style in a Lincoln limousine with bud vases and a bar and a chauffeur in a turban. He is quaffing something bubbly from his bar, and he holds up a bottle in salute. "You must," he says to us, "must, must come back with me to my house. So distressing. Climb in." The padded, gray-leather-lined door of the limousine is held open in invitation.

Daddy is thrilled. He is completely ready, once again, for Egypt Regained. He says he needs to look at his coffin lid. No arguments from me that he saw it five hours ago make any difference. "That man," he says, "is gone; I know he is. Oh, I need to see."

Cherie is fulsomely invited, but she declines. She announces that she has to get back to file a brief, and she and Susie drive off, hair flying.

So Daddy and I are buckled into Egon's plushy vehicle, supplied with pillows, bottles of water. "A green drink," says my parent. "I appreciate that."

"*So* glad to have you," Egon tells him. "Because today was regrettable, totally regrettable." He punches some buttons on his cell phone and has a discussion about dinner. "Aram sandwiches. Plenty of pâté. Moroccan chicken."

"And now," he says. "Oh, what a terrible day you have had, Dr. Day. If only I can make up for it just a little.

"Dr. Day is one of our most outstanding scholars," Egon continues, addressing me. "We are so proud to have his coffin lid. So history-making."

The coffin lid has been in Egon's museum ever since Daddy managed to wangle it away from Cairo on an indefinite loan. My father preferred Egypt Regained over other, more prestigious museums because of Egon's expensive climate control.

"I have a wonderful treat," Egon says now. "Dear Dr. Day, are you all right?"

My father says that *all right* is a relative term, but Egon goes on talking. "Scott Dillard is staying with us. So intelligent, so fine. You know him, of course you do . . . So prestigious. You know, Scott has new publications and a new appointment to Yale and—rumor has it—the Hartdale." He half whispers this name; it's a magic one, that of a famous grant. "And he is here! At our just-established Scholars' Institute!"

He pauses for emphasis, to which Daddy says, "The past is encroaching."

"Oh, not at all." Egon sounds defensive. "If you mean this terrible event today. Or the thefts. The disappearances of artifacts. I told you about them. So distressing. We have been so troubled. Artifacts disappearing, when we are sure they are well guarded. But we are taking steps."

My father says he is worried about the artifacts, and Egon says, No, no, he should not worry. After which Daddy says he is concerned about his coffin lid, and Egon says, "No, no, completely attended to."

Meanwhile I sit caressing my cold drink-bottle and wondering what Egon's house will look like. I've been to the museum several times and was involved in a scary confrontation there once. But I've never seen the house itself, never been asked to a meal.

Egon's mansion is low-riding and is latched on to one side of the museum. We enter through the museum's Great Hall with Egon preceding triumphally, like Pharaoh leading a procession.

"And now," he intones as a new person appears from some distant marble depths, "you've been waiting for this, I know, Dr. Day. Here is your wonderful colleague, someone you know of old. Dr. Scott Dillard, Yale University's newest shining star."

Egon stands aside and beams, as if he has produced an especially sleek rabbit out of his hat.

Scott Dillard looks reluctant.

He's one of those handsome, sturdy men, about forty, stocky and energetic, with watchful gray eyes. He wears blue jeans and a black turtleneck sweater and a gold chain. Right away he bothers me. He looks familiar. He looks like one of my old boyfriends.

This boyfriend and I parted badly. I abandoned him back in Baker's Landing, Tennessee, where he was the head of a Habitat for Humanity project I worked on.

Scott Dillard and I stare at each other. The atmosphere seems tense. Of course, today is an uncomfortable day, but maybe I also remind Scott of somebody. He holds a hand stiffly out to my dad and says "Oh, yes," and "Hello." Finally he projects a hand at me.

He has a surprisingly wiry handshake.

"Wonderful revelations from this young man," says Egon. "History-making."

I know something about Scott Dillard's history-making-ness. In car, I was reading Egon's newsletter, *Egypt Regained for You*, and sandwiched between appeals for contributions, he provides news items about the museum. "Record Attendances in March," et cetera. There's a major story about Scott Dillard, "One of our two wonderful Resident Scholars. Dr. Dillard, newly hired at Yale to be Focus Professor of Ancient Egyptian History. He will be with us for two months. We are eagerly anticipating his revelations about NEFERTITI. A big celebration for this. Tickets soon."

The other Resident Scholar, it seems, is Rita Claus, the crazy lady who thinks my dad is a murderer.

Scott looks at Egon. If I knew Scott better, I'd say the glance was pitying.

We go on into Egon's house, which is big and overstuffed. Like the museum, it contains a lot of slate and marble; it also has wall paintings that resemble tomb wall paintings, chairs that look like the ones in a tomb, couches copied from Tutankhamen's collection. Everything is red, gold, or peacock blue; straight-backed; and signaling, *I am ferociously uncomfortable*. Tomb furniture was designed for the next life, not to be sat on by living people, or at least not modern ones. The Egyptians seem to have had better posture than we do.

The room is bathed in pink light from recessed overhead fixtures. I glance at Scott D. under this romantic illumination. He still looks handsome and I remember how much I hated that Habitat guy.

"How very fortunate," Egon enthuses over dinner, "to have my two foremost scholars here together. And how much I hope to compensate, dear Dr. Day, for your awful experiences. I cannot explain. The sheriff is usually a perfect gentleman. And Rita—Dr. Claus—well. She has been feeling ill."

Daddy is bland. He takes another piece of chicken, he wipes his hands on a linen napkin. He says that he would like to see his coffin lid.

And eventually, everyone being sated on chicken and fried doohickies dipped in powdered sugar, we form a short trail behind Egon, headed for the museum and its Edward Day Room.

My father likes having everyone's attention. "Someone was trying to kill that man," he announces as we start walking.

"Dr. Day, you *must* tell me," and "What exactly did you see?" Egon tries, reaching for Daddy's arm.

But Daddy shrugs him off. "The ways are strange," he declaims.

Egon is plaintive. "Oh, dear. I feel so very lost."

The museum is approached from Egon's house by an underground passage.

Egon cheers up when he gets to demonstrate this. "It was a special idea of hers." *She* is his grandmother, Gudrun Rothskellar, a lady whose portrait appears on bottle labels as lantern-jawed, ferret-eyed, and wearing a lace cap with ears. Gudrun, I have heard, made a bundle off a restorative tonic for women and left her fortune to Egon. "Very interested in Egypt," he says now. "Very spiritual. In touch with meaningful forces." He gestures. "The niches were her idea."

This section of the underground passage is lined with open apertures that look like the ones in the catacombs in Paris. The Paris catacomb niches contain bodies, most visibly skulls. These openings hold Egyptian pottery plus some objects that look like skulls but are, I hope, ceramics. The walls are calcined an attractive shade of blue-green. There are candleholders at intervals whose candles end in crimped electric flames.

Scott gestures at the pottery. "A couple of good things here, Egon."

"The ka will be distressed," my father says.

Egon says, "I worry about earthquake."

My father says he is on his way to see his coffin lid.

Egon says, "You know, she is buried in the basement." I gather that we are back on the subject of his grandmother. "In a special sublevel. A truly beautiful tomb. A marble structure on top, but inside many aspects of the New Kingdom. We must do a tour. I don't usually invite people for tours."

We pop up inside the museum's main gallery via a flight of stairs and a mahogany coat closet. Egon produces a remote that gets the lights on.

I decide I like the museum better when there's nobody else here. The mummy and decayed wrappings exhibits seem less staged minus the lines of schoolkids making remarks like, "Yech. Where's his eyes?" and "I bet when they take that glass lid off, it really smells." The museum has some decent art objects that show up now. I stop to admire a bronze mirror with a handle shaped like a lotus plant.

"Excellent proportions. New Kingdom," Scott remarks of the mirror.

He has begun acting interested in me, that business of looking to see if I'm listening, aiming his remarks my way. But he doesn't get too close, which is a plus. I dislike men who stand too close.

We proceed at a leisurely pace through the big gallery, where I stop to admire a cartonnage of a cheerful fat lady, a great favorite of Daddy's. A cartonnage is a mummy encased in plaster and painted to look like the person inside; this one has black bangs and a jaunty smile and sports too much mascara. She's cheap and appealing. She looks like a cocktail waitress.

"Late. Not very fine," Scott pronounces, smiling my way and missing the whole idea.

I start to explain that the lack of finesse is a big part of the charm, and am deciding not to do this when we're interrupted by a commotion in the next room, Egon's voice and my father's voice. Daddy sounding like his old professor-self, "An intrusion. Appalling," and Egon making birdlike squawks.

When we get there, Egon has become articulate. "No one had access. No one."

We're in the Edward Day Room; I can't see anything

amiss except for Egon jittering and waving his arms and my father standing erect and angry, like the captain of the ship.

Egon gesticulates, "Truly, Dr. Day, I do not understand."

"Undo it," commands my dad.

I look at my father's coffin lid case and then inside it; I'm at first baffled. Everything seems okay; the coffin lid itself inclines in its usual place, appearing old, scratched, and unimpressive; the transparent shell above it shines. "There," Daddy says, pointing.

And yes, there, on the lower corner of the lid, certainly is something that ought not to be present. A little intruder. A creepie-crawlie. "Oh," I offer cheerfully, "a bug."

This is met by silence from Egon and cries of "No, no," from my dad.

"It crawled in there to die," I continue. And then I look more closely. This little thing is not a bug but a snake, small and tightly curled, more a worm than a snake, except for a very definite snake's head. And it hasn't crawled anywhere for a while; it's encased in plastic. It's one of those stupid charm souvenirs they sell at tourist stands in places like Fisherman's Wharf. A tiny red snake in a blob of plastic. A strip of paper is Scotch-taped onto it. By squinting, I can see that the paper contains hieroglyphs. I identify a couple of them; I remember that the bird with its tail down is a negative image.

"Red is bad," a voice says from behind my shoulder. "Bad fortune. Red is the death color."

The voice is not Scott's, being an octave higher; I turn and identify. The voice belongs to Rita, the crazy lady who thinks my father is a killer. Also, one of the museum's Resident Scholars.

She wears a purple sweater and silver leather pants. Her black hair stands up almost straight.

"Oh, hell," Scott says in her direction.

Egon gives her a thoughtful glance and turns back to the display case. "But how on earth . . ." He points at a shiny, professional-looking lock. "The case is secured. The guard and I have the keys. She is a reliable guard."

"A house is open to him who has goods in his hand," my father offers in a tight voice.

"Dear Dr. Day." Egon sounds alarmed. "What *can* you mean?"

"Do you know, a person was trying to kill him?"

"You were," Rita says.

Scott puts his hand on Daddy's shoulder. "What person?" he asks. "Is the person here?"

My father says, "We must get my coffin lid case open."

"What was the person wearing, Ed?"

Daddy doesn't answer, but he pats Scott's hand where it rests on his shoulder.

Scott turns to Egon. "You've got the key on you?"

Rita says, "Y'know what? Somebody should do that case for fingerprints."

I've been thinking this, too, but now, looking hard, I can see that the surface is squeaky clean.

It comes up easily. Apparently, it's very light.

And inside sits the nasty little plastic souvenir.

"Hey, hold it," I call out, fishing in my pocket for a Kleenex to protect any fingerprints on the snake thing.

But already it's too late. Egon, who is grasping the case with one hand, has reached under it with the other hand.

Rita mutters about a setup.

I'm not going to slip into suspecting Egon, who probably hasn't even heard of fingerprints. He shakes the plastic blob to get the paper extended and starts trying to read it, moving his lips and frowning.

"Apep, the evil god," my father says, watching the plastic snake. "Very strong. Dangerous. There should be a talisman against it."

Scott takes the snake blob out of Egon's hand. He squints at the paper. "*Arhoo*," he reads. "Pain." He starts waving one hand, something I guess he does when he concentrates. "Yes. A familiar inscription. A vulture, a reed shelter, a quail chick, a sparrow with tail feathers down; this denoting pain because . . ." He stops and looks at me. "Sorry. There I go again."

I think at him, *Someone, back in your past, has objected to your lecturing.*

I want to say, No, keep it up, so I can hear the story. What happens? The vulture hides in the reed shelter and catches the quail chick?

Those hieroglyphs are a lot more interesting than our predictable, straight-line, easily-carved-on-monuments Roman alphabet.

Rita says, "Pain? Brilliant, mister, what do *you* know about pain?" Her eyes are half-closed. I think maybe Rita takes medication, and has been getting the dosage wrong.

The protective shell is now lying on the floor, upside down. I start to circle the coffin-stand, scanning for other nasty things left inside. The room is silent except for the hiss of the climate-control machine and a low intermittent recital from Egon: "Truly, Dr. Day, I cannot imagine. Believe me, we will do everything . . ."

"Very bad," says my father. "Red, especially. Someone

sending pain." Question crimps his face. "But Carla, I already have pain."

I look at him, my gentle, distressed father. What do I say? *No, you don't. It'll be okay. Maybe you'll forget about it*? I walk over to hold his hand, which dangles at his side.

And then after about a minute it happens. I get a bolt of inspiration, straight from the goddess. "But you *can* do something. You can say a spell. You know a lot of spells, good ones, spells against sorrow. You could recite a spell against the snake." I'm squeezing his hand as I talk.

Daddy's face starts to clear. "Why, of course I could."

"You can say one now," I emote. "It will cleanse everything."

Egon latches on to this. "Oh, this is going to be so interesting. I feel so privileged."

"One of the *Book of the Dead* spells?" Scott asks. "Of course, they were for the other world, but that should be okay."

"And it will protect the whole collection. The entire museum." Egon affects a singsong intonation. He gets excited. He tosses his white mane.

Rita sits down on the floor.

I seem to be the only one who notices that my father has deflated, shoulders slumped. I understand why. He's having an Alzheimer's fugue, reaching back into his foggy gray memory bank and finding nothing. No spell. No words. Just shifting space.

Well, I used to know some spells. I learned them just from listening to him and a few stuck. I try a few beginnings: *Oh you who wait at night . . . oh you out of the darkness . . .* Not right.

Most of my knowledge of Egyptian poetry dates back to our night sessions in the camp in Thebes. Daddy, me, and

Rob (I was fifteen years old) sitting around a little fire, launching Ancient Egyptian poetry quotes at each other, trying to make a story of them. Ancient Egyptian poetry is good for this sort of thing, being very free-form and surreal; our stories were versions of comic book serials or science fiction movies.

The quote I want now would have been at the end of the story we were inventing, at the time when the good forces are getting rid of the evil ones, cursing them out, the way Daddy did Sheriff Munro earlier today, and got arrested for it. And now he can't remember that power he evoked against the sheriff just this morning.

"Bullshit," Rita fires up from her seat on the floor. Maybe that's a pretty good spell.

I squeeze my eyes shut, trying to get the right setting to bring back a quote. It's evening, along the street is a Theban ruin, night drops down suddenly; there's a smell of cold decayed buildings but the sand's still warm under my butt; the fire spreads its tang of singed wood scraps . . . And yep, I have it.

"*Get back! Crawl away! Get away from me, you creature!*"

That's a spell to overcome a rerek-snake, a special divine being with a special history, but it will do for this occasion.

Scott backs me up. "Hey, great!"

"Why, yes," my father says, "why certainly." He stands up straight; his face comes alive; he picks up the recitation. "*Go, be drowned in the lake of the abyss, in that place where your father has set aside for you . . .*" He pauses here; obviously there's another problem. "But I should be doing this outside. It is for a cleansing of the whole building. All of the surroundings. I should be outside in the sunlight."

"Wonderful, wonderful," Egon says.

It's almost eight o'clock, late for sunlight. But there was still a bright glow in the west last time I looked. That probably will keep my dad happy.

"And we need some powerful water," he adds. "Water that has been poured over a sacred talisman."

That's a stopper. Egon looks distressed. "Oh, dear. *Sacred* water?"

Everybody looks at everybody. But Scott, after a minute, comes to and smiles. "Right here. In my Thermos," which he produces from his pocket.

The Thermos isn't a Thermos, not to my eye. It's a small curved silver flask, one of those upper-class antique doodads they advertise in the back pages of *The New Yorker*. Probably made for whiskey.

"Yes," Daddy says, looking satisfied as the gurgling little receptacle is handed over to him. "I think that is necessary for this spell. Otherwise we can't be sure."

I'm wondering what the flask contains. Whiskey? Vodka? Probably not water. I hope it'll be okay with my father, who has picked up the snake-blob with two fingers and is heading through the main hall and toward the side door, flask and snake-blob in hand.

Rita gets up, protesting, "Stud, I know what you put in your flask. And maybe I'll tell. I could tell a lot of things."

Egon does some digital clicking to unlock the side door and then rushes ahead for further unlocking. Daddy stands at the closed portal like the seeker at the gates. Finally the door swings wide and he leads us outside. We follow onto a wide cement platform above a garden where green and gray plants contend for space with native grasses and Egyptian-type statuary. Steps lead down into a garden; the residue of a sunset pulsates at the end of a pebbled walk.

My father says, "Ah!" and "A good setting." The rest of us make similar murmurs. We're all looking out, across the garden, toward the lighted evening sky. Daddy raises his arms high, holding aloft the snake, the magic water; he starts out, "Listen to me, oh you powers." It's a mystic scene, a ridiculous scene; it commands attention; my father the hierant; no wonder we don't look down, right near our feet, where something is very much the matter.

"Daddy, stop! Oh, my God. Honey, stop." That is me speaking. Carla, yelling at her father the spell-binder. I am the one who has finally looked down the steps into the garden and seen what's waiting for us there. Something we can't avoid anymore.

At the side of the cement platform, partly in a stand of oleander, partly in a patch of lavender, a man. Or a man's body. The same man as before, I think, wasn't he stretched like this before, legs splayed, and wearing the same cashmere sweater, the head turned like that before, though I'm not sure about the head; the face now partly hidden by some broken oleander branches.

Egon says, "Oh, dear God." My father and Scott are silent. Rita says, "Je-sus." I am the first one down the stairs.

He's alive, I'm telling myself. Last time he was alive; he's alive now; they took him away and examined him; I don't even know what was the matter with him.

I know I'm not supposed to touch him, but I think maybe his legs are twitching, a sign that he's alive. He needs help. I take his left hand and feel for the pulse. He hasn't any. I try again. No. His flesh is cold, damp, and pale.

He feels very inert to be alive.

His head is back, half-buried in a clump of bushes, but one eye is visible, a gray-blue eye, not staring at me, looking at something behind my shoulder. His lips are pulled back and the teeth are together; I see that there's a bright blue object in his mouth, loosely resting on his teeth. A bright blue something small, about the size of a quarter. I reach toward it and it falls off to rest on a clump of lavender.

It's a modeling made of blue glazed clay, a representation of the ankh, that loop-shaped symbol of eternal life that the Egyptians were so fond of.

He was holding an ankh in his mouth.

My father has come up behind me. He has watched the blue shape and follows its progress into the bushes. "Yes," he says in a resigned voice, "I am much too late.

"I told you, he was trying to eat life."

⌐ Chapter 5

Four hours have passed since the discovery of Marcus
Broussard, the dead-again trustee.

The sheriff has been here and has been obnoxious; he has
once again accused my father of sinister involvement in fatal
events. And I have been obnoxious in return; I have mentioned lawsuits, legal appeals, newspaper stories, injunctions.
The sheriff has finally retreated, looking harassed and promis-
ing to schedule a recorded session with my father.

"Great," I tell him.

It is ten-thirty at night, and I am ready to leave.

I am not ready for what Egon Rothskellar does now, which
is to proffer an invitation to come live at Egypt Regained.

"For at least a month," he says. "Dear Dr. Day. As part of
our Resident Scholars' Program. And you, too, Miss Day, for
as long as you like."

I do not say, "My God, no," which is what I think. More

time at this strange place? I am dying to leave. I simply decline.

"No," I tell Egon Rothskellar, with impolite directness.

Unfortunately he isn't inviting only me; his true invitation is to my father. He must have thought carefully about this. He does it in the perfect form. "Edward, I would like very much for you to stay here. For several weeks. As part of our Resident Scholars' Program. We really need you."

Daddy is Johnny-on-the-spot. He doesn't say, "Why so sudden?" or "What's the Resident Scholars' Program?" or "What's the meaning of the word *resident?*" or any of the other remarks he could make. His response is simple and heartfelt. "Yes." After a minute he adds, "Good."

This is followed, very emphatically, by, "It is good to be needed."

I waste twenty minutes arguing that he is needed back at the Manor, that he has good friends at the Manor who will miss him, that he has a lovely apartment at the Manor and duties there to the classes he attends in art, macramé, concert appreciation. That he thinks the food there is good. That Susie is coming to see him.

I do not point out that the museum is an unstable environment, the setting of a death that I suspect of being a murder and of a crazy lady (Rita) who has it in for my father, and also the setting of minor pilferings that I suspect of . . . I'm not sure what I suspect of those little thefts. They seem peculiar. I don't say any of this to my dad, but I think it.

Daddy is so adamant, so insistent, and so fired by unreasonable hope . . . things have not been good, but now they are going to be better; this is a turning point, once again the world will recognize his coffin lid for the discovery it was . . . he has been feeling bad, yes, he knows that, but now he is going to feel better. All this is so moving and up-setting that I finally haul out my cell phone and call Rob.

Rob knows my father very well. I'm thoroughly in the habit of talking to him in any crisis.

"Hey," is his first response to my story. "That's great."

I answer with a flock of *yes, but*'s and he says, "Oh. Uh-huh." There is a moment of telephone silence during which I guess he is thinking. Then he confers with someone beside the telephone, "Hey, what do you think, mumble, mumble."

The person who may think something isn't really audi-ble, but I get a weird feeling that there's a Southern accent involved.

"Hey," Rob says, confirming this perception, "guess what? Cherie is here and I asked her what she thought and . . ."

Cherie apparently thinks it would be wonderful for dar-ling Croc to stay and be an expert at the museum. "Yeah," Rob says. "Like, I think she has really good perceptions about people? We had dinner together and we've been talk-ing all evening and we really hit it off, isn't that great? Wow. It's not often that it happens like that. And she really loves your dad. And I took her around the hospital and . . ."

This is the point at which I turn off my imaginary hear-ing aid. There's an exercise where you pretend you're stuff-ing your ears up with those round white foam stoppers.

"So," Rob is saying five minutes later when I come back to earth, "we both feel pretty good about that. About meet-ing each other. And I certainly think, yes, Ed should accept. I'm in favor of taking on every option that life offers."

I tell him good-bye and thanks loads, and when I'm back

in the museum setting, Egon informs me that everything is all arranged. He will come to get us. Tomorrow? Well, then, the next day.

"There, dear Dr. Day. That is all settled."

Among the many things I don't understand here is why Egon is so anxious to get my dad, who is vague as to what century it is, into his think tank.

And it's an exaggeration to say that I agree to the arrangement just because I'm furious with Rob. But for certain that's a contributing factor.

🦉 Chapter 6

Daddy and I leave the following Monday. He's good about helping me pack. He looks like a new man, a younger one. He helps me find the right socks to go with his blue plaid shirt; he remembers his special shampoo; he collects some Egyptian figures that need to come with him.

"Oh, this will be interesting," he says.

And he is sociable during the drive over in Egon's limousine, chatting with the driver about the quail families we see en route. "The ancient Egyptian bird of this type was the guinea hen," he volunteers.

Egon's Resident Scholars' quarters are on the third floor of his handsome house. We are conveyed there by an elevator. The predominant color of everything—elevator, doors, halls, outside grasses—is a golden beige. There is stained glass. There are passageways with indirect light and bathrooms with spas and warmed towel bars. I've been expecting Egyptian funerary beds and chairs, but no; Egon's guest quarters, resplendent in (I immediately check this and count) six bedrooms, an upstairs parlor, a library; these quarters are almost Egypt-free except for the carpets on which endless processions of tan people parade bearing libations.

This is, in fact, an excellent hotel with the usual hotel extras. Exotic fruit—pineapple, mango, et cetera—is offered in a silver-plated basket; chocolates adorn each pillow. I'm sure someone will be around in the morning to remake the tousled beds.

"What a delightful accommodation," says my father. He sits on the edge of his new bed with its Ralph Lauren spread and arranges the stone and clay figures he's brought with him, plus a knitted representation of the Sacred Eye. Susie gave him this; she has a friend in Berkeley who makes them.

"I can tape that up on the wall for you," I suggest. But he clutches the object. "I can do it," he says accusingly, as if I'm telling him that he can't.

I drift off. Today is not Carla Day's Day, nor was yesterday. I won't offer to help him unpack his leather suitcase. I'll be good; I'll be supportive and nondirective. I'll let him unroll his socks all by himself.

Half an hour later I ask Dr. Scott Dillard, "Am I a nag?"

"Huh?" inquires Dr. Scott, who has just wandered into the library, where I am attempting simultaneously to listen to a Leadbelly tape and read a mystery novel set in first-century B.C. Rome.

When I pull the earphones away, the strains of "Good to

the Last Drop" detach and Scott raises an eyebrow. "*What are you listening to?*"

"Egon has some great tapes."

"I never before met a girl blues fan."

"Woman. Woman blues fan. Blues enthusiast. All my best friends say I'm a nag. But you wouldn't know."

"Damn right not. What are you keening about, Woman Blues Fan?"

"Some facts would be nice. I'd like to know why we're here. Egon won't speak straight. My father can't. I'm forgetting how."

"Je-sus," says Scott. He's been balancing in front of me holding a couple of books; now he settles slowly into a recliner, watching me. He tilts the back of it and tents his legs.

"So," I pursue, "am I a nag?"

"How in hell would I know?"

"Why are you here, Professor Scott? At Egypt Regained?"

"Me? Here?" Somehow I've hit a nerve. "I belong here, Miss Woman Enthusiast. I'm a scholar. An Egyptologist. A linguist. I'm a specialist in . . ." Maybe he's listening to himself; maybe it sounds overimportant.

"I read one article you wrote," I say. "It was about sandals."

Scott gives me a dirty look. I personally liked the eighteenth-dynasty Theban sandals article. Those sandals sounded just like last year's Venice Beach items, with the same strap between the big toe and the rest of the foot. But I guess Scott is ashamed of the whole idea—not scholarly enough.

"And I hear you're getting a Hartdale Grant."

He doesn't answer, but he pinks up. His sturdy tan face looks better when it has some red color.

After a brief pause I ask, "So what killed that man?"

He clears his throat. "You *are* a nag."

"Just persistent. I have a father to feed."

He surveys me. I remind myself that I do not like this Scott Dillard, that he reminds me of an old, unsuccessful boyfriend. And that I am flirting with him. This verbal poking I'm doing is a kind of flirting. It says, *Look at me.*

"Did he die twice?" I ask.

"Why not? Some famous people died more than that. What the hell is this?"

"What did he die of?"

"How would I know?"

"You know everything. You're a fact-bank."

"I don't know what he died of."

"I saw you romancing the guard. She's *into* everything."

"She says he died when his heart stopped beating. She says she had a cousin who died that way. No, sorry, it wasn't her cousin, it was her husband's cousin or maybe her husband's brother's cousin. But she's a well-informed lady. In fact, a world-class expert. You're right to be pursuing her knowledge. She knows."

I ignore Scott's sarcasm. "She was talking to the first-aid guys."

"Oh, Christ."

Scott isn't going to tell me what the guard said. I guess I can ask her myself. "But you," I say, "have an opinion. You've been trained as a doctor. What do you think?"

He stares at me. "Whoa."

"I looked you up in Google," I tell him modestly. In fact, I've just finished doing that, here in Egon's library. "And Google quoted the *Brooklyn Intelligencer*, which asked you about your education, and this was long enough ago that you were really flattered to be asked, so you put it all in, which maybe you wouldn't do now. After all, people don't go to The Medical University of the Virgin Islands because they had high MCATs. They go there because they took so much pot in college they couldn't get into school here." I grind to a halt and wait.

Scott doesn't say anything. His mouth turns down.

In the flip of a minute I decide I've been mean and underhanded. There's no basis at all for my accusation about his MCATs, just some long-ago experience with my ex-friend Habitat. What apology can I offer?

"It wasn't pot," Scott says finally in a strangled voice. He clunks the recliner forward and struggles to his feet. Some papers spill out of the file he's holding. A whole batch of them land in my lap.

I start shuffling his stuff up into a little pile. I make it clear I'm not reading, just organizing.

Maybe that assuages him some. Maybe he has a need to justify. "It was a girl. Her name was Danielle." He hits her name hard and his face pinks up again as he says it.

I think, Oh, a girl who took pot. A girl who got pregnant? A girl who went to the Virgin Islands for a divorce? Romance, interesting. I love stuff like that. I'll be here for the rest of the week. I can get this story out of him.

Danielle. My father mentioned a Danielle sometime or other.

I hand up his stack of papers.

"I was only there a year," he says.

I decide his story isn't true. Whatever it is. I'll find out.

He's still standing, looking irresolute. This idiot doesn't want to talk, but he's standing with his feet glued to the floor. Definitely, Danielle was important.

"A year is long enough," I say, pulling the conversation

back on its trolley. "You'll remember some of that med training. What could Mr. Broussard have died of? Twice?"

"The nine-one-one guys said he had very low blood pressure," he offers finally in a strangled voice.

"And what would cause that?"

"Shock. Trauma. Blood loss."

"He wasn't losing blood."

"Internally."

I try to imagine the man struggling around for a whole afternoon with something bleeding inside, not telling anyone, bumping into walls. "Wouldn't that make you sort of crazy?"

"What are you? Madame Hercule Poirot?"

I say, "Oh, shit," and try to organize myself for an exit. Now if he had just accused me of being Tempe Brennan or Kinsey Milhone or any one of the other thousand successful woman sleuths of the last fifty years. I am caught in the listening equipment and can't get up.

"Egon left a printed welcome on my dresser," I say. "It talks about our distinguished roster of scholars. It lists you and Rita and my father. Everybody's history gets reviewed and their publications listed. You've got tons of those. And your field is Egyptian history. Specifically the history of the Middle New Kingdom. Dr. Scott Dillard, Memphis State University, Memphis, Tennessee."

He interrupts, "I'm at Yale now."

"Oh, is that better than Memphis State?" (Actually, Memphis State gives a degree in Egyptology; I checked that in Google, too.)

Scott stares. We've had a brisk exchange of insults this afternoon. I wonder if he has a sense of humor. Not about his career, I betcha.

I have finally gotten myself loose from the wires and am struggling up with my book. "We're going to have a good time, aren't we," I ask, "talking about our work histories and our study histories and our articles? Of course, I'm not listed in Egon's welcome document; I'm not a scholar, just the daughter of a scholar. They don't make a category for that. But it's very important, too. Don't you think?

"Incidentally, did you know him?" I ask.

"Did I know who?" Scott stares and the muscles in his tan cheeks flex. I suspect that he's perfectly aware that I mean Marcus Broussard.

"You're not exactly making sense, Lady Blues Enthusiast."

"See you at dinner." I leave feeling that I've learned a couple of things, but I'm not sure what.

I'm on my way down the hall toward Daddy's room when I run more or less head-on into Rita. I brace myself, preparing for another hysterical confrontation. But no such thing. Rita smiles. She says, in a high, little-girl voice, "Oh, hey, sorry."

"Huh?" I ask, amazed.

"I mean, hey, I ran right into you."

She is clutching a large purple orchid in a clay pot. She wears a silk turquoise shirt with a sequin outline of a swan on the front. Her hair is newly moussed, her face is washed; she sports one turquoise earring and a delicate smile. This Rita is a new person and not hysterical. Dressed, coiffed, trimmed. Changed, you could say.

In fact, an altered and reconstituted Rita. Remade and a bit scary for that reason. Because it's been only a few days since I last saw her, screaming "Help," and accusing my dad of murder. And here she is, someone who has altered her entire outer envelope. She wears a pale tasteful dab of lip-stick and blusher, a tiny hint of eyeliner. Has she been having charm sessions with Cherie? She wears pale green pants. It seems that all this time she's had pale green eyes. She is still plump, which looks sweet.

"My God," I say.

She agrees, "Oh. Yeah."

"You look great."

"Kind of a surprise, huh?"

I remember that I was on my way to my dad's room and turn to go in that direction, but she falls in beside me. She bounces the orchid on her hip. "This is for your father. I had it, but now I'm giving it to him. Does he like orchids, do you know?"

I can feel myself staring, mouth open.

"Unprecedented, right?" she interprets. The orchid gets shifted. "Well, I have manic-depressive tendencies. And I take meds. And sometimes I need help to get back on track."

I'm sure there are appropriate responses, like, "I guess we all do, some," or, "I had a good friend that had that." But I'm still too astonished to say anything.

We arrive at Daddy's room side by side, but can't go in that way, because the door isn't wide enough.

Rita enters first, orchid held out straight. "Here you are, Ed. Honest, I'm so sorry."

"Why, my dear," says my father. "What a beautiful color. Are you on your way to your plane?"

"No, Ed." She positions the orchid on a table and stands back appraisingly. "I guess I was real bitchy, right?"

"I don't think so," Daddy says. "Let us sit down. What do you mean by *bitchy*? Isn't that a handsome flower?"

Rita sits, exposing silver socks and turquoise strap sandals. Definitely, she's been getting schooling from Cherie.

My father silences the television with the remote. He turns; he smiles a delighted smile. "My dear. What plane is it?"

She says, "No, Ed."

"So hard on us. Travel. There was a book where they talked about simply putting you in a capsule. You could sleep the whole way. Wake up in Kazakhstan."

Rita waits a minute. She digs something out of her pocket, a silver and ivory comb, and twiddles the comb-teeth to make it sing. "I guess I'm finding this interview sorta upsetting?"

Yeah, I think.

She snaps and unsnaps the comb.

"I would sure like it if . . ." Kazoom, a fingernail down the edge of the comb.

Maybe what we're getting here is the original precollapse Rita. Low-key, nervous, anxious to please.

"Oh, hell. Everybody's entitled to one bitch-day once a month during a bad PMS bout. Am I right? Right. The hell with all you clones." Kazoom some more.

Well, not *that* anxious to please. "Rita, cut it out." She flashes me a good smile and sticks the comb in her pocket.

My father says, "I think someday there will be an implosion of undifferentiated factoids."

"Seems likely," Rita examines him. "Some of the basic Ed is still there."

"Much, my dear."

"You always were a handsome bastard."

I do a reassessment. Daddy is sprightly, trim, sturdy. Is he handsome?

Rita fixes on me. "This the way it usually is?" She flexes an eyebrow in Daddy's direction.

"It varies."

"Boy, did I ever adore him, once. When we were on the dig in Thebes. A great scene; maybe I should tell you. But maybe not."

I wait.

"Ah, the hell with it. It'll wait. You'll be around here awhile?"

I tell her yes and she says, "Dinner calls, acid reflux falls, keep cool," and exits in a flurry. Her hair still wants to stand up straight.

It is going to be an engrossing few days at the museum.

Chapter 7

A hassled Egon Rothskellar is trying to induce the right atmosphere around his dinner table.

The right atmosphere would be one of sophistication and intelligent discourse, rising above the fact of Marcus Broussard, whom everybody at this table saw spread-eagled and, we are told, finally dead in Egon's garden just three nights ago.

"Any news, Egon?" Scott asks.

Egon jumps. "News, Scott? I don't think so. What kind of news would that be?"

"Studly is fishing to find out if you heard something about Marcus," Rita says, jabbing a piece of lettuce. "Like, what did it to him? Who did it to him?"

Egon is desolate. "Marcus. Oh, dear. So dreadful."

"Stud is Mr. Energizer Bunny," Rita says. "He never stops, you know, on the intellectual quest? You've heard of it? Fill up your brain with facts?"

"Hey, Rita, cut it out, huh?" Scott says.

Rita says, "Why?"

Egon says, "Oh, dear."

"Any more little tchochkes missing, Egon?" Rita asks. "Maybe Stud's been collecting them." She turns to me. "You heard about it. They've been disappearing at the rate of—oh—one a day. Right, Egon?"

"Alas," Egon says. "Yes. And we are so careful. Rita, dear, settle down, please."

Rita, who has been poised on the edge of her chair, surprises me by subsiding. Maybe it's the presence of the extra person at the table, Mrs. Bunny Modjeska, that does it. Bunny is the guard. ("Just call me Bunny. It sure is easier than Modjeska.") She leans forward now, exhibiting fat shoulders and flattering interest. She views the visible enmity at the table. "Wow."

Rita settles back. "Pass the mashed potatoes, please." Egon waves a hand over his beautiful table and its crystal, china, linen, platter of tasty-looking roast chicken. Tonight's menu is American. There is a printed menu card, labeled AMERICAN DINNER.

"Congrats, Rita," Scott tells her. "You look sort of like you some more."

Rita ladles out mashed potatoes and pours gravy.

"I didn't like that other stuff," Scott says. "The lost Goth look. '*Shifting of face is the name of him who*' et cetera—remember those lines, Reet?"

Rita eats a forkful of food and stares at Scott, eyes narrowed.

"And, chicklet, I bet you never looked in a mirror once. Not to mention the invective. Hey, Rita . . ."

Egon intervenes. "Scott. Please. Bygones, and . . . well, please. This is *Rita* back."

Rita has been eating potatoes stolidly, her head straight forward. The platter of chicken sits in the middle of the table, untouched.

"Rita is back?" says Scott. "How do you tell? Rita, the bleater, are you back, my darling?"

Bunny puts her fork down with emphasis. "Listen, mister. Cool it some, okay?"

Rita is still unresponsive. Back straight, even though the shoulders are twitching slightly.

Daddy says, "Oh, dear. Perhaps some of us have been out in the sun too long?"

And I'm fired to action. "Scott, for God's sake, what's with you? Let it go. So Rita wasn't feeling good for a while; now she's better. Why're you keeping at it? I just don't get it."

Somehow the spectacle of Rita's stolid back and shoulders is more touching than crying would be, or seeing her with her head in her hands. She doesn't do any of that. She eats for a while and then raises her eyes and says at Scott, "Quit pretending like I'm dirt on your shoe. There's plenty of times you wanted it different, if you can scrape your brains together enough to remember. And quit pretending Ed here is some kinda new acquaintance. You've known Ed since the flood. For Christ's sake. You look at him now like you never saw him before."

A sound intrudes from the outside, a train whistle. That's from the weedy triple railway line on the other side of Route One. "Hear that lonesome whistle / Sounding on the trestle," says, or rather, sings, my dad. He has a nice tenor voice. He supplies the chorus, "Ah—whooee, ah—whooee."

Egon bangs a little gong for more wine.

"I really like those trains," says my father.

I'm inspired to a speech. Maybe this isn't a good time, but I need to make it.

"Scott, you're being mean to Rita; she's off-base but she's vulnerable, she's like . . ." I'm about to say, *Like a snail without a shell*, when Rita turns such a poisonous glance my way that I cancel that. "I don't care about your history with her. Nobody cares, so cut it out. And cut it out with my dad, too." I'm not sure what I'm talking about here, so I slow down some. "If you knew my dad sometime in the past, it's unkind of you—not just unkind, cruel—not to act like you know him. You don't understand how often he stumbles along and doesn't say things because he thinks maybe he's wrong. I'll bet anything he looked at you and wondered, *Hey do I know him*, and then he just . . ." I'm amazed to hear my voice faltering. I don't want to emote for these people.

"Okay," says Scott, sounding muffled. "Point taken. I apologize. And I guess I better have some of this chicken, because nobody else is going to."

We chew for a while, until Egon announces that cappuccino and dessert will be served in the small exhibit hall.

"Well, another eventful day at Sunny Dell Acres," says Scott, rising to fold his menu into a neat square and stash it in his pocket. He looks thoughtful. "Can you pluck from the mind its rooted sorrow?" he asks.

I say, "Oh, shut up." I'm irked by people who revert to literary stuff in tense moments.

* * *

Apparently I've found a way to become the most popular girl in the dorm.

Raise a fuss during dinner. But I doubt if it always works.

My first visitor tonight is Bunny. She taps on my bedroom door and says, "Hello, dear, I wanted to tell you, I just had to say . . ."

I have to urge her to come in. She is a large lady and she fills up the whole door.

"What I mean," she exhales, settling into an ivory-slip-covered armchair. "Boy, these rooms are real nice, aren't they?"

She says no, she doesn't exactly live at the museum; she has a room down the hall for when she works late, but she *lives* in "one of those houses in Conestoga, in back of Main Street, y'know?"

But that's not what she wants to talk to me about. "I thought you were great for tackling that asshole," she says. "And he is one. A real sure-of-himself bastard. And if he knew your little dad. And didn't admit it. Well. That is real bad.

"And your dad is someone you got to side with. Know what I mean?"

I tell her *uh-huh*. I wait. Bunny has the look of a lady who wants to go on talking.

"Anyway, dear, you're a smart girl. College girl, I guess, right?

"And you're stickin' with your dad, which is great. And I haven't really been able to talk to anybody, y'know?"

She looks at me triumphantly.

Apparently she thinks she has piled up enough criteria to make me a confidante. "So I just thought I'd come here and . . ."

She shifts and tries to find something to delay action. She moves her legs. Long ago, I guess, when she was thinner, she would have crossed them; now they are too wide to get one thigh on top of the other.

"Do you want a cup of tea?" I ask. Tea was the conversation-priming device at the Manor; Egon has supplied all the necessaries, including a professional display of tea bags.

"Dear, you just let me do that." Bunny won't listen to my protests that I'm the hostess here. She sets out, being extremely efficient, which cheers her up.

While she's pouring hot water, she says, "What makes it kinda hard to say is, well, I don't know exackly. I mean, it's about him, that trustee. When I went to help him that first time. When he was supposed to be dead."

Each of us sits down. There's a rhythmic clink of stirring.

"I dunno," Bunny says. "Something was weird."

"Well, sure," I say. "He looked dead. But he wasn't. That's weird."

Bunny grunts and takes a large slurp. "Sure, but. Like, when you remember back and say, this happened and that happened and then, whoa, peculi-ar."

After a pause she adds, "I gave him mouth-to-mouth, y'know."

"I remember." I'd been especially impressed by the mouth-to-mouth.

"It was somethin' special," Bunny says. "It keeps hangin' there on the edge of me catching it, like what happens when you want to remember a dream. Y'know?"

Yes, I do know. "Try to think," I say. "Think about how his face looked. What color sweater he had."

But this gets us nowhere.

We veer off into talking about dreams and then about Bunny's two girls, one of whom dreams a lot. She's fifteen. And then we talk some about living in Conestoga, which I'm interested in, although Bunny claims it's just like living anywhere. "I mean, it's the place where you are, know what I mean?"

We have a good visit, and when Bunny leaves, she says she's glad she talked to me; it made her feel better. "I kept thinking I ought to do something, know what I mean?"

After she leaves, I go down the hall to check on Daddy, who is wrestling with the details of the new television remote. "Ah," he says, when I drill him on its procedures, "the little *quiet* button is *here* instead of *there*." He likes the TV set, which has a bigger screen than the one we left behind at the Manor.

I scan him for signs that this move has been disturbing, but the signs all point in the opposite direction. He looks good; his eyes are bright; his hair stands up, fluffy and white.

A year ago I thought he was on the verge of something bad, a steep Alzheimer's slide, but now he seems stable. They tell you Alzheimer's is like that. There are plateaus; there are moments of brightness. Hang on to them, the books all say. Be in the moment.

Back in my room, I think I'm ready for bed, but I'm wrong. I have a second visitor. Rita.

Rita isn't tentative about wanting to see me. The minute I open the door, she slips in, heads for the ivory-colored arm-chair, and curls up in it, feet under her. "Do you smoke?"

"Nope."

"Neither do I. Do you mind?" She pulls a small gold cigarette pack out of her pocket; it opens to expose black cigarettes with gold tips. She lights one with a cigarette lighter and looks around. Of course, there are no ashtrays in Egon's good hotel. I get a saucer for her.

"This is so damn much trouble." She waves a hand at the cigarettes and lighter. "Special stuff all the way around, fags, lights, too pain-in-the-neck; I hate it; I've quit."

She flips her head back, and her dark hair bounces; she exhales a neat smoke ring. "So next I'll have to start drinking. A lot. Vodka with brandy chasers."

She exhales another smoke ring and practices crossing her eyes as she watches the smoke ascend. "Neat, huh?

"What I wanted to ask you," she says, "is, what do you think Scott is up to?"

"Something," I agree. "But he seems like a guy who usually has an agenda."

This time she lets the smoke come out through her nostrils. "Believe it or not, he and I were extra close. For a while. A while ago."

"I thought maybe."

"That was in Thebes, where your dad was. I guess maybe now Scotty's ashamed of it, but he's had some other tarts since then he could be more ashamed of. Know what I mean?

"I mean, I'm a prominent woman. Crazy or not, I've done things. Degrees all over the fucking universe. I teach at Brown, for Christ's sake. That's way better than Yale for some stuff."

I agree with her that Brown could be better than Yale in some areas. Academic gossip is funny. I don't remember the details, but the general feeling of it has rubbed off on me. I understand about Yale, and Brown, and Chicago, and UC Berkeley. UC Berkeley was where my dad was.

"And what in hell is Scott the Stud doing here?" she asks. "I came to get away from the world for private personal psychiatric reasons—a suitcase full of meds and my shrink on the long-distance phone every day and Egon kind of protects me. Better on my record than the Menninger Clinic. But I don't think Scott's faced with a psychiatric meltdown. Do you?"

"No."

"Which leaves, why is he here? It didn't just happen; he engineered it. This Scholars' Institute is an invented entity, like we say in criticism, and Scott invented it and then invited himself to be in it. He wasn't figuring on Egon inviting me, too."

She taps off her cigarette ash. The room is getting full of smoke. "So what do you think?"

"Does it have anything to do with the Hartdale Grant?"

Rita sits up. She looks triumphant. "Socko!"

"You mean it does?"

"I dunno. But I thought it did. And then I couldn't figure out how. Because, believe me, that Hartdale Committee, whoever they are—Archbishop Tutu, Einstein's ghost, and God, whoever—they met a long time ago and whoever gets tapped for this year is already chosen and no terrific thing anybody discovers now is gonna change that. So."

"And Scott is supposed to be one of the recipients?"

She scowls. "Wanta bet he started that rumor?"

I shrug. Yes, it seems possible Scott started the buzz about himself and the Hartdale. But I'm having a Junior Moment of feeling guilty about Scott. I've been on his case, nagging him about everything for a whole day now. I've told myself the reason is my bad history with the Habitat boyfriend, but a likelier reason is Rob. Or Rob and Cherie. I get another throb of righteous fury when I think of them. Rob. Cherie. How can he?

Rita squashes out her cigarette.

The room now stinks as bad as our apartment in Santa Cruz used to. Rob's and my apartment.

"Rita," I say, "what made you so sure about my dad? That he was trying to kill Mr. Broussard?"

Rita frowns. She reaches for another cigarette, and then seems to think better of it. She pushes the top of the package down, firmly stows it in her pocket. "You ever been seriously depressed?"

I think about this. Of course I've been depressed, but not the way she means. Not the completely gone depression that sends you to the hospital. "No."

"Well, it louses up everything—the way you sit, how you stand, breathe, think—everything. What you hear, how you hear it, what you see. And especially what you read. It all seems terrible. So maybe most of it is, anyway, terrible. But if you're depressed, it's extra, super, drag-down awful. Take just one phrase. *Walk, don't walk*. That thing they flash at intersections. The epitome of neutral, you'd say. But if you're depressed? Whammo. Not neutral. Seems like a command from outer space. Negative. Controlling. Sinister. Threatening. Got it?"

"Yes."

"So I was like that. Everything's awful; everything's a threat; along comes this little poem on the Internet: *Day is death / Day is destruction*—got it?"

"Well, I guess."

"It was presented like a couple of lines from that series of Middle Kingdom prediction poems—you know the ones, the *Prophecies, Complaints,* and *Admonitions*, about how awful everything is going to be . . ."

I don't tell Rita I'm flattered by her assumption that I know the poems. I'll take her word on them.

"For me," she goes on, "that *Day* in the poem was your dad, Edward Day. He had just come here to the museum and I'd seen him. And I used to love him a lot, back when. We used to joke—me and the other people on the dig— about his name, Day, and him being so sunny and bright. Most archaeologists don't have much personality."

"And you thought the poem meant something about him?"

"Well, it was crazy; I was crazy. I thought it meant he wasn't a saint anymore; he was the devil. And then, while I was thinking that, I saw your dad on the floor with Marcus.

"I was crazy then, remember?

"But what was really weird was that poem. It was printed up like a page from an Internet site where people exchange versions of Egyptian poetry. But when I tried to check it later, it wasn't there."

"I don't get it."

"That's a real site about Egyptian poetry—new versions, new translations—but there wasn't any little 'Day' poem on it the second time I looked.

"So at first I thought somebody was gaslighting me. And then when I got better, I was perfectly sure that there really had been a poem. But I couldn't find it.

"So go figure."

She reaches for the cigarette pack and says, "Oh, shit . . . Hey, I really am going to quit smoking. Save this in remembrance of me." And she tosses me her cigarette lighter.

"That stupid verse didn't even sound like an Egyptian poem." She scrambles to her feet. "I knew that."

Pausing by the door, she says, "That was one of the best times in my life, that spring in Thebes. Five years ago. One of those bouts you get only once. Know what I mean?"

Five years ago would have been just before Daddy began to lose it to Alzheimer's. I guess he was still okay then.

I don't tell Rita that I have memories of Thebes, too, but this was a while before she was there. I was fifteen and Rob was eighteen. And my dad, who still had every one of his marbles, was seventy-five.

When Rita leaves, I start getting ready for bed. I've opened the windows and stowed the cigarette saucer in the hall and am brushing my teeth when the phone rings.

It's Scott. "Greetings, Lady Blues Enthusiast," he says, as if he and I were old, close, amicable buddies.

"Hello, Scott." I'm still suffering from my Junior Moment of guilt, so I probably sound nicer than I am.

"Hey," he says. "Lady Blues Enthusiast: How about going out for a drink?"

"Now?"

"Sure."

"Scott, it's quarter of eleven at night."

"Great hour for a drink."

"No."

"Try it. Just once."

"We're in the middle of no place. You gonna raid Egon's refrigerator?"

"We aren't, as you so elitistly put it, in the middle of no

place. There's a Best Western Motel, with a bar, ten minutes away."

I open my mouth to protest about the Best Western bar and then realize that I'm painting myself into a corner. Scott will now suggest another bar, a better hotel . . . "No."

"Tomorrow night?"

"Uh-uh."

"Night after that? Lunch? Afternoon trip to the big city?"

"Hey, Scott, cut it out." I don't sound as nasty as I ought to sound. This man has a smart-aleck, acid side to him. *Firm up, Carla.*

"I'll be back."

What on earth is the matter with me? "Listen, bro, you haven't a chance," I say. I tune in on myself, and I sound flirtatious.

"Okay. Sleep well. Long empty night ahead." He signs off, sounding pleased.

Obviously, I feel guilty at having stiffed him so consistently for something he didn't do.

Nuts.

I get a towel and fan the room to get rid of the rest of Rita's smoke. I go down the hall and listen at Daddy's door; the only sound is the quiet susurrus inside of peaceful elderly breathing. I proceed farther down the hall to the library, where I take down a book of Egyptian poetry. Then I realize that I'm outside in my pajamas and will surely meet Scott if I stay around a minute longer, so I beat a hasty, controlled retreat.

Flapping a towel again doesn't help much with any of my

problems. I still feel cross at myself. And the room continues to smell of those black cigarettes.

Before I go to bed I make the mistake of accessing my e-mail.
    Oh, hell.
    The fifth visitor of the evening.
    It's Cherie, gabbling away in a schoolgirl e-mail shorthand:

*Hi dd u no I'm stil in ur bakyard things poppin all ovr lkg
frwrd 2 hang tt sherf up by hs tiny bals Wt a treat & tt
other thing mr Broussard rely bothrs me ts s pretty wird stuff
cant wait 2 c u & talk luv luv cheri
Njoying t scen ard here luv luv luv*

Yes, Cherie, the scene around here is super. I bang the
delete button so hard I awaken the Microsoft Word Office
Assistant.

¥ Chapter 8

"That is one classy-looking lady." This is the opinion of Bunny Modjeska, viewing Cherie Ghent. Cherie, complete in pink pantsuit and Mustang convertible, has just arrived at the museum with a *Chronicle* reporter in tow. The *Chronicle* reporter, a man, is young and sweet-looking, with floppy hair and pimples. Cherie is gorgeous and determined. Her short blond hair is newly layered.

She and the reporter are cruising the museum, but the purpose of their visit is for the reporter to interview Daddy about the sheriff. "I am going to splash that story all over this paper and the rest of the papers in the U.S.A.," Cherie says. "It'll be a national scandal. People making speeches in Congress." She is walking between the glass cases and viewing the displays as she talks. "Hey, I really like this weird guy with the falcon head, handsome, huh? And a dynamite great shape" (a statue of Horus, king of the gods).

"Darling," she picks up, addressing me, "boy, have I missed you. A helluva lot going on."

I tell her that I gathered as much, and try to sound sarcastic, but she's far beyond me. "Guess what? Me and your little friend Rob got together; hey, how's that? I guess you don't think much about him anymore; well, he turns out to be a really sweet guy, and you might not believe it because he seems kinda stiff at first and you're used to that, but after you know him some . . ."

Here, thank God, she's interrupted by the arrival of my father, the ostensible object of this visit, who has come down from upstairs. "Darling Crocodile, am I glad to see you. This here is Steve, he's a reporter for the *Chronicle*, isn't that great? And he is going to talk to you about what that sheriff did to you."

And Cherie, Daddy, the reporter, and I head for the elevator, where we are whisked up to Daddy's room for an interview.

The *Chronicle* reporter doesn't seem to mind that the interview consists almost entirely of comments from my dad, which are enthusiastic, gentle, and have nothing to do with the questions he's being asked, and interpolations by Cherie that answer the questions.

"How very lovely to see you, my dear," Daddy addresses Cherie. "I know you've been on a dig; how did it go?"

He asks the *Chronicle* reporter if he is one of his students. He tells both of them it's too late now to go into the Valley, but if they can arrive earlier tomorrow, preferably just before sunrise . . .

Meanwhile Cherie is describing the tight grip that the sheriff had on Daddy and the handcuffs that he twisted on him, and makes Daddy put his hands up and behind to illustrate the position this forced him into. My father is complaisant about this, although at one point he asks, "Are you thinking of the position the seeker adopted under the tree, my dear? He wouldn't have had to reach so high."

"Stevie here," Cherie says, "is a newer reporter, but he is way sharp. He is going to be one of their ace guys. Steve, I have a great eye for that stuff, I can always tell; you are going to do some world-beating news stories. Now you know that the sheriff did that attack not once, but twice. To this gentle, distinguished old gentleman? The second time, Croc, he accused you, didn't he; he practically accused you of being a murderer. Just because you were there?"

Surprisingly, Daddy cues in for this question. "I said a spell for the occasion. But I don't know if he understood that."

"Highly unlikely. He accused you of murder and forced you down into a chair."

The *Chronicle* reporter seems to have filled up several pages of notes. He looks a little puzzled, but also happy.

Cherie says that both of them will stay for lunch, but after that the reporter, who has his own car, must get back to the city. She, Cherie, will remain awhile longer. "I am fascinated by this place. The museum. It looks like something I've seen before."

I say, "Well, Egon tries for that," but she disagrees. "No, I mean *really* something I've seen before, not just in pictures. I know this architecture is partly fake Egyptian and partly fake Greek, but that's not what I'm talking about."

Cherie, of course, is brighter than I want her to be. She's not just a cute curvy blonde in a pink pantsuit. She's quick, intelligent, manipulative. Probably Rob is crazy about her.

I go down to lunch feeling mad at myself.

*   *   *

"How delightful," Egon says. "I am so glad you decided to stay for lunch. Edward's lawyer, you say? What a fine idea." He beams and passes a plate of curried mushrooms. This noon's menu is Vegetarian Near Eastern.

Egon says he would be honored to take Cherie on a tour of the premises. "Wonderful. To get your opinions. I can see you have excellent taste."

Scott wants to interview Cherie on how she got to be a lawyer. Rita asks about shoes and nail polish colors. "I mean, hey, that shade is terrific," she tells her.

Daddy says Cherie is going to take him on a walk down to the railroad track. "Absolutely," she says. "I adore trains."

Stevie the newsman volunteers that Cherie handled a case against Southern Pacific, and Bunny comments that, wow, that is big time. And Egon talks about the stolen artifacts and wonders if Cherie can help him with his insurance problems.

Scott starts a couple of lectures about intercoastal American transportation and about travel during the reign of Amenhotep III. He lets both of these lectures trail off, with a throwaway of, "Oh, hell, there I go again."

Lunch is lively. I'm the only unhappy person at the table.

And now I'm headed upstairs to the library, where I plan to hide with some of Egon's blues tapes and a low-caliber poetry book. But Cherie stops me.

She does this with an arm around my shoulders. "You got to come along, honey bun. Help me out."

"For company," she half explains, squeezing a shoulder

blade and glancing at Egon. I'm puzzled. No one would suspect Egon of being unsafe to be alone with.

I've had enough of Cherie for a day. For a week. But also, I want to find out what she's up to.

We start out, with Cherie holding my hand. She does this firmly; she's surprisingly strong and exerts some muscle.

First we do the museum, Egon leading and chanting, "Wonderful, just look," and Cherie asking questions, about the difference between Akhnaten's reign and his father's, about Amarna art, with its elongated figures and faces. Her questions are smart ones. She likes the Amarna better than the traditional. She's right.

I have a moment of rebellion. I am not going to end up liking this woman, I decide.

"Hey," she asks when we pause to admire a statue of the Apis bull, "who was the handsome cat at lunch? The one who couldn't finish his lectures?"

I explain that Scott was probably too impressed with her to be coherent, and she turns an amazed turquoise gaze at me. "Me? It was you, sweet cakes. You were the one he was watching."

I think I've misunderstood. "Huh?"

"He was tracking *you*. The whole time."

"No he wasn't."

"Carla, tune in. You don't like him? He thought you *did* like him."

"Nuts." I tug loose from her hand and listen for a while to Egon, who is telling us how the Apis bull is a creation god. Yet another fertility symbol.

*   *   *

At the end of this gallery, after we have passed my friend the cheerful plump cartonnage lady (and Cherie admires her appropriately, exclaiming, "Great mascara"), Cherie turns toward Egon. "Sir," she says, "is it all right to call you Egon?"

"Oh, my dear. Of course."

"Well, you know, I think I remember that Croc said—that is, my darling Ed—did he say something about a crypt? I mean, some special place that you built downstairs? I love the architecture here and I would really appreciate—not, of course, if it's private—but if I could maybe see it . . ."

"My dear," Egon interprets, "you want to see the crypt? Just for special people, of course. But yes, for you. A special person. Of course. And Carla, too."

Egon calls for Bunny Modjeska and asks for the electronic remote. "Keys and electronic signals," he says. "All these devices. Things get difficult.

"That's why I can't understand. The thefts—and they're getting worse—how can they be happening? Ms. Ghent, you couldn't help us a tiny bit, pressuring the insurance company?"

Cherie smiles noncommittally.

The crypt is approached from the underground passages. As we are entering them, Rita joins us, carrying a flashlight.

Egon must have had fun designing this system: it's full of mysterious convolutions. The result is half Alice's rabbit hole, half *Passageways of the Lost Kings*. Cherie loves the blue alcoves with the urns. "So damn suggestive. Egon, I do hope there's nobody in them?"

Rita announces loudly that there's nobody there; she checked.

Egon gestures ahead as his button-pushing makes a section of fake marble wall roll up into the ceiling. Lights come on, revealing a psychedelic mix of columns, murals, sculptured finials, solemn erect figures, and in the middle, the monumental construction of a double marble coffin on pilasters, one coffin container below, one above. There is an interesting smell of cold, incense-flavored stone.

I want to say, "Wow," but don't. Cherie says, "Egon, absolutely fab. My God."

I also want to ask who the second coffin is for, but Egon answers my question. "I, of course, will rest here later."

Should we say, "Much later?" I guess Egon assumes this.

There is a reverent silence. "And your grandmother is below," Cherie says.

Below? Cherie catches my eye and winks. Rita aims her flashlight at the roof, where a parade of people is led by the hawk-headed god.

"The whole thing was her idea," Egon says reverently.

Bunny has come in behind us. "That sure is gorgeous white marble," she breathes in appreciation.

"Genuine Parian," Egon says. "You see that there are Egyptian murals, but under them is the marble. Not exactly consistent, you know. I mean the Egyptian tombs have terra cotta walls, not marble ones. But the Egyptians loved marble. They used it any time they could. I felt it got the spirit . . ."

Our backs are turned and Egon is gesturing at the wall scene, a handsome depiction of the outfitting of the mummy, with the jackal-headed Anubis leaning over the recumbent figure.

But I have very good peripheral vision and I can see Rita behind us. She has begun poking at the carvings on the sarcophagi. She isn't using her flashlight, but she appears to be looking for something.

Beside me, Cherie's brisk little shoulders flex. I think she also has noticed Rita. And I think she decides, like me, to cover for her. The two of us fix on Egon and make a lot of noise about the fascinating mural and does he maybe remember the source, perhaps one of the texts of *The Book of the Dead*; of course he, Egon, will know.

To which Egon agrees enthusiastically, "Why yes, my dears, yes." And he's off into chapter and verse about which text, which page, his whole speech interpolated with comments of, "Wonderful!"

Meanwhile Rita, behind us, appears to be doing a Braille search of the carvings on the sarcophagus. Her nose is very close, her hair stands up very pointy. I'll interview her later.

There's an interlude while Egon bleats along about mummification and the cult of the god Anubis, and Cherie supplies admiring Southern comments. Bunny says, "Wow."

"Hey, Egon," Rita finally calls out from behind us, "way to go; that was super. God, have I forgotten a lot."

Cherie squeezes my hand. She announces, "Oh, I just feel so stupid."

One of Cherie's methods of dealing with the world is to act dumber than she is. This is disarming and makes people like her. Perhaps I should try it.

"Now," she says, "we'll go up into that bright upper world and suddenly we'll just be sitting under a date palm with a mango drink. Am I right, Rita?"

"Never happened to me." Rita sounds suspicious. But then she usually does.

"So." Cherie bustles an arm around Egon and an arm around me. She doesn't have extra arms to put around

Bunny and Rita, but she turns a multimegawatt smile their way. The five of us leave the crypt, the best of friends.

I half hate Cherie for stealing my boyfriend and half am attracted to her for being sharp and interesting. I'll bet she has a good theory about what Rita was up to.

And I wish I didn't have to ask her about her theory. When this is all over, I'll never speak to her again.

"Sweetcakes," Cherie addresses me at the door of the museum, "we got to talk; walk out to my car with me."

But right away we pick up an admiring following of both Egon and Bunny.

"Call you later, darlin'." Cherie has one foot inside the Mustang; she leans forward to kiss me on both cheeks.

I hope she wants to talk about what she saw in the crypt. If she's planning a heart-to-heart on Rob, I'm not interested.

☥ Chapter 9

"Well hel-lo. And how are we this A.M.?"

Scott has fallen into step with me beside the wisteria bush, which is as far as I've gotten on a tour of the museum garden. The sun is bright; something with a chirpy call is sounding off in the tall skinny bushes beside the walk. Egon has tried to decorate his landscape with a few plants that look Egyptian—as does the statuary positioned in and among these bushes, all stiff-standing gods and monsters. "Not very good, I'm afraid," my father has judged them.

"*We* are okay," I tell Scott. "And how are you?"

"Oh, hell." He reaches for a wisteria leaf. "Caught again. Sententious, pretentious, yes? Don't say yes."

I squint at him. He has posed himself against the bright sunlight, but even without that electric surround, he gives off a kind of energy. A stocky man, vivid, anxious, a little pugnacious.

Was Cherie right, was he really staring at me all during lunch? He certainly is doing it now.

I keep on walking and he does, too.

"Are you settling in all right? No nightmares, sudden alarms? No figures glimpsed around shadowy corners?"

"I'm doing okay."

"And your dad? . . . Listen, I wanted to tell you . . ." There's a sizable pause, while we walk and crunch gravel.

Maybe I should say, "Proceed, proceed." People threaten to tell me things a lot lately.

"I'm sorry if it seemed I was ignoring your dad. Sure, I knew him. Knew him well. We were all together, you know, good friends, one of those intense adult summer-camp kind of deals. That time was a good time, and now it's hard to re-member. And it was extra hard, seeing your dad . . . I just didn't know how to take it."

I turn to look at Scott. Now he seems embarrassed. I shouldn't ask myself if he really feels all this, or if he half believes and half embellishes.

I say, "A lot of people don't know how to deal with Daddy's illness."

"Yeah. Well, that's no excuse." Scuff, scuff. He does the bashful penitent act well.

We scrape gravel, moving forward for a while. Finally, I ask the question about the past that I've been poking at lately. "Thebes. That's where you were all together, isn't it?"

"Thebes? Yeah, sure."

"When was that?"

"Like, five years ago? Yeah, four, five. But listen, enough of that, too much harking back to the past. You owe me a drink."

"No, I don't."

"Okay. You owe me going out with me to get a drink. You pretty much promised."

I didn't pretty much anything, Scott, I think, but I guess I'm flattered. I know I'm flattered. I don't have time now to stop and analyze how much of that is because I'm mad at Rob and jealous of Cherie and how much is because he is, I guess, attractive. Not my type, of course. Neither was my Habitat friend.

"Tonight," Scott suggests.

"Nope."

"Tomorrow night?"

"Okay."

What in hell is the matter with me?

Let's face it, it will be interesting to go to the Best Western, where Cherie is staying and, presumably, where Rob hangs out now—it will be interesting to go there and see Cherie and Rob together. Or interesting to have Rob see me and Scott together. Really, really interesting.

"Eight o'clock?" Scott suggests, and I agree, "Absolutely. Eight o'clock."

We walk back to the Museum Residents' building with Scott talking about how the sheriff mistreated my father. "I was there. I saw it. You need somebody to testify? I'm your guy."

He'd be a good witness, eager, alive, verbal. A genuine Hartdale Grant prospect. I guess he's good at a lot of things.

I am standing on the steps of the Residents' hall, brooding about Scott and our prospective evening at the Best Western, when the building's double cedar doors pop open with a suitably tomblike squawk and Rita bursts forth.

She is all gotten up in a denim pantsuit with spangles and a denim bow in her hair. She wears her silver sandals and no socks and black toenail polish. It's a look I would never attempt, but on her it does okay. "Well, hey," she says. And, "Hi." She grabs me by the arm.

Lately I am the Object. People keep zeroing in on me and grabbing.

"Rita, hi." *Yes, I want to talk to you*, I think. "Come for a walk."

"Right on. Like, exactly. I got this bottle. See?" She has one of those slouchy over-the-shoulder bags; a bottle neck sticks out of it. "I'm sorta drunk, y'know? No cigs; I'm giving them up, right? So, a lady has to do something."

A good moment, I think. Rita is the impulsive type. We fall into step on the graveled walk, walking in unison, my Teva sandals contrasting with her silver ones. "Listen, Rita, what were you doing yesterday in the crypt?"

"Yesterday? In the crypt?" Her voice is loaded with total incomprehension.

"We saw you inspecting. Feeling around at the sculpture. We covered for you."

"Covered? Wow, how sweet! But like, I wasn't doing anything. I mean, I was just looking, y'know?" She waits. I feel her watching me. "I mean, totally nothing. I was counting Egon's mistakes. That sculpture is so off. He can never get it straight. He doesn't understand about Egyptian architecture, nothing, no way. He gets it mixed up with Roman and Renaissance."

Rita, come on. I know what I know. I'm bored with people not telling me things. "I was watching you. I could see what you were doing. You were looking for something; it was pretty clear."

"Clear?" Rita stops to examine her wine bottle as if an answer hides inside. "You think I had an ulterior motive? For sort of, in passing, looking at a tomb carving?"

"It wasn't sort of in passing. You were heavy-duty interested."

Rita says, "Duh," and takes a swig of her wine. "I'm an archaeologist, remember? Of course I was interested. That stuff is my business. It's what I do."

"And in this case you don't want to talk about it."

"Who said so? We're talking now."

And we're walking. Slowly down the hill. Merrily, merrily. "I'm getting just a particle frustrated lately," I say. "There's a whole list of things people won't talk about. That you especially won't talk about, even though you cozy up to me and make like you're my new best friend.

"First, there was Marcus Broussard you wouldn't talk about, and then that spring in Thebes thing, and now this."

Rita says, "Hey, I am your friend; really I am." She puts intensity into her assertion. She cares, the way people do who've been through a bad spell and are coming out of it. It's underhanded of me to attack her now. You've heard about baby ducks and how when they're first hatched they get imprinted by the first moving object that comes by and then they follow that object? Well, Rita got imprinted by me. When she was coming out of her depression, I was the moving object that came by.

"I am so your best friend," she protests. "You want me to tell you about something? Okay, I will. Thebes, I'll talk about Thebes, then, okay. Not that there's anything much to tell."

Well, I guess so, if that's the only subject you can manage this morning. "Okay."

Rita says oratorically, "Thebes." Off in the middle distance is something that makes her giggle. "Oh, hell."

We continue walking, with her occasionally extending the bottle in my direction. It's a white wine, not too sweet.

"It was a real wild scene," she says contemplatively. "Hard to boil down. Lots of sex."

She pauses. I spur her on. "Yeah. Right."

"Sex and archaeology. Did you know they go together? Like, dig, dig, and then, sex, sex?

"Me and Scott," she picks up. "Me and Marcus. Everybody and everybody. A lot of people named Fatima and Aisha and Naomi.

"Oh, yes," she answers my slightly surprised shoulder motion. "Too much testosterone. Too many vitamins, too much archaeology. Gets into your privates. Marcus and me, Marcus and . . ." Rita screws her face up. She looks as if she has bitten into something sour. "Marcus and all the Fatimas."

"And Scott?"

"Sure. Scott and a Fatima or two."

"Rita, that sounds racist."

Rita is a little drunk.

"It is. They were. I am, when I think back at it. Oh, shit."

"And Danielle," I supply. "Marcus and Danielle."

"Where'd we get her?"

"She's around. Everybody sort of walks around her."

Rita turns a shoulder. "Walks around? Well, not exactly. You ran, one direction or the other. But yeah, she kept popping up.

"A bitch," Rita adds.

"What kind of bitch?"

"The man-stealing kind."

Egon has supplied a red marble bench at a turn in the path. We stop to sit on it.

I press for brighter lights and wilder details. About Danielle—where'd she come from? But Rita just shrugs. "Who knows? That was a hairy time. Like I said, bed, bed, bed. And dope. Not just pot, real stuff. Hard stuff.

"Yeah," she says, appraising my expression of discomfort, "not good."

"Why doesn't anybody want to talk about her?"

"*I* especially don't want to talk about her. She stole my guy."

She holds the bottle up and squints at the light it catches. "She stole both my guys. First she stole Marcus and then she stole Scott. Or the other way around. First she was Scott's and . . . well, nuts."

"First she was Scott's," I interpret, "and then she left Scott and took up with Marcus. And then she went back to Scott again."

"Sort of. I hated her."

"Was she gorgeous?"

"Well, I guess. If you like the type. Something for every-body. Oh, *shit*."

"So why won't anybody talk about her?"

Rita shrugs elaborately.

"Where was Egon in all this?"

"Dithering around. Waving his hands. I think Egon is asexual. One of the few cases. I think he really is."

Now I have to ask it. "And my dad?"

Rita sort of laughs. "Oh, your dad. He knew some of it; I couldn't tell how much. He'd start quoting from the ancient Egyptians when things got hairy."

The ancient Egyptians thought sex was fine. But they also believed in marriage. They were sensible and nice. Even if a little obsessed with the afterlife.

"This dig lasted how long?"

"Two and a half months. We found a lot. Lots of stuff in my area, lots of textile scraps, pictures of whatever; I did notebooks and notebooks full. That spring is the only reason I have a job now. See, they had this tomb that was explored, like thirty years ago. And then, much later on, they found this extra passage, under a lot of rock and rubble. And when it was cleaned up, there was a long tunnel and a room that was bigger than all the rest of it. We were the third team there. They're probably still doing it, still cataloguing and sifting and brushing. Well, you know."

"And Scott did okay."

"Studly did wonderful. That was one reason the testosterone got so dense. His field is supposed to be history, so he's a dynamite whiz on hieroglyphs and he nearly had a seizure over some of the stuff he found; he was taking impressions and translating and talking and making casts and jumping up and down. And falling in love with anything that moved."

Rita clinks her teeth against her glass and appears to brood. "Y'know, he's not too irresistible usually, but when he was fired up like that . . . Well. It was like getting the battery back into the rabbit."

"And Danielle thought so, too."

"She sure did. At first. Y'know she was his girlfriend from back in college."

"I heard."

"And then they started up again in Thebes. And then they had some really great fights. But not about sex. At least, I don't think. They fought about his hieroglyphs."

My surprise shows in my voice. "Really?"

"She was a pretty good Egyptologist. Oh, damn it, she was that kind. She could do anything."

Rita doesn't know exactly what it was about the hieroglyphs that they disagreed on. "But he was blathering about how they changed history."

"And she didn't think so?"

"Well, she yelled at him plenty."

The wine is gone. I have had about a third of it, which is an awful lot for eleven-thirty in the morning. I suggest a walk in the garden. "I saw a statue of Hatshepshut down there. And if you keep on going, there's the ocean. And farther south some railroad."

"I like the ocean," Rita says.

At the Hatshepshut, which has been prettied up some, Rita snorts, "Y'know, I think it's Egon's fake pharaohs that make me hate money."

I'm sufficiently drunk to skip the *oh, so you hate money* response and go on to suggest that maybe inherited money corrupts and she says no, institutional money corrupts; she knows this from working in universities. "First they start out with, they think, principles. This money is going to cure AIDS, solve poverty, educate kids, and then in three years they're dithering around with godawful fake art or fake cures or ghastly publicity. Look at Studly and his world-shaking discoveries."

Something in her voice makes me say, "You've done okay, Rita. How old are you?"

"Thirty-nine."

Only thirteen years older than me. "You've done great."

"Scott's a year older and look at him."

"Quit thinking like that. Think about you." I don't ask how she's feeling lately with her depression. She seems to be managing okay.

Rita says, and maybe it's a non sequitur, "I think in a way he really loved that bitch. I mean, like, it was easy to be fascinated by her, so I'm not sure."

We stare down at the beach and watch the waves. "It does something to you, y'know?" she says. "That rhythm. It replicates the human heartbeat."

"What happened to Danielle?" I ask after a while of listening to the waves thump. "Do you know where she is now?"

Rita shrugs. "I heard she was at the Luxor Museum. She's the kind who always lands on her feet."

⌐ Chapter 10

It's evening, and I am out in front of the residence, washed and scrubbed for my outing with Scott.

His car is a red convertible. Of course, it's a rental, since his home now is at Yale, in New Haven, Connecticut. "Since last September," he says as he helps me into the BMW. "A weird place to live—crowded, dangerous, slummy, elitist. And boy, was I excited to get there."

"Well, Yale," I agree. "Pretty okay."

"In my wildest. The answer to every farm boy's dream."

"You're not a farm boy."

"Oh, but I am."

We have already turned onto Highway One and are zipping along with the ocean off to our left, below some cliffs. "I grew up milking cows in Pennsylvania."

I don't pursue this. Scott's aura makes me want to argue and question. I don't really have any reason to assume, as I'm doing, that the farm he means is the one with the eighteenth-century stone house and barn and fifty-five acres of graded woodland inherited from dear old Grandpa who got it from his dear old Revolutionary-hero ancestor.

"Why were you so mean to Rita?" I ask.

"Yeah. Sorry about that."

"Well, why?" Which is none of my business.

"Reet and I go way back."

"I guess. That's not really an excuse."

He seems to brood for a minute, capably managing oceanside highway curves. He drives too fast, as you'd expect. Finally he says, "People that know each other well . . ." And he warms up into a lecture about familiarity dulling the edge of perception and forgetting about the sensibilities of someone you know well and so on. It's not exactly blather since he does some quoting of experts and a paragraph or so of dipping into psychology texts. After which, at the end of a sharp, rock-enclosed hairpin, he expels a loud breath. "Hey. Another lecture. I do that too much, don't I?"

I mutter uh-huh and he says, "Anyway, Reet was mean to me sometimes, too."

I can believe that, all right.

I decide he's been pretty good so far about turning the other cheek on my Rita-bashing accusations. A red-and-white highway placard tells us we've almost arrived at Conestoga. I open up my other subject—the Thebes one. "And you were a cluster—a set. Everybody that's around now. Marcus Broussard, too. That's when he really got interested in Egyptian archaeology."

"Marcus was interested in everything. He was a wild man. Everything that came along. Wanted to be it and do it. Interesting as hell. I hated his guts.

"But," he adds, pulling into the Best Western's parking lot, "I didn't kill him. If anybody did. Do we know yet?"

"He's dead, all right."

"Okay, but did somebody make him be dead? Or just the old heart again?"

"Earlier, you said internal bleeding."

"Did I? Boy, what presumption." He holds out his arm for me to emerge from the Beemer, which hugs the ground and is hard to get out of.

The Welcome Bar at the Conestoga Best Western has a Western theme. Conestoga is a hamlet of, the sign says, 412 people, and the Best Western Bar is the only entertainment for thirty miles in all directions.

A cowboy boot outlined in red neon overhangs the bar; below it is a red neon message, HELLO PARDNER. Boot-shaped glass doohickies to hold peanuts are lined up along the bar counter. The rest of the scene is too dark and too red for other thematic touches to show, but I know they're there. I waste a minute being inwardly snide about the way this Texas motif has been mercilessly dumped on an innocent California landscape.

Really, I'm feeling snide about arriving here with Scott, who is acting okay. But as if he's discreetly triumphant. "I told myself this would work out."

"What would work out?" I ask.

"Our date." He stands away from me. I've just handed my coat to a hatcheck person. "*Great* dress."

It's a dark blue sheath that I inherited from my Habitat roommate, who was a South Carolina pork heiress. They grow a lot of pigs in the South.

I debated wearing this outfit tonight; it's far too dressy for the Best Western. I guess I wanted to impress Scott.

"You know you look sort of Egyptian?" he asks.

"Right. Angular, one-eyed, and all profile."

He ignores this. "There's a gawky grace they get sometimes in those drawings. The ones of dancers. Long arms and long legs."

I could add a few witty remarks here about backbends and no clothes, but I don't. The room is very noisy and dark, and as we hover at the door, they dim the lights to even darker. Scott, who has been leaning against the hatcheck stand, takes my arm; we follow a sequined person wearing a cowboy hat toward a table. I stare up at Scott, wondering if the compliment really is a compliment, and decide that it is. Those dancing houris are graceful. If just a tad uncoordinated-looking.

"What'll it be?" Scott shouts over the noise, nudging my chair toward a postage-stamp-sized table.

My usual drink is red wine, but I've decided to be ridiculous tonight. I'll try Rita's recipe from the other night. "Vodka, brandy chaser."

He thinks he hasn't heard and brings his head closer. "Say what?"

I repeat my order and we do an act where he says, "You jest," and calls me "Lady Blues," and I say that no, I do not jest, all of this delivered in minishouts, because a small orchestra is warming up, in honor of which the lights are muffled some more to the point where I can barely see my fingernails.

He tries again. I think he says, "You can't be serious."

"No, that's it." There's a pause while he asks something else, and I realize I'm supposed to be specific. "Smirnoff and cherry brandy. Any brand."

He shouts, "Oh, cut it out," and I shout, "No, I mean it," and he shouts, "Shit," and gives the order.

We're off to a good start. Cherry brandy is one of the most awful drinks there is. I'll have to carry it away into the restroom, or something.

That about finishes it for the conversation, at least for the time being, because the band has hotted up and has started playing, in dirgelike tempo, something that I think is "Sentimental Journey." And the lights, in tribute to the music, have been turned down to nada. It's impossible to talk and almost impossible to see each other, should anybody want to communicate in sign language.

Our drinks arrive. The waitress must have echolocation, to get around in this shrouded room. I taste my brandy. Oh, God. Why am I doing any of this?

When Scott touches my wrist and gestures in the direction of the dance floor, I agree right away.

The band is still dragging itself through "Sentimental Journey." Slow and with lots of beat.

Scott's hand around mine feels pretty sure of itself. He leads us successfully on a pathway through tables and out into an apparently free space where we start to move.

He's a good dancer, with a sturdy, energized body. He finds the right place in my back, and doesn't hold me too hard. It's been a long time since I danced like this, face-to-face, fifties style. I'm able to do all the stuff, breaking and coming back, at first in pitch dark. That's fun, too. Finding a skill you didn't know you had is always ego-boosting. Then I guess somebody in the really bad orchestra notices us, or maybe it's the lights person; anyway, suddenly we have a spotlight on us and we're doing an exhibition.

The orchestra saws its way out of "Sentimental Journey"

and starts on "I Love Paris." Scott and Carla do three minutes of Fred Astaire and Ginger Rogers. The house lights
come on; there's a lot of applause. "Wow," I say.

We're leaving the floor, with me trying to look modest.
"Somebody's waving," Scott says.

I say, "Oh, yeah. Of course."

Of course, I think. Cherie, on cue. Cherie and Rob. I'm
partly irked and possessive: Cherie. In this bar. With Rob.
How dare they? And partly triumphant. Sure, I expected
this. And how do I appear for the occasion? Triumphant.
Dancing with a handsome man. Getting applauded for my
skill. How great is that? The goddess who arranges such
things did right by me; I send up a thank-you to her.

Except that Scott intervenes, deflating my balloon.
"Well, guess what? It's Rita."

"Rita?" I bleat, as if I had never heard of such a person.

"And she's with . . ." I brace myself, prepared to hear
that Rita is with Rob. I'm still aimed in that direction. And
you never know.

"She's with your dad."

Surprise of surprises. Yes, there they are, as the lights
continue to get higher, a couple at a table near the door,
Rita with something glittery in her spiky dark hair, my dad
in what I think is his best tweed jacket. Rita is waving with
both hands. Now she stands up. My father just sits, looking
pleased.

And Cherie and Rob aren't here at all. Not present, when
I was expecting them. I find that I'm feeling disappointed.

Now Rita is bearing down on us, arms outspread. "Hey,
fellow art lovers. Scott, old stud." She moves forward into a
kiss, both cheeks for me, one cheek for Scott, while he mutters, "Oh, shit."

"We have got to sit together," Rita says. "Your dad is so excited." My father is waving now. "We'll bring all our junk over. Oh, this is going to be great. It'll be such fun."

"Hey, Reet," Scott says, "you look nice." Which surprises me. Scott hasn't been heavily into complimenting Rita, who does look nice. She sparkles, Rita-style, with a sequin bird, wings outspread, across the front of her white dress. Like my outfit, this is too formal for our setting, but it looks great on her, with her tan arms swinging free and wild black hair standing up above.

Rita and I will go to the ladies' room. "Hey, a lady-act, right?" She puts a matey arm around my shoulder. "I read somewhere that's what ladies do when they want to talk about the men.

"I can talk about your dad just fine," she expands, pushing me ahead of her into the corridor. "He is my best guy and I don't care if he remembers anything or not. And I'm sorry I was mean to him. That was the nuttiness speaking. Scott, now . . ."

Rita is behind me, with a finger in my back. Now she drops farther back, which means she has to yell, since the band is hotting up again, preparing to assault another Golden Oldie. They signal this with a couple of percussion booms and some saxophone squeals. The lights begin fading.

"This is crazy, but confession's good for the soul, right?" Rita shouts into my shoulder blades. "I mean, I'm here because I got suspicious of that Scott. Maybe about his intentions with you, babe. And then when your dad wanted to come along . . . Well, that was sweet, right? So here we both are. And oh, hey, Carla, guess what . . ."

I think it is after "guess what" that it happens. But maybe not. Maybe she says another couple more words and I just don't remember. It's possible that what happened then is partly wiped out by what comes now.

A noise. Not terribly loud. From someplace behind us. Pretty much covered up by the band's boops and squawks, but not entirely, if you have good hearing, which I do.

Why I think that noise is meant for us, I'm not sure. Maybe I'm just editing backward. Maybe all I remember is Rita smiling back at me while I looked at her over my shoulder, seeing her, and part of the room beyond, and Scott waiting for us, and Rita saying, "Carla, guess what," and then this noise, which is a sharp one—no, two sharp noises—from someplace behind. And Rita looking kind of surprised. Or apologetic. I think she moves her hand around toward her breast, but maybe not.

I recognize the noise before I understand anything else. That noise is the smothered pop that a gun with a silencer makes, being fired. I heard gunfire, every kind, plenty in Egypt and later in other places. The sounds here are louder than they would normally be—that's the enclosed space; there are some echoes; they're followed by the beginnings of a burned smell and maybe by a savor of smoke. One gunshot, then perhaps another gunshot.

Rita turns, arms out, and looks at me pleasantly, her remark stuck somewhere behind her teeth. She makes an embarrassed gesture as if to say, "Hey, it's not my fault." She opens her mouth; a waterfall of blood jumps out and cascades down her sequined front. She pitches forward. She's plump, and she makes a noise as she falls.

I make a noise, too. I'm screaming. I think I'm screaming incoherently, but Scott later tells me that I was yelling for him. What did I say? Something like "Scott, come, Scott, come," he thinks.

Whatever I said, it brings people, a lot of them. I'm aware of them as shapes jostling and crowding in; by that time, I'm kneeling beside Rita. "You were trying to give her mouth-to-mouth," Scott says.

I don't remember that, but I must have been doing mouth-to-mouth because later I have to wash the blood off my face as well as off my hands and my knees.

Now I'm on the floor on my knees and holding on to someone who is standing. This person is saying, "Okay, okay." He says, "Carla, listen, let go of me for a minute, I have to try something here." He bends over Rita, who is stretched out, half on her side, her face resting in a big dark patch.

I look at the person who says this and he turns out to be Scott. There are a lot of other people here, too. The lights come on, very bright, and I say, "She's hurt."

He doesn't pay attention. He's bent over Rita. I think he's saying, "Reet, honey." And "Baby, no."

When I focus on him again, he's on his knees, doing something.

"She's hurt," I say.

He's saying stuff that doesn't make sense, like, "Rita, don't," and, "You can. Try. Try really hard."

"She needs a *doctor*," I say.

He starts to straighten up. "Oh, Christ." He has to sit down again. "God."

After a minute he adds, "A doctor is coming.

"Now try to move over. Sit with your back against the wall."

I move over, sliding along. I notice the pattern on the rug, which is orange and tan diamonds. When I am lined up with my back against the wall, I see that Scott is sitting beside me. He has his knees up and his face on his knees.

"Oh, yes, that would feel better," I say about Scott's posture. I think he's crying, but I don't want to cry. I raise my knees and put my head on them.

More people (I see them as legs) have pushed in, and I remember that there's something I have to do. I pull at Scott. "My father. I'm worried about my father."

I think he says, "Okay, okay."

"And she needs a doctor." I wonder if I've said this before. Scott says, "Yeah."

"Soon?" I ask, and Scott says, I think, "Yeah."

The racket around us increases. Someone tries to help me onto my feet, but I resist.

"She's gone," Scott, beside me, says.

This doesn't make sense. I think about it for a minute. Then I hear myself tell him he can't be sure and he says, "Oh, yes, I can. She's gone."

I stare down at my knees and at my right hand, with the blood still running down it.

I can only sort of see. But I think about my father and lift my head and squint, and yes, there, off at a table in a corner, is my dad. He has a glass.

I'm halfway up onto my feet. What should I do? Get him, bring him along into this scene of chaos? Go sit with him? Somehow that doesn't seem right. Shouldn't I be here? I can't leave Rita; she needs me.

She has a set of small holes in her back. But she must have a very big hole in her front, because she has gushed blood all down her front and into the orange-and-tan carpet. An awful lot of blood.

Now I am coming out of it. I can hear what some people

who have just arrived are saying to each other. These people have black shoes and dark blue pants and have laid a canvas stretcher on the floor. They say things like, "Put a mask on her," and "Easy now," and "May not matter, that mask." One of them says to the other, "Hey, reach in my back pocket, will you? I got a clean handkerchief there." Now Scott is talking to somebody; he has his face raised and is talking up; he says, "Try anything. Everything." And the person answers, "Sure, guy, sure."

I scramble to my feet, holding on to the wall for support.

My father appears by my side. He has settled the question of who goes where by doing the moving around himself. He's holding his glass. He has managed, in his Edward Day way, to squeeze through the mob of people.

"Come with me," he says.

"Can I?" I have the feeling that I'm supposed to stay right here.

He doesn't bother to answer, but grabs me by the elbow and leads me out of the corridor, and then slowly, between tables. There is a chair.

"Well, my dear." He pats my shoulder. "Are you scared?" He leans and tries to put his arms around me. "Darling, it's going to be all right."

After a few minutes he talks, in an elliptical way, about his coming here. "She was very worried, you know? She is a lady who worries a lot. And I wanted to come. It was nice of her to include me. I am so sorry this happened to her."

"Daddy, did you see anybody? Somebody trying to shoot her? Did she say anything about somebody . . ." I let this question sag off. What am I trying to ask? Did Rita say anything like, "Someone is going to shoot me tonight"?

"Would you like a taste of my drink, dear?" He is having

white wine. At first I say no, and then change my mind. The gulp of wine is a help. I can feel it straightening the clogged snarls in my brain.

I sip and watch the corridor, where I can see Scott. He staggers to his feet, leaning against the wall. Now he is talking to one of the blue-outfitted guys, heading toward the fire door with the litter. There's a figure on the litter; I guess that's Rita. It's hard to be sure, there's a white sheet over most of her.

The sheriff arrives. He comes in through the side door and pauses there; maybe he's trying for an overview. The Best Western management has been attempting to keep people in place, but with zero success. "Sorry, I gotta go." "Baby at home." The room is now a sea of angled tables, dirty glasses, dropped table napkins.

We at our table have been good and have stayed put; we turn our faces toward the sheriff. He squints at us. He's holding an armful of books; he fixes on my father. "Dr. Alzheimered Day, right here, king of the action again."

The books are bound in red leather and look legal. "You're not supposed to leave this room," the sheriff says in an uncertain voice.

Scott has his head in his arms. I am clutching my wine in one hand and the table edge in the other. My father seems almost okay. He looks up at the sheriff and suggests cautiously, "I think you're supposed to ask us where we were."

"Goddamn it to hell, you interfering old buzzard." This man is scared. I remember Cherie's analysis: he doesn't know what to do.

I have an idiot recollection of the schoolgirl fantasy about the exam when you haven't read the book.

"She's dead," the sheriff says loudly.

Nobody answers.

"Everybody in your group gets a skin test. For firing a gun."

I start to say, "She was shot in the back," and then don't say it. I'm the only one of us who wasn't behind Rita. I was the one in front; everybody else was back here with a good chance for a shot. A dark room. Dark corners. A lighted corridor with Rita outlined in it.

I'm grateful to the med crew for not bundling her into a black plastic bag.

And so we move shakily along Sheriff Munro's part of the evening. I think he wants to open the law books and look things up, but he doesn't. He squints at us sideways. He delivers instructions in a scratchy voice. He contradicts himself. "We'll find a room and question you now. No, later." The deputies sidle up and say, "Hey, boss." He tells them to shut up.

We do not get the skin test for firing a gun. There are some mutters with the deputies about, "Tomorrow? For God's sweet sake." I'm guessing that this means that the skin-test equipment isn't available to Del Oro County until tomorrow; Sheriff Munro klunks one of the books down and says, "What a jerkwater place." He tells us to go away. No, don't go away. Yes, leave. He promises to be in touch.

Sheriff Munro has made my father worried. He stares after him with his lost Edward Day look. "That man was in Thebes. I haven't been in Thebes for years, have I? You would remember."

"That's the sheriff, Daddy. He wasn't in Thebes."

"Yes, yes. But I haven't been in Thebes for a long time, have I?

"Thebes is the center of the remaking," he adds. "*I will go down into Thebes and be made whole.*

"But a place of death, perhaps," he adds. "Oh, dear."

Much later that night, back at Egypt Regained, I am still not alone.

First I have had to drive us home. Pretty much against my will. In Scott's little low-slung rental.

I'm an all-right driver, but I'm not anxious for this duty. And at first Scott assures me, "Sure I can do it. Of course I can." After which he climbs into the driver's seat and can't turn the key. He tries twice. His hand is shaking too hard to get the key in the slot. He doesn't even object too much when I take over.

On the trip home my father talks about Egyptian poetry and Scott tries to answer. "*I shall cross over to the mansion of him who finds faces,*" Daddy says. And Scott responds, "Yeah. Right. Good." Just before we get to the museum Scott says, "*You have your blood*; that's a quote." He throws the remark into the night, where it warbles idiotically and hangs like an accusation.

It's a bright night, with a lot of the brilliant overhanging stars we get when we're fog-free.

Upstairs in the residence my dad says, "Well, I'll go to bed.

"Yes, I'll be all right." He looks surprised at my question. "Of course. I am sorry about that young woman. I knew her, yes, of course. A very smart young woman. I am sorry she was hurt. A problem." He stops, and for a moment seems to understand something. He looks at me, a contortion crosses his face. "Oh, *dear*.

"But now I will go to bed. Good night, Carla."

And he kisses me on the cheek and tells Scott, "That is a bad worry. But it will get better. You realize that?"

He pads off down the corridor to his room.

Scott and I look at each other.

He looks really terrible. He stares at me unfocusedly, his face streaked with blood, his brown hair hanging, mouth lopsided. He keeps trying to pull at his chin with an unsteady hand.

"Listen," I say. "Vodka. I've got a big bottle. And coffee and a couple of kinds of tea. And I think Egon has some bourbon in the library cabinet."

Scott says, "Vodka," and agrees that he should go wash his face. "You, too." He tries for a smile.

Seated in a library armchair, Scott chews on his vodka and says, for the third time that night, "God. Why does everything always turn out shitty?"

"Does it?"

"Anything I touch."

"Anything?"

"Everything . . ." He holds the glass up and stares into it. "Seems like I got the world by the balls, right? Well, wrong. Oh, God." He has to put his glass down and crumples as if he has a cramp.

I think I have been really good so far. I haven't told Scott that I didn't think he cared that much, that I thought he really didn't like Rita. I haven't said I'm surprised that he is hit so hard. But I am surprised.

Surprised and touched. Sort of. I've discovered that Scott can be really upset by someone else's disaster. Scratch it that part of his problem is that he thinks it's a disaster for him. Also.

I'm surprised at that, too.

He refills his vodka glass and says, "That poor, silly, ditzy kid."

I nod.

"No bad in her," he says. "Well, not much. Not a hell of a lot." A long pause and more vodka. "Oh, shit."

"You were good friends?"

"In a way. Kind of." Another pause and he reaches for the bottle. "Do you mind if I get drunk?"

"Be my guest."

"And finish off your bottle?"

"Go ahead."

"It's not going to help me much."

"She didn't have any sense," he volunteers, after a pause. "Not a scrap. Good archaeologist, real perceptive about relics, good eye for artifacts. But for human relationships?

"She was crazy, too," he adds after a minute. "Have I said that?"

"Uh-huh."

"Everything I do turns shitty. I've said that, too?"

I could tell him, "Why is it everything *you* do, Scott," but instead I say, "Listen, bro," *bro* being something I used to call Rob when I was feeling matey, "what you need now is bed, how does that sound?"

"Not too bad . . . Reet was good at that act. Being nice when you were down . . . Oh, my *God*.

"We knew each other really well," he adds, unnecessarily.

Maybe in my wilder fantasies I've imagined Scott spending the night in my room. Probably I have. This is an attractive guy, with a contagious animal energy. But I didn't picture anything like this, with him climbing unsteadily onto one of the twin beds and pulling the coverlet up over his clothed body, shoes and all, and saying, "You don't mind, do you Carla? I'm out of it."

If he were a woman, he'd tell me, "Listen, I just can't face being alone tonight." But he's not a woman.

Eventually I climb into the other bed. I'm not as drunk as Scott and apparently not as miserable; I take off my shoes and squeeze into some pajamas.

🐦 ,Chapter 11

Morning, that is, 10 A.M., finds me and Scott still in our respective beds and my father, in the guise of the Morning Greeter, balancing a tray containing bagels and coffee.

"Oh, dear," he says.

He's interested to find Scott here. "I know this young man. A good friend. It will come to me. That lady sent these."

Is the lady Bunny?

"She has a leather belt." Yes, Bunny.

We eat our breakfast off a teetery table. Daddy bounces on the bed and offers questions.

"Why is it raining outside?" He thought the rainy season was over.

"Why has the room containing my coffin lid been locked?" He needs to go see his coffin lid.

"Are you sick, Carla?" He certainly hopes not. There is a lot of illness going around. He was discussing this with the man downstairs. A man who was asking questions. This is a man he does not much like.

Suggestion and prying elicit some facts. This man is not Egon. He is not one of the chauffeurs, all of whom are named Haroun. Yes, he does wear a uniform. Perhaps he has a star on his pocket. Perhaps he wears a tan cotton suit. And a dark brown belt.

He is, in fact, Sheriff Munro.

I say, "Oh, Jesus," at Scott.

Daddy volunteers further info about his chat with the man. There was a thought-provoking discussion. (Was he mean? You asked that question some time ago, Carla. Well, was he cross? Not precisely. There is a word, perhaps you don't know it, *peremptory*. We discussed Nebutol.) Scott and I eye each other, questioning. Is he really saying he talked to the sheriff about Nebutol?

We're interrupted by a set of knockings at the door, rat-tat-tat, machine-gun fashion, followed immediately by the entry of himself, the sheriff. He doesn't say howdy-do or please; he strides in, like a Boy Scout on parade, face fixed in what he possibly thinks is an expression of command.

"So. Late risers. And Dr. Edward Day, the forgetful genius. Dr. Day, I know all about you. I am on to you. The Alzheimered Dr. Day cannot remember his own name, ha-ha; inventor of the coffin lid cannot answer any questions at all."

Scott and I look at each other.

The sheriff is providing the symptoms of someone caught in a nervous breakdown. He tries to walk in big strides. He tries to lower his voice. He laughs inappropriately.

"Dr. Alzheimer," he starts out. Daddy doesn't respond, so it gets amended to "Dr. Day."

"Now"—fixing him with an unsteady eye—"tell me all about Nebutol."

My father looks sad. "Would you like a cinnamon-raisin bagel? I think it's the last one."

The sheriff bleats, "Dr. Day. Nebutol."

Scott has been watching the exchange. "What are you trying to get him to say?"

"You stay out of this. Go back to playing musical beds with your lady friend."

"Listen, you officious creep, I won't stay out of it." Scott looks more like himself today. The bags under the eyes and sag in the shoulders could almost be a normal hangover.

I interject something weaker, some reproach like, "You are browbeating an old, disabled citizen." It's about now that I realize that Scott and I present an unusual picture, I in my PJs and he fully clothed.

Scott says, "I hear Miss Ghent has you up on a complaint. Browbeating. Undue pressure. Deliberate harm and pain."

At which point the sheriff implodes. Yes, this man teeters constantly on the edge of a Big One.

"Fucking A, all of you are gonna be in trouble. Every single one of you . . ." He stops here. He doesn't finish his sentence. "Your little friend was careless." He backtracks. "She was a real weird girl and she got herself caught in . . ." He doesn't finish this sentence, either. He looks amazed, as if he's wondering how he got into this mess.

Scott waits a minute. When he reacts, his response is physical and kinetic; he's off the bed and almost on top of the sheriff, his hands outstretched. Then I guess he thinks better of this. He backs off and lets his hands hang down. "You got something to say, Sheriff? So say it."

The sheriff stares, his little mouth sewed tight.

"I think Nebutol is advertised on television, you know," my father says, in a wavering voice. "For acid reflux. It is purple."

Daddy is wrong here, since Nexium is the purple pill advertised on TV. Nebutol is a sedative.

The sheriff turns, managing his body stiffly, shoulders straight and flat, like the Tin Soldier. He aims the whole weapon of himself at me. "I want a recorded session with him. You'll get him downtown. My office will call you." He's at the door when he turns and looks at me squint-eyed. "This nonsense can't go on," he says.

At least he directs his ultimatums at me now, which means he has stopped pretending Daddy is a free agent who moves successfully around the world on his own.

It is the afternoon of the same day, and Scott and I are in Rita's room going through her stuff.

It was my idea that we should do this. Scott seemed at first too distracted to think about it.

Though as soon as I raised the plan, he was gung ho. "Sure. Absolutely. I come, too."

Now I wonder if I shouldn't have just gone in and raided Rita's territory all by myself.

I'm trying to find out things. What, I'm not sure.

Having an observer won't help. And he and Rita have a history . . . "Are you sure you're okay with this?" I ask.

He says he's okay. "Last night was . . . well. Jesus. Shock. Somebody you know real well." He stops briefly. "I want to do this. Maybe find out . . ."

"And you're okay reading her stuff? She probably had lots of other friends."

"Hey, don't we all." He tries a smile. "That's not what I'm afraid of; I'm afraid of Egon maybe stopping us. I mean, it's his institute and his room. Does he really want us snooping into Reet's recent life? Maybe she learned something about the museum's slimy doings. And that's why she got topped."

"You think they have slimy doings?"

"Wouldn't surprise me." He reads my inquiring look and responds, "Sure, I go along with Egon, let him wine and dine me and make a fuss, why not? Doesn't mean I'm gonna marry him. Or pretend he's a decent scholar . . . Or hook up with his idiot Egyptian-Spiritualist religion." Scott lowers himself to the floor cross-legged and reaches for a pile of papers.

Rita was messy, as you'd expect. Books and papers wobble in hamster heaps against the room's walls and in its nooks and crannies.

"I know Reet felt the same way," he says in a minute, more quietly.

I tell him that I liked it that he got upset about her death, and he shrugs and reads assiduously. He doesn't answer.

For the first time I really put it to myself: Where was Scott when Rita was shot? And the answer is straightforward: I don't know. I thought I could see him, sitting at our table, but I'm not sure.

Rita has left a laptop, an overnight bag, a lot of clothes on hangers, and piles of shoes on floors, plus the teetering stashes of papers. I start to suggest that Scott do the computer stuff and I the papers and then I get a look at Rita's handwriting, backhanded and spidery. Scott apparently is used to it; he has already started reading.

Also he seems wary of the computer. "Don't you need a special password?"

"You do, but I have it." Rita was the sort who taped her password on the underside of her computer table. When she forgot it, she could climb under there and refresh her wobbly memory. She wasn't planning to get shot.

"So what are we looking for?" I ask.

"How the hell, how do I know, Reet was into a lot of stuff. Just pass on anything that looks interesting."

Okay, okay, I think. *Interesting stuff is what I myself will hang on to.*

So I settle down to punch buttons and try to translate file names. What does GAGS mean? Or VIGILACE? How about CIRCLES?

Rita didn't mean to go off and leave all this to be puzzled over by a stranger. She meant to come back and maybe put the N in her VIGILACE file and then to laugh and fall in love some more and have a couple more nervous breakdowns and publish some articles about her Egyptian specialty. I find I don't even know what that is.

"Oh. Shoes," Scott says.

"Shoes? *You* did a piece on shoes."

"I stole it from her." He reads my expression and says, "She helped me with the research. She was good at that kind of thing—sociological exploration, who wears 'em and who doesn't, what the degree of decor tells you about the society. She did all kinds of clothing, but shoes especially. New Kingdom."

"That sounds good. Interesting. It's the kind of stuff I'd like to do. If I did it."

Scott says, "Yeah," and goes back to his reading. I attack the computer again.

*   *   *

It is jammed with records that look like research, backup for research, correspondence about same, notes, speculations, references to buried issues: "Perfume—Dioscorides re balanos ??? query jeordie."

"Jeordie?" Scott asks. "Oh, sure. At the BM." He doesn't explain what BM is. Not bowel movement, probably.

Plus, since Rita didn't have the kind of sequential, organized brain that I'm sure Scott does, copies of personal letters (which she saved—some people discard theirs right away; Rita liked her effusions) are stuck in the same file as research notes. Jeordie (who's at the British Museum—that's BM) gets a message with a fond reference. "Hey, Jeord, great evening. That is some place, wow, and good conversation, great company. Thanks a bunch. You're a pal." I try to limit my attention on the files talking about shoes, clothing, perfume, ornament. Scan them, forget them. But this is hard to do; they're interesting.

VIGILACE does seem to be Vigilance, as I've been suspecting. But it's just a couple of news items about some other Egyptologists who are researching shoes.

And the lady did have a sense of humor. *Me vs. You*. That's a love poem or, more accurately, an "I Don't Love You Anymore" poem. No date, but it sounds recent. Was her depression due to a rebound romance?

There are lots and lots of letters, confusing, boring: "Tom, you dreamboat, can you possibly get your drug-dealing outfit to pay me a little faster?" (*Drug-dealing?* I think. *Oh, migawd, alert, alert. But no. It's a joke.* Later on in the letter: "Anyway, tell them I tried their aspirin-*bulti*-fishoil mixture and, sweet-cakes, it's nowhere as good as straight aspirin.")

"Rosie, how is the snow at Aspen?" "Sam, Tchaikovsky is soupy, please change tickets." "Hey, Aunt Margery: It isn't fair that someone as nice as you . . ."

Partway through, I find tears smarting my eyelids. This is all that's left of Rita, who was too damn much alive. So much in the now, so curious, puppylike, incautious, that somebody picked up a gun, sighted along it, or whatever you do, and performed all the rest of that cold, calculating process that ends with somebody's life being bled out on a Best Western rug.

Scott is shuffling papers rapidly. He takes from a pile on his left and adds to a pile on his right. Occasionally he makes a subterranean remark.

"Hey, Scott," I intervene.

"Huh?"

"She knew everybody here, right? I mean, like you and Egon? Shouldn't she have a file on each of you?"

He says, "God." And then adds, "Listen, you come on a file about me, hand it over, will you?"

"Oh, sure. Did she write to you?"

"Not for the last five years."

"Five years ago was Thebes, right?"

"Why do you care about Thebes?"

"I just do. Big scene. Everybody together, wild nights. Rita talked about it."

"She would. Better let *me* try the computer."

"Forget it. There's nothing about you here, not unless she has you hidden in her perfume research. She knew Marcus, too?"

"Very, very well." He reaches a hand toward the computer. I guess he's sorry he let me get involved in this, but he couldn't very well have said no, it being my idea. I keep on through a few more gushy personal letters and some research notes on turquoise jewelry and kohl eye makeup.

I'm looking for some really personal files, ones that will include Scott Dillard and Marcus Broussard.

What was it Rita called Scott? Studly?

"Hey, Scott, was there an Egyptian fertility god?"

"Everybody was a fertility god. Or goddess. The whole religion was about the Nile."

"No, I mean like the Greeks and Romans had the little guy with the fat erection."

Scott says, "Min," and when I say, "What?" he repeats, "Min. An agriculture god. Why?"

I think fast and invent a poem that Rita was quoting, involving wheat fields.

This discourages Scott, so I can scramble around some more in Rita's Documents file where, yes, there is a MIN folder and, yes, it contains two subfiles, M and S.

Bingo.

I open M first. M would be for Marcus.

Six or seven letters of the *Hey, baby, what a dynamite night last night* variety. A couple that refer to Scott with tender remarks like *I guess we showed Scott the Stud a thing or two, am I right?* And surprisingly, a whole batch of records of stock transactions. Pages of printouts of sales. Letters of thanks (*You always have the right info*) and short notes saying, *Wow, you are the best*, along with pages of reports from Pricewaterhouse showing very nice profits.

And finally, unexpectedly, some copies of biographical reports from Google on MARCUS BROUSSARD.

I gobble these up. I'm getting really curious about

Marcus Broussard. I should have Googled him myself before this, but I didn't think of it.

I read. Then I read some more. Then I say to Scott, "Guess what, there are two of them."

"Two what?" Scott asks, looking up, alarmed. He has been getting edgier as I've kept reading.

"Two Marcus Broussards. Rita printed them from Google. One is a banker and one makes adult films. I guess your friend, her friend, our dead trustee, is the banker. Because, from what Egon says, I don't really guess . . . although it's possible . . ." I trail off because I'm reading again.

"What do you think?" I ask. "Was he the banker?"

Scott says, "Yeah, I guess. And other stuff." He's stopped reading and is watching me.

Rita's computer is already hitched up to a printer; all I have to do is punch some more buttons. The adult film maker has an illustrated description. The banker has just one brief, pithy, boring statement, one paragraph long.

"Does *adult film* mean what I think it means?"

Scott shrugs. "I guess."

"I mean, like, in-your-face, close-up, scorchingly lit photography, women with legs spread, guys with dicks out, tits, ass, group fuck—"

Scott interrupts me, sounding muffled. "I guess."

"Well, this isn't exactly . . . Maybe you'd know."

"How in hell would *I* know?"

"Listen to this: 'Marcus Broussard, cutting-edge director-producer of the voyeur-film movement, late 1990s, organizer of the group Casualty. His company, Directionless, based in Tenerife, made six films combining reality with anime, art, painting, Picasso, Chagall, Stella, Arbus, comic-huckster Tradu. *Wild, intense, way, way out. Unzip. Adult Industry Revu.'* "

"Son of a bitch." Scott waits a minute, then asks, "Surreal sex movies. So where does that get us?"

"And here's for the good, boring Marcus: 'Chairman of the Board and Chief Executive Officer of the Central California Land Bank, founder of that bank, founder of the Stockton Credit Association, the Stockton Loan Group, Central California Title,' and more and more and blah, blah. 'Mr. Broussard is active in many volunteer organizations . . .' and it lists a whole bunch with names like Jobs Ahoy and Growth into Management. The only faintly interesting one is the Cross-Cultural Museum; he was a trustee of that. Oh, and 'Trustee of Egypt Regained, a museum devoted to Ancient Egypt.'

"Which Marcus would you rather be stuck in an elevator with?"

Scott is silent, and I wait, staring down at the page. "Do you think Marcus Broussard was a double personality?" he says.

"Yeah, I sure do."

"He was a writer, too," Scott says after a minute. "He talked about the writing as if it were a joke on all of us. Like he was especially planning to write up the story of the dig."

Scott sounds thoughtful. "I sure would like to get my hands on that, but I'm not sure he ever really did it. More, just threatened to."

The S file is not as interesting as the M one. Most of it is earlier and includes several *Hey what a hot night* notes. There are two breakup notes of the *I should have known about you, you rat* type. There are a couple of *I hate Danielle* missives. And there is a recent note. (Yes, Scott lied. Or forgot. Or something.) I memorize it: "Scotty: She'll never go along with you. Never. Give it up."

Below this there's a fragment of what looks like Google information. Or maybe a biographical line from a catalog. "DANIELLE BERTOLUSCI has given lecture courses at Oxford, University of London, and Yale. She is the author of nine articles on the historic placement of British Museum Egyptian texts and is a consutant to the Luxor Museum."

Danielle. Rita had a thing about her, and she gets put in the S for Scott (or for Stud?) file. I don't say anything about that to Scott, sitting on the floor facing me.

I wish I could print out both MIN files. I look over at Scott, busy shuffling paper, and decide I can't.

"Did you find anything?" I ask as we prepare to quit. He is stacking his papers into a neat bunch and fixing them together with red plastic tape.

"Some messy research notes. Nothing to get her shot, for sure. And you?"

"Nope. Not unless you're suspicious of perfume cones."

"Jesus." He flips the edges of his red-bound pile of paper. "So here's Rita. Oh, Christ." He lowers his head. "Some people you don't think will ever get it; they should just go on and on being peculiar; know what I mean?"

When I don't answer, he picks up, "That daffy quality. We weren't ever in love. Not exactly. But we were okay. I liked that irrepressible . . ."

"Uh-huh."

After a minute, he says, "Let's go out to dinner. Some place ordinary. No printed menu or Middle Eastern theme."

"*Not* a Best Western."

He asks me if I've ever been to Penitentia; it's inland and dusty and there's a Mexican restaurant.

"Bring your dad along if you need to," he says.

But Daddy wants to stay here. He likes the new TV program where the four young men help you redecorate your house.

Scott is cheerful over dinner. Almost, I think you could say, hectic. "Hey, what do you think about that Marcus?"

"It's interesting. Strange."

"Like I told you, a wild man. Am I right?"

"I didn't know him."

"Oh, sure. I forget. Just because you and I . . ." Some shared ordeals make you feel you've had a lot of other stuff together.

"I guess Marcus was a strange cat."

"Tell me."

He consults the menu. "Stuffed chile with mole." He fires this in the direction of the waitress, who is departing, before he turns, looking surprised. "Unless you don't like spicy?"

"What happens if I don't?"

"Oh, hell. Sorry."

"I love spicy. Tell me about Marcus."

"You saw. He did everything and tried everything."

"But he was a banker."

"Sure he was a banker. And a stockbroker. And a whole lot of different kinds of speculator. It was a game. Life was a play."

"And he was successful?"

"Way successful. Totally off the wall, like a bundle of exploding firecrackers. He made the rest of us look pale beige."

Our baskets of chips and salsa arrive. Scott is finally telling me about the crowd at Thebes and I want to keep him there. "You weren't a beige crowd."

"Not likely." He realizes where I'm pulling the conversation and stops himself. "But listen——"

"Tell me about his stock deals."

"Oh, God, the stocks. They were stuff you wouldn't ever dream of. A company that made a stair-climbing toy. Another one that processed avocado pits."

"And they always paid off."

"Every single time. The stair-climber got sold to the army. The avocado oil——Jesus, it was awful——I think Heinz took that. We got so we bought anything he said. He was making all of us rich."

Scott looks wary again, he's been listening to himself; so I pile in quickly, "What besides finance?"

Our food arrives. It's wonderfully spicy, steamy, and greasy. With that weird chocolate tang of real mole. I tell Scott thank you for ordering it and try to steer the conversation back. "But you think he could be the filmmaker, too."

He shrugs. "He could be anything. Now, let's talk about . . ." Maybe he can't think of a neutral topic fast enough. "Boy, I sure would like to see one of those movies."

"I bet we can find one." Susie is an old-film buff. She gets them from a special Berkeley video store and she tends to favor Buster Keaton. But she'd be thrilled by this assignment.

"He did sculpture, too," Scott says, looking reflective. "Mostly, he took Japanese model figures——"

"Japanese model figures?" I can't picture it.

"Yeah, you know, like Godzilla and Dragon Man . . . and he pasted stuff on them. Crucifixes and halos."

I say, "Oh," which seems about to cover it.

"And he was a dynamite welder. *That* kind of sculpture, too."

I'm silent here, which is good, because Scott is caught in retrospection. "Danny—that is—Rita—couldn't make up her mind. Was he a genius or was he nuts?"

"*Danielle* couldn't decide," I say, pouncing.

"How'd she get into this story?"

"You just said."

"No, I didn't."

Instead of getting into a *yes, you did* and *no, I didn't*, I say, "This was in Thebes, at the camp in Thebes, and Danielle and Rita were both there. Did Danielle look like Rita?"

He's been wanting to deny more and change the subject more, but this stops him so cold he has to protest, "Oh, my God, no."

"So Rita was your girlfriend and then Danielle was your girlfriend?"

"Hey, cut it out."

After a minute he picks up, hesitantly, "You don't understand . . ."

"Oh, but I do. That was one active scene."

"Okay, okay. I guess you never—"

"Sure I never." I think about the Habitat camp on a weekend night. "So Danielle didn't look like Rita."

"Danielle looked like . . ." He clamps down on this idea. "Yeah, that was one wild scene, but Marcus was the one. I mean he was the center. He had all the ideas and every sort of other idea. And the resources. He spoke three different kinds of Arabic. He got us the digging site, which was terrific. He got us drugs."

"Drugs." I had forgotten about that.

"Everything. Pot. Meth. Heroin. Hash. Hash was his special deal."

We're silent for a minute. I guess Scott is remembering, and I'm feeling sad. All that liveliness and talent, splashed around so recklessly.

"Danielle didn't look anything like Rita," Scott says. "She looked like you."

This is a stopper, but after he says it, I can't get him to talk anymore about Thebes. He wants to discuss my dad's health and my relationship with my old boyfriend—what's his name, Rob?—and why Cherie is now Rob's girlfriend and why the sheriff is pursuing my father. He's concerned about me. What am I going to do with my life?

And he talks about the Hartdale Grant. "Maybe it's a crock of shit, but I sure wanted it. I'd have given anything. If they said, 'You lose everything in your whole life except your brain and the Hartdale,' I'd've agreed straight off, 'Okay, right.' I'd've donated my left nut. That Hartdale is a lot of money, but that wasn't the point. It's a symbol. It's your life all in one, everything you've been working for."

I pick up on the tenses in this lecture and ask, "And not so much now?"

"Now I'm not really sure of anything."

Scott is mostly silent on the way home. He stares at the dark road with its many curves. An owl flies right across our windshield.

* * *

But inside the museum residence, as we're waiting for the elevator, he shifts again. "Carla, you've been a big help. Really."

When I don't respond, he picks up, "Christ. This whole thing hit me hard."

And after a minute, "Can I kiss you?"

I put my face up. If he had asked in the middle of talking about his Yale appointment, I would have told him sorry. But this is a Scott that I partly understand. I feel sorry for him.

The kiss lasts for the elevator ride. It's a good kiss, better than I'm prepared for. Too good, one of those that you sense all the way down in your gut. This man packs a lot of animal energy.

We part as the elevator doors open. I don't have any trouble breaking away, though maybe he hangs on to my shoulder a minute too long. I depart toward my room, shoring myself up with the idea that I have a secret. In my pocket there is a copy of one of Rita's notes to Marcus:

Hey, Marcus, you wily Roman, thanks for the info; I'll be watching. And watching. You're the best in the world with the inside awful secret. Loveyoualways.

I'm not that great with spotting secrets. It could be on a computer or on the Internet or on the inside of Rita's dead wrist. Well, shoot.

There are people that are probably good with that stuff. I don't want to think of Cherie, but I do.

ᒧ Chapter 12

And Cherie is very much with me and on the spot.

First of all, I get a veritable information storm of e-mails, each written in Cherie's patented text-message shorthand, and needing translation. The first one dates an hour after the shooting:

O drlings drlings jst hd I fel 4 u o migwd how r u luv luv Cher.

Fifteen minutes later:

R u any btr ds it gt btr wn ur usd 2 it o drlngs I tk of u.

Half an hour later:

cdnt gt a bt of slp lst nit tkg of u luv u bth so mch.

I get a headache and can hardly think (tk) and know that
I have lost the ability to spell (spl) after dealing with ten
(count'em, 10) of these effusions, with more popping up
every few minutes and my assiduous computer ringing a bell
for each one. Cherie, of course, really wants to text-message
but I've lied to her about the text-messaging capacity of my
phone. So, of course, she calls.

"Hello? Darling? Oh, my God, my God."

We do that for a while, with Cherie wanting to know
how is her darling Crocodile, and how is her darling Carla,
and have I any idea who could have shot Rita, did I see anything, does that feeble-minded asshole of a sheriff have any
idea at all?

"And Rob and I are both feeling so guilty, we were set to go
down to the bar that night; we go most nights for just a spot
of dancing, but then we got involved and got too lazy . . ."

My stomach does a neat flip here. I understand this rhet-
oric and enjoy a mental picture of Cherie and Rob locked in
a long languorous embrace. Hasn't Cherie said about Rob,
"He seems kind of stiff at first, but when you get used to
him . . ." Oh, hell and damn. I summon a counterimage of
me and Scott in the elevator.

"So, darling," says Cherie, "when should we come over;
we are dying to see you; of course, Rob is on duty today and
also tonight and I actually do have some cases that are nip-
ping at my heels, but if you need me, I'll be there in a flash."

I assure Cherie that we can live without her, and she assures me that if we need her, she's there, spot on, right away,
and she hates to be just thinking about me from a few miles
away and Rob is so worried.

"He cares so much," she says. "For your dad. And for you.
He really cares about you, Carla."

I restrain myself and insist that we are fine.

"And that little sweet Rita," Cherie picks up, "that poor child, I keep thinking about her . . ."

Amazingly, she trails off for a minute and something makes me want to try for a reality-injection. "Rita wasn't exactly sweet, Cherie. She was an interesting woman. Educated. Good in her field. But not sweet."

"Oh, girlfriend, I know that. *Sweet* doesn't really mean that. It's just the Southern in me coming out. Just something to say."

As usual, Cherie proves herself smarter than she lets on. Smarter than I think she is. I'll bet that surprise quality is attractive to Rob.

"But listen, sugar-bell, about Rita. Somebody shot her? In the back? And killed her? Have you any idea who?"

"None."

"That little girl didn't look like she had an enemy in the world."

"Yes, she did."

"Oh, God, there I go again. Sure, she looked like she had enemies. She was off-the-wall crazy part of the time. She said your dad was a murderer."

"He didn't kill her."

"Oh, I *know* that." She's silent for a minute, and then says to me in her professional voice, "In my experience, people don't get really, permanently mad about something somebody does when they're in the down cycle of bipolar. The average person can recognize that. And know it's not the true person.

"That's in my experience," she adds dismissively.

We actually have two seconds of telephone silence before I remember to jump in with my question. "Cherie, tell me. In the crypt the other day. What was Rita doing?"

There is a pause. Cherie says, "Hmm." She waits. "Now that is a question, isn't it?"

"Yes, Cherie, it surely is." I let some irritation creep into my voice.

"Well, now darlin', of course I don't rightly know."

I wait.

"She looked like she was just interested in that beautiful carving."

"No, she didn't. She looked as if she were looking for something. Getting her nose up to it, feeling it with her fingertips. We both thought so. And we kept Egon busy so he wouldn't notice."

"Is that what we were doin'? Oh, my God, naughty us."

"Cherie, cut it out."

There is another pause. I hear Cherie exhale. "Well, darlin', since you are so observant, I guess I'll tell you. There is a history for that crypt there. It's the setting for a movie."

I say, "Oh."

"Not such a bad movie, really. Sort of porn and sort of weird artsy. If you know what I mean."

"I have an idea."

"I didn't say a word about that to Egon. He's such an unctuous bastard. I don't know—did he produce the movie? Does he maybe not know a thing about it?"

I'm quiet, thinking about Cherie's news. Yes, I can imagine both these possibilities. Egon Rothskellar, porn producer. Or Egon, complacent oblivious dupe.

The whole thing, of course, says Marcus Broussard.

"What happened in this movie?"

"The usual. Gasping, groping, penises, vaginas, whips, vampires."

"Oh," I say. "Vampires."

"Well, natch. This is in a tomb. Real well photographed and weirdly lit and gorgeous costumes with holes in them. What I don't know is if the crypt ever gets opened. The movie was underground, not to float a pun; my friend only had half of the video."

I brood about this for a while. Very interesting news, which explains why Cherie wanted to see the crypt.

"Was Rita in the movie?"

"Maybe. Masks, costumes, you couldn't be sure."

"And so what was she doing the other day while we were there?"

"Sweetheart, I don't know. Messing around. But I figure it's real important."

I figure that, too. Someone had better try to find out.

This part of our conversation ends in an uncomfortable suspension. I wait for Cherie to say, "Let's work on this together," but she doesn't.

I'm about to sign off when I remember that we have more business. "Cherie. The sheriff was threatening to call us in."

She sounds relieved to have a new topic. "Oh, absolutely, you can count on it. I'll be there. I scared that little slimeball sheriff up proper; he won't dare proceed without me.

"I'll bring Robbie with me," she threatens. "Now, Carla, you sure you're okay? And your dad? He's fine? I think about the two of you all the time . . . Hey, I got a new bottle of grappa that a client gave me, made in some little village of Tuscany; I'll bring it along, just the right thing for those tense moments. See you, don't forget now."

Cherie, you can count on it; I won't forget.

*   *   *

Talking to Cherie upsets me. I hate to admit it, but it does.

I go out into the garden for a change of venue, and right away Egon is after me. He pursues me down several garden lanes and finally catches up with me, triumphantly gloomy. "I have brought you a cheese-filled doughnut."

He has two of them, two cheese-filled doughnuts, one for him and one for me.

"Yes," he says. "A beautiful morning. Sad. Ironic."

"I say ironic," he expands, balancing a mouthful of runny cheese, "because of the dichotomy between the beauty of the scene and the tragedies around us. Possibly you feel it."

I accept my doughnut and mumble, "Two murders."

Actually, I do want to talk to you, Egon. Just, not right now.

He is alarmed. "Murders? Well, not at all. That is, we aren't sure. For Rita—poor, tragic Rita——yes, certainly. Shot. That was murder. But for Marcus? There is no sign of murder."

I look at him to see if he's serious and decide that he thinks he is. I mention the ankh.

"Ah, yes. The ankh. The life force, the symbol. Many of us had them. Carried them, you know? For good luck."

I mutter something about its not helping much, which Egon ignores. "And what could be more natural"—he gets almost enthusiastic—"than, at the last minute, when you feel the life force ebbing, all that you love going from you"—he waves a hand to indicate the things he loves dissipating into the atmosphere—"what could be more natural than that you thrust the potent token . . ."

(*Potent token,* I think, *good, good.*)

". . . than that you thrust it into yourself."

An unpleasant image, don't carry it further. "So you think he swallowed another ankh, that first time?"

He looks dumbfounded. No, he didn't mean that.

"What did he die of?" I ask, veering the conversation some.

Egon sounds defensive. "They're still testing." The defensiveness makes me decide he hasn't been told the cause of Marcus's death and doesn't want to admit it.

Of course, maybe they still don't know. Don't those forensic studies sometimes take ages?

"Well," I suggest, "they said something about low blood pressure."

Egon says, "Ah."

"And someone has suggested internal bleeding." Actually the person is Scott, but for some reason I don't mention that.

Egon just stares.

"I mean," I remind him, "staggering around for a whole day."

He fishes for a remark. "Terrible, terrible."

We give that some space. "What I really wanted to talk to you about . . ." Egon starts off.

Yes, I thought you were chasing me around the garden for a reason. And I won't be deflected just yet. "I'm curious about Mr. Broussard. What was he like?"

"Oh. Charming."

"What did he do for a living?"

"He was very rich. Very generous. Listed in the Fortune 500. Other places. I think it was . . . banks?" Egon offers this with furrowed brow, as if the subject is a bit vulgar. Mr. Broussard was so rich that one didn't inquire.

Now *I* get to say, *Ah. Egon, did you know he was making porn films in your crypt?* "Was he here often?"

"Oh, yes, certainly. Yes, often." For some reason this question makes Egon uncomfortable.

"How did you meet him, Egon?"

"How did I *meet* him?" I observe that a question, even a repeated one, is a good way of stalling. "Why. A prominent man. Interested in the field. Well."

"You were together in Egypt, weren't you?"

"In Egypt? Why. Well . . ."

"In Thebes. In a camp in Thebes."

"Ah. *That* time. Why. Of course." A concerned crease has developed between Egon's eyebrows. He fiddles with the doughnut paper.

"Egon, I'd really like to talk about that spring in Thebes."

"*Spring* in *Thebes?*" Egon asks, making it sound like the title of a musical comedy. "Oh, my. But, you see, I was there only a few days. Perhaps everyone had a good time. Perhaps you should ask your father."

That camp in Thebes is a hot topic. Everyone has to be cajoled, pushed, bribed into discussing it.

". . . And it is Dr. Day that I really wanted to talk to you about," Egon picks up. I've waited a minute too long and have lost the initiative. "He is such an admirable scholar."

I think, *Oh, God, I know what's coming.*

I want it, what he's going to say. But on another level, that of keeping my dad from being hurt, I very much don't want it.

I wait, thinking at Egon, *Come on, get going.*

He's going to tell me that Edward Day is acting disturbed. Egon has finally caught on—Edward Day is a damaged example of Alzheimer's. Egon will say, regretfully, that Dr. Day can't help with the topics the museum is trying to research.

He will extend his sympathy, but he will say that perhaps my father and I should leave the museum by the end of this week.

"I was wondering"—Egon opens his little blue eyes very wide—"if we could get Dr. Day to take a more active role in the doings of the Resident Scholars' Program." He chews on his doughnut.

I stare. *Yes, he is serious.* He radiates sincerity. *Egon, you take my breath away. Furthermore, I don't understand. You've got to be faking; I can't imagine why.* "Active role? What kind of active role?"

He brings his nervous horse-face, wiggling nose and all, close in to mine. "We're going to do a newsletter. Perhaps an article?"

I don't answer this, being struck dumb by the idea. Write an article? Some days my dad can't write at all, and has to deliver anything he wants to put down on paper in wobbly block letters. Other days he can sign his name beautifully, in ornate Victorian script. But to translate some idea in his head into sentences on paper?

"I would be proud to work with him on it," Egon suggests. "I could interview him. Something about the earlier days of Egyptology?"

After a minute's silence he adds, "There may be wonderful matters he knows that will get lost. Reminiscences. Views of people. Little facts. All those fascinating details that are so helpful, so important, but that we don't . . . well, that nobody is sure of. Anymore."

His voice dies down. He looks reflective, as if he's listening to what he's just said.

"After all, your father knows circumstances that . . ." He pauses, clears the throat. He has started on a sentence he doesn't quite like. "He knows things other people don't know. Egyptology things."

Okay, Egon, I think, *I don't understand this and it makes me itchy, but sure, you can interview my dad. He'll love the attention. You think he knows something important? Something connected with the tangle we're in right now? Maybe. I've not had any luck questioning him.*

The Memoirs of Edward Day, edited by Egon Rothskellar. I access that ridiculous image for a few seconds.

But if my dad is going to hang around here for a while longer, I want the place to be safer. Egon can look doubtful all he wants, but I know there have been murders. Not just one murder, two. Plus a lot of little thefts. And a sheriff who doesn't know his ass from a posthole. "Egon, I think you should hire a detective."

"What?" He sounds absolutely flabbergasted.

I detail my points. Murder. Theft. Chaos. Inadequate law enforcement.

Egon is disbelieving. "Inadequate? Oh, my, oh, no. We have a new sheriff. A fine man. This sheriff is a gentleman."

"No, he's not."

"Much different from the previous one. Sheriff Munro is interested in Egyptology."

No, he's not. And he's also not interested in solving the crime under his jurisdiction. "He seems completely inadequate to me," I say. I start listing for-instances. Egon blinks and says, "Oh. No," a lot.

A few more minutes reveal that we are stalemated. Egon is happy with Sheriff Munro. He will not hire a detective.

We stand staring at each other, and Egon changes the subject. "I truly look forward to working with your father."

I do not understand anything at all. *There must be something in it for you, Egon, maintaining my damaged father on your elegant premises. But I don't have a clue what that is.*

And meanwhile your museum is not safe.

I think of approaching Cherie to do some pro bono detection. She would be okay at it, but having Cherie around all the time? Oh, my God.

The only available detective is me.

"Right," I tell Egon. "I guess my father would enjoy helping the Institute."

ᛏ Chapter 13

"Hello," Rob says at the other end of my cell phone. "I mean, well. Hi."

I wait, long enough that it gets embarrassing. Obviously this is a conversation that he thinks will give him trouble. "Hi, Rob."

"I got, I mean, I made this appointment. Well. I'm going to San Francisco to see Rita's boyfriend. And I thought maybe you'd come, too."

I manage to keep some of the complete startlement out of my voice. "Rita? Boyfriend?"

"Yes. Well, you know, I treated her."

No, I didn't know. I keep learning new things. It makes my head hurt.

"She came into the trauma clinic. I was on duty." Rob's field is tropical medicine, but Rita, in spite of her years in

Egypt, didn't have a tropical disease but a worldwide one: depression. And from somewhere she got the common sense to go to the clinic with it.

So Rob was the one who got her back on track.

"She listed this guy as her next of kin," he says after a minute. "She and I got to be friends, sort of."

And here I was, thinking maybe it was Cherie who had helped Rita back to sanity.

"Cherie should go with you to visit this guy," I say.

There's a minute's uncomfortable silence. "Cher says you should.

"She says you're in the situation. And you're good with people."

Actually I do want to talk to Rita's boyfriend. I just don't want to do anything Cherie has told Rob I ought to do.

"My dad comes, too," I say, inspired. Daddy will provide a buffer between me and Rob. And he loves to go to San Francisco.

Rob, too, is relieved. "Oh, hey, great." He says it with almost too much enthusiasm. Rob and I, buddies since I was six, have reached the point where we need a barrier between us.

Rob will pick us up this afternoon. It seems that Rita's boyfriend lives in the Mission.

"Going to the city," my father says. "Oh, I am so pleased. Now, dear, exactly which city is it?"

Careening up Highway One in Rob's little car (Rob is a usually careful driver who gets undisciplined when he's under tension), he and I alternate between being antsy (that's me) and superficially matey (which is Rob). He says he is concerned about me. How am I, do I feel better, have I been having bad dreams, any flashbacks? And how is Ed . . .

We are all jammed in the front seat, with my dad between us, straddling the gear shift. He says, "Ed. That is me. I am Ed."

I say, "What do you care, Rob? That's ancient history, right? What's past is past."

Rob is appalled. "Carla, we're a team. You are important to me."

I let that resonate for a few blue California miles. It's a bright, achingly clear day. I think even Rob in his present mood of euphoria and denial must hear the echoes his words fling out.

"I am fine," my dad announces. "Why do people always ask that? It is not very interesting."

After a while Rob picks up again. His voice is still cheerful, but a teeny bit forced. "Well, I called this George; Rita listed him on the treatment form as her next of kin. I didn't even know if he knew." (He means about Rita's death.) "But it turned out he did; the sheriff called him. And then we talked . . ." His voice trails off. He's silent for a half a mile; the Toyota clunks quietly. "Like, he and I talked. People that have lost someone will talk to anybody. It doesn't matter whether they know them or not."

"I am always happy to talk to people," my father offers. "I have been conversing with the man in the museum. Doing that is relaxing."

I ask him what he's saying to Egon and he acts interested. "Oh, is that his name? Egon? I knew someone else with that name."

"Carla," Rob says, "I hope you're not distressed about Cherie. You and I are still good friends. We'll always be good friends."

"Oh, yeah," I agree. "Sure."

"I mean, it's not as if you also haven't had . . . other friends. There was that Chinese guy. At the Manor."

Wayne Lee wasn't Chinese; he was an American of Chinese ancestry. A handsome sweet stud who worked at the Manor and with whom I had a three-month flirtation. But that's been over for a while now.

I think Rob doesn't know about my Habitat boyfriend. Rob was in his last year of his internship at Davis. Come to think of it, we corresponded steadily during that one. I sent him matey letters about nailing sheetrock and going to neighborhood potlucks.

I say aloud, "Oh, for God's sake."

"Anyway," Rob says, "this George sounds like a really nice guy."

"Sure." I'm beginning to get curious. I can ask this man questions; that will take my mind off wanting to strangle Rob. And it will be as if I'm constructing Rita out of some new bits and pieces. She gave me a few; her computer offered some others. Scott did, too. Scraps of the bright materials she liked to wear.

A quarter mile of knockout California scenery unreels around us, coves and blue water and wind-tossed grasses. After that we hit civilization in the form of square white cardboard houses plastered against the hillsides like an invading robot army.

"He lives in the center of the Mission," Rob says. "He works in a bookstore."

I grunt. It's a mistake to try for a clear picture of people before you meet them; I always do that and it never works out. But up 'til now I was getting a George in my head who's nothing like the boyfriend that works in a bookstore. The imaginary boyfriend was suave and older and quirky—another version of my imaginary Marcus. I've been trying to reconstruct him, too, out of bits and scraps.

We fight our way along the freeway and down into San Francisco, in and out of the narrow streets of the Mission District. Rob is asking my dad concerned questions about his health and his interests, and my father is answering with a lecture on the history of San Francisco, which seems to be conflated with the history of some Near Eastern city. "There is a more indigenous area to the west," Daddy says. "Tourists have preempted the central neighborhoods."

And every now and then, over my dad's head, Rob tries to alert me to my sins. The ones against my father. "Carl," he begins solemnly, "I wonder"—flicking a glance down at the crisp white head between us—"enough attention here? Are you really paying attention? To your dad, in the middle of everything? Do you think . . . ?"

Rob, what I think is that I will swat you and wreck this car full of people.

"I dunno." Rob squeezes his little blue vehicle into a parking space that magically appears in front of a vegetable stand. "You say it's one hundred percent okay with him, all this commotion. I don't believe that for a minute. He's compensating. I mean, think about it. Be real."

He has parked so close to a crateful of plantains that I have to scramble over the gearshift and out the door on his side. My dad has no trouble doing this. He thinks it's fun.

Rob and I, despite Cherie, are practicing for our old favorite script: telling each other what to do. "You have a
colossal amount of nerve," I say to him, scraping my shin on
a plywood carton.

George Marziano lives in a gray-and-pink Victorian with
arched windows and a round shingled towerlike protuber-
ance out front; entry is up a flight of cracked cement stairs.
George's name appears on a list beside the green-painted
front door. A note pointing to his name reads, "Ring twice";
this is crossed out and amended to "Knock Real Loud."

Rob does the loud knocking on the door's glass panel; I
lean against the warm splintery housefront and try to take
in street scenes. Assorted interlocked couples pass by; after
that there's one woman in an undershirt and purple skivvies
pushing a stroller holding a fluffy white dog, then there's
another woman in T-shirt, sweatshirt, gold lamé shoes, skirt
on top of jeans, and playing a recorder as she walks. Typical
Mission District scenery. The door crunches open to reveal
George Marziano, who is skinny, long-haired, and a little
breathless. He wears a blue-stained undershirt with gaping
armholes.

He is so much not what I've been picturing as Rita's
boyfriend that I'm struck dumb. I guess Rob is, too. And
George takes a minute to get enough wind to greet us.
"Well, hi there. Wow."

Well, hey, wow.

He greets my dad with enthusiasm. And Daddy says,
"Yes, of course, young man. You're an old friend; I'd know
you anywhere."

We follow him up a steep staircase. Early San Francisco

builders economized by making staircases too narrow and too abrupt.

At the top of the stairs George's apartment is a long hallway with rooms branching off. There are lots of rooms; this was once a spacious house. Someone has painted the front space, which maybe used to be the parlor, black, but George doesn't take us in there; he leads us into another room with lipstick-pink curtains.

"Welcome to my humble abode." I guess he's trying to be funny.

We sit on furniture that looks like the stuff Rob and I had in Santa Cruz. Goodwill or left-in-the-street, primarily tapestried, shiny, and gray. Cats have been sharpening their claws on the chair arms; that's a big feature of this kind of furniture.

"Well," we say, and "Hi," and once again, "Wow." George gazes at us anxiously. He is hollow-chested, which shows up painfully with the kind of undershirt he's wearing. He has a long, sincere, worried face and circles under his eyes.

"I guess it's hard to believe," he says.

Rob and I nod.

"I mean, when you called. Of course I already knew. Hey, it was really nice of you to do that."

Rob nods again. "Glad to."

"I mean, Rita was special. Know what I mean?"

Et cetera. We do this, him emoting and us agreeing, and my dad saying things like, "I think I understand the system behind that sculpture there" (a mobile made out of plastic strips) for about five minutes. I listen and try hard to get a picture of how this weedy little man fitted into Rita's life, but I don't succeed. George is sweet, tentative, insecure. He's about thirty-five years old. About five years younger than

Rita. Maybe she liked younger men? No soap. Marcus wasn't younger and neither is Scott. Maybe she liked losers? That certainly doesn't work, not with those two as evidence. Even this guy, with his ropy chest and anxious eyes, isn't exactly a loser. He's just hopeful and sad-looking, and maybe the sadness is for her.

He says he is writing a novel.

I revise my analysis. You can't tell with writers. Rita would have thought writers were in a special category. I can hear her saying something about how if you're really creative who measures your machos.

Although that lady really liked macho a lot, I think.

The novel, George says, is about a wolverine. His eyes get a little life in them. He says, "Hey, *great* of you to ask."

Wolverine. I struggle with this; it's strange and uncomfortable but it might be interesting. The wolverine is not the central character, exactly, George elucidates, it's the alter ego for the guy who is the central character.

Rita liked the novel. She also made fun of it. "That lady had a true critic's eye. She could do anything. She was so goddamn talented." George appears to choke up.

Rob says we are interested in Rita and what she was like, but we're especially interested in her death; who might have killed her. We think her death is related to a death at the museum, but maybe not. We'd like to know what enemies she had.

George appears amazed. "Rita didn't have enemies. She was all light and bright and sparkling."

We are silent for a minute, digesting this. Do you remember the Japanese movie where you get four different views of a crime?

I finally say, "But she was excitable, don't you think?"

George agrees, "Hey, absolutely; a basic part of her charm."

"Do you think," Rob gently suggests, "that could have been misinterpreted?"

"No way." George is steadfast. "Everybody could see. Right off."

Rob and I spend about five minutes saying, "Well, but . . ." and "Don't you think maybe . . ." and "Did you notice that . . ." with almost no effect.

George remembers a Rita who was sunny and responsive. "Yeah, awfully energetic," he finally concedes. "I guess it's possible that someone or other . . ."

He's not saying that someone or other killed her for being too energetic. No, no, he thinks it was a plot of some kind.

George looks like a guy who might believe in Martian invasions or worldwide schemes to redress the wrongs of the Boer Wars. He doesn't say anything like this, though; he begins to act distressed and puts one hand in front of his eyes. "God, was I ever lucky. Of course it couldn't last."

I decide to be ashamed of myself.

My father tells George that he should not have been up on the ladder so long. "The bat droppings. They're piled in drifts on the floor and they rise and affect your balance."

"Rita was really fond of you," George tells my father.

We take a few minutes off to lean back and stare out George's window, which holds a view of a eucalyptus tree.

When George takes his hand away from his eyes, he agrees that anybody can get mad about anything. He's read about that happening. But he doesn't remember anybody ever calling Rita up, middle-of-the-night, threatening. Yeah, he's heard of that; he just doesn't remember it with her.

Sure, he'll give us a list of people that possibly could have, maybe. Sure.

People maybe from archaeology.

But he really thinks it had to be something in this last week. It all ties up, doesn't it? "Listen. She was a child of light. Everybody loved her."

I say, "Right. Yes, we, too, think it was something that happened recently. In the museum. For her to be shot near there. Was she in touch with you while she was there?"

George says, "Oh, sure. All the time."

"Did she have . . ." I pause and rephrase. "Was she feeling bad part of that time?"

"She was. And she mentioned Rob here. She said he helped her."

There's a pause while Rob and I wait for elaboration.

"She never let feeling bad affect other people."

Do I want to leave behind me a lover who's as blind to my faults as George is? I guess not. I certainly haven't taken any steps in that direction.

What did she say about her adventures with us?

George agrees the adventures were interesting. "She was with great people." He interrupts himself to ask if we'd like a beer. A lemon Crystal Geyser? "Hey, sorry not to have offered sooner, kind of upsetting, you know?"

We follow him down a long gray hall and into a minute kitchen that looks out onto a sea of wooden back porches. I resist thinking about a fire in this area. The whole neighborhood would go up like a pile of Presto logs.

George has one of those refrigerators where, when you open the door, everything falls out on the kitchen floor. "Well, hey, I guess there was one thing," he says. "Well, two

things. Or maybe three. First of all the sheriff." He tries unsuccessfully to open a Crystal Geyser with his thumbs and
ends up handing it to Rob. "That's an enemy to almost anybody, that sheriff, but you know about him, you know all
about that.

"The rest aren't enemies." He finds only two other bottles of Crystal Geyser, which go to me and my dad. He takes
a beer for himself and sits us at a wobbly oblong table,
bathed in light reflected off the other back porches. "Kind
of nice here, right?"

We agree, yes, nice.

"Well, it was things that happened there at your place.
Not the big things, but the little ones. Of course, all of it
was real dramatic. Out of synch. It all sounded like it belonged in my novel. Not in real life. Y'know?"

Yes, we say. We know.

"First of all, the guy that died twice. Marcus. He did
that?"

This, of course, is hard to explain. It takes us a while.

"Well, she knew him. Real well. You knew?"

We agree, yes, right.

"She knew everybody there. Except, of course, you." He
squints in my direction. "This Marcus was her lover. Sounds
like a real interesting guy."

Rob and I are silent. I put my energy into not blinking.

"And Scott and she were lovers, too. She was real good
about that. About keeping on being friends. She liked Marcus and she liked Scott."

I say, "Oh." What was it Rita called Scott? Studly?

Scott was hit hard by her death, though.

"She talked about both of them."

I look at George, who gets an A-plus at the moment for coolth. Can he possibly be as okay with all this as he seems? The only sign of stress is that his beer is going down fast.

He revolves the glass. "Had a lot of stuff to say about them." He takes a big final swig and puts the empty glass down.

"Hey, don't stop," I tell him. "It's nice sitting here. Kind of . . ." What phrase would George like? "Bonding." I get up to find him another beer.

He agrees, "Bonding.

"I've never been the kind to be jealous," he picks up. "And one of the great things about Rita was her frankness. Y'know?

"She could talk about those past relationships. That was so cool. Made me feel I was with her then."

This is beginning to be creepy, but I nod agreement. I want to keep George talking.

"This Marcus—she said he was a dynamite moneymaker when he felt like it.

"She made a lot of money one month in that place. Thebes. Just on his recommendations. 'Big wads of profit,' she said. 'Along with all the digging and identifying and bonking.'

" 'Wow,' is how she put it." George looks nostalgic.

I want to say, "It can't be that okay with you." But I just repeat, "Wow."

"I guess he was some over the top sometimes," George reflects. "Like with drugs."

We're silent, letting the word *drugs* hang around.

"Marcus was an artist, sort of?" I suggest. "Sculpture, maybe?"

"Oh, yeah, I guess. Like collecting Japanese tin toys and something or other with steel welding. And painting."

"Did he make movies?"

"Hey, come to think of it . . . Rita said something . . . I guess this guy could do anything."

"A good archaeologist, too. Though Scott was the one there. Scott and your dad."

"She *revered* your dad."

We're back to the different versions of reality.

And Scott? What else about him?

"Oh. Like I say, she was friends with them both." George swigs his beer and lets a troubled frown dent his high pale forehead. "Well, a couple of times she seemed almost, you know, cross?" He stares, troubled, at the sun and shadows on the neighboring back porches. He doesn't want to admit any small negative emotions into his Rita-memories. "Something or other about Scott and a lady named Danielle."

I pounce. "*Danielle*. Tell me. What about her?"

"Rita had a picture of her."

This is a stopper. It takes me a minute to get hold of it. "A picture. My God. Why?"

"Well, it was kind of odd. Because this Danielle was the only person Rita ever spoke real harshly of."

I'll bet she did. The Danielle that stole both her boyfriends. I can imagine Rita's comment: "Card-carrying bitch." And that's the expurgated version.

"George, I'd love to see that picture."

"She threw it away. It was a big picture." George makes squaring-off motions. So Rita had a studio picture of Danielle. I do not get it.

"What did Danielle look like?" I ask. "Was she pretty? Tall? Skinny? Oval face?"

George is completely stymied. "Lots of hair," he finally volunteers. "Oh, and Rita felt something about that picture, know what I mean?"

George, a novelist is supposed to notice detail; nobody ever told you that, huh?

Silence descends on our back porch. George drinks beer and broods. My father begins softly, "She was lying on a long white table . . ." Rob smiles at a blue jay on the porch rail.

George adds, "It was a nice picture. A nude study."

Oh, for God's sake.

That even wakes Rob up. He turns to me, and for the first time in a while he tries to share a moment.

George misinterprets our reactions. "Hey, I don't feel anything about that. I mean, the naked body is beautiful. A temple."

I let this percolate for a while. "But why did she *have* the picture?

"Other than for an art object," I add quickly, forestalling whatever pious remark George is hibernating. "Was it for some personal reason?"

George says oh, and uh. I can tell that he does have an idea. "Well," he admits finally. "I guess she had some kind of a plan.

"Because when she threw it out, she looked at it for a minute and said, 'You know, Jidge'—she called me that sometimes—'you think about doing something mean and after a while you get bored with it. That ever happen to you?'

"And then she chucked it in the recycle bin."

George won't respond to my further proddings about motives and plans. He doesn't like talking about this; it shows a possible flaw in his ephemeral Rita.

But Rita did have a plan, which I am interpreting as follows: Danielle is an archaeologist. She has a job at the Luxor
Museum. The Luxor Museum, Arab-managed, would hate a
nude picture of a female staff member.

After a minute, George finds a way to change the subject.
"Well, yeah," he volunteers. "I thought of something. Almost a threat; maybe it figures. Nothing about an enemy,
but, well, she telephoned, I guess the night before . . . no,
two nights before . . ." He has to pause; this gets to him;
he's choking up again.

I look at Rob, who is back to admiring the blue jay, his
face smooth. He looks like the nice American boy he is. My
father has arrived at, "Let her go, God bless her."

"And she said, 'There's something that bothers me. Something not great, Jidge. I guess I was real dumb. I don't always
get it.' She used to say that about herself: 'I'm real fast with
archaeology. Not other stuff.'

"And then she wouldn't tell me what she meant. She said
she hated to say and she wasn't really sure and she'd been
wrong about something else lately—something about you,
Dr. Day . . ."

My father stops singing to turn a pink interested face in
George's direction. "I doubt that I can help."

"And when I tried to push her, she just said, 'This friend
gave me a serious secret. It started back in Thebes. A deep,
deep secret. I think I'll try to check up on it.'"

George adds, "Not that it's anything about an enemy.
But it's strange, don't you think?"

"George," I say, "if you think of anything else about that—
any clue about who may have said something, or if Rita read

something or noticed something somewhere—anything else she said that might tie in—please call me. It's important."

"Yeah, I guess." He's dubious. "I'm not real good at that kind of stuff."

"Listen." I try for a strength infusion. "It's vital. It could tell us who killed her."

He looks upset. He says he'll try. He takes my phone number.

I want to get George to talk some more, but he has other ideas. "Wanna see my clay figures?"

The answer is no, but of course, we say yes.

George's clay figures are the kind where you're not sure whether it's a dog or a tree or a model of your fist. I tell him they're suggestive and he seems to like that.

On our way out of the Mission, Rob asks, "Have we been there, Carla? In Thebes?"

I'm disbelieving. "Are you kidding?"

He shakes his head no. "When he was talking, it kept sounding familiar. But I couldn't picture it."

"Robbie, we were in Thebes for six weeks. In a camp. We had a tent. We cooked stuff over a fire. We were there when Daddy found the coffin lid."

"Oh," he says, in a tone of discovery. "That place. Yeah. Okay."

I don't follow up with *what do you mean, that place,* and *what did you think the name of that place was,* and *what in the hell gives, Rob,* and all the other questions I could ask. I decide to be quiet and stare sullenly at the scenery.

Rob is so taken up with Cherie that he has completely abolished the part of his past that includes me. *Good-bye, Rob, good-bye, old playmate.* Everything passes, right, chum? Right.

My father fills the sound gap by singing. He finds a new appropriate song: *Where it all goes, the dear lord only knows.*

Dinner tonight is one of Egon's theme meals. The theme is Ethiopian; there are carved wooden platters in the middle of the table, which Egon announces are from Addis Ababa. And the food is roast lamb served with flabby hunks of pancake.

Egon makes an announcement about Daddy. Egon looks around proprietarily; he pauses; he is pleased. "He will be helping me recover some of our memories of earlier archaeology."

"No, there won't be Western silverware," he asides to a complaining Bunny. "You pick the lamb up by wrapping the pancake around it. Anybody can do it."

"Yeah? Well, not me." Bunny turns toward my father. "What's this about Pop?"

"He'll be helping me with his memories."

"Hey, Mr. Rothskellar, memories? Pop and memories? Come on."

Egon levels a mild gaze her way. "Surely you agree that Dr. Day can be a help."

Daddy looks up from his lamb. He is the only one who has kept on eating; he's good at this hands-on method. "Dr. Day," he says cheerfully, "that's me; I'm Dr. Day."

Bunny agrees. "Yep, you sure are."

"I've been waiting," Daddy says, "for further material. There's a sign out front."

The banners advertising Scott's new discoveries have been augmented during the last week; Egon has had two new ones painted. One of these reads, THE SUN QUEEN'S SECRETS. Nefertiti is the sun queen. The other one says, WONDERFUL NEW DISCOVERIES. TICKETS NOW.

"New discoveries," Daddy says now, apparently recalling this slogan. "I don't know. There is a poem about the new; Perhaps I can quote it, *Now the shadow of the new comes across* . . . No, *now the threat of the new comes across* . . . Re may not be terribly happy."

Scott says, "You're remembering the poem right, Edward."

My father says, "Ah. But the point is that when we are . . ." He founders here and quits trying to deal with his lamb. "There is an image of . . . what am I trying to say . . . perhaps of radical coherence . . ." He stops and sits with his head bent, staring at his dish.

Bunny is the one who states the obvious. "Dr. Rothskellar, listen, I mean, do you think that Pop . . ." (When did Bunny started calling my father Pop? This has snuck up on me.) "I mean, Pop's memory isn't all that great. Do you really think he can, well . . . How long ago archaeology is it you want?"

Scott says to my father, "That's okay, Ed, you're doing great."

Egon agrees enthusiastically, "Scott, you are right. Absolutely."

Bunny's question of what period in archaeology my father is supposed to help with still hangs around unanswered. All of us return to our lamb. We seem to have gotten better at managing the pancakes.

*   *   *

Now, after dinner, I find Daddy in the museum office, sitting in front of a computer.

I stare at him with my mouth open. I don't want to think about the collision between him and a computer.

But then I notice that there are pictures on this computer and that by hitting a button he's able to get a new picture whenever he wants. The five-year-old grandchildren of my Manor residents can do this.

The pictures all seem to be ones of Egyptian scenes or Egyptian art.

I ask Daddy how he's getting along with Mr. Rothskellar and he says, "My what?" and then says, "Mr. *Rothskellar?*" as if he's never heard of such a person. After a minute at his Egyptian website he says, perfectly coherently, "I am rejoicing at feeling needed."

"That's wonderful," I say. "I'm glad."

He gestures at the computer screen. "Most of these were photographed in a museum. Where you can't make a mistake on what it is. But they are good clear images."

He looks okay, body erect, shoulders back. I ask myself if he could have followed a computer website this closely before he came here, punching the right button each time, and for a minute I'm not sure. Then I realize that of course he could; he used the TV remote at the Manor; he could summon up *This Old House* and *Antiques Roadshow*.

But still, it's a nice sign of adjustment, I tell myself.

So it was okay about his coming here, I also assure the anxious me. It was an okay thing.

Stop feeling wary, I tell myself. Stop following him around. Quit worrying that he, or you, is riding for a fall.

It's perfectly normal that Egon wants him to talk about the past.

The minute I state that to myself, I feel peculiar again. I have to come hang over Daddy's shoulder and look at his website pictures. One flashes up now, an image of Hathor from the British Museum, stately, perfectly poised, balancing her unwieldy horned crown. Daddy greets her with enthusiasm. "A queen indeed."

But then the next page has no picture, just the website's address, and he asks me to go get Bunny. Bunny, he claims, will be able to get him a new set of pictures.

♟ Chapter 14

"Hello, darling," says Cherie's voice over the phone.

Do not forget that Cherie is deeply Southern, and that the word *darling* comes across as *dahlin'*! A pronunciation that sometimes, when I remember that this lady is efficient and feisty and my father's lawyer, I start to find appealing. At the moment I'm still smarting over my afternoon with Rob, and Cherie does not seem appealing.

I tell her *Hello, Cherie* and she says that that asshole has just gotten around to calling her because she told him she would sue the *cojones* off him if he didn't keep her in the loop, and the asshole (meaning the sheriff) is going to question my dad this afternoon.

"And, darling, I don't know what he was planning, maybe to send a squad car and drag your daddy in there by force; but that, believe me, is not going to be. So would you get him down into Conestoga at two today and dear, believe you me, I will be along with all my guns ready."

The sheriff's office is on Conestoga's Main Street. My friend the old sheriff had his office in his house, but Sheriff Munro has liberated a storefront. It says SHERIFF on its plate glass window in a curved arrangement that looks as if it belongs on *Deadwood*.

Daddy is thrilled that we are going into town to talk to the sheriff. He likes any outing. He thinks the sheriff is a peculiar man, but he's not afraid of him. "Only a little," he says. "And I will have you and that pretty woman with me. I am wearing my gray tweed jacket. And my dark blue shirt. This dark blue shirt is fashionable."

He thinks the dark blue shirt is fashionable because there was a whole school full of men wearing dark blue shirts. And these men listened to a lecture by him, while he talked about Tutankhamen.

"Yes, you look great." I bend over to kiss his cheek, at which he says, "My dear, how nice!"

When we arrive at the sheriff's office, Cherie also kisses him. She leaves a pink smudge on his cheek. "Oh, my goodness, darling Crocodile, I have branded you. It is so wonderful to see you, and you just wait, we will distribute this slimy creature in little pieces all over his floor.

"And darling Carla." I get the full benefit of a wide-open, turquoise-eyed inspection. Only sometimes, when she looks at me in this assessing way, do I understand that Cherie, too, worries about the emotional triangle she and I are in. "Carla, dear, how are you, how is it going? Do not worry about a thing here with this creature; he is all threat and noise and nothin'. And that little *Chronicle* guy finally got his ass in gear and the story is going to run maybe tomorrow."

While she fires all this at me, Cherie has a hand behind my shoulder and one behind my father's, and she is shepherding us through the door of the sheriff's office.

It is an ordinary grocery store door that rings a bell when you enter.

Inside there are three desks, a Formica picnic table with a small plaster statue of a grizzly bear, some desk chairs, some folding chairs, and a file cabinet. The sheriff is behind one of the desks. He waits for a while, as if he's deciding whether he has to do this, then finally stands up.

"Sheriff Munro," Cherie says, "I do not know what you thought you were up to, getting us down here like this. But believe me, I have the full force of public opinion on my side and I am not about to take any nonsense."

She zeroes in on two chairs into which she guides me and my father. "There, darling Crocodile, are you comfy? Not too hard on your old back; this is sort of a nasty chair? It is just too bad that a prominent gentleman of your age has to be dragged around . . ." She interrupts herself long enough to find a nasty chair of her own, into which she gracefully subsides. "Yes, sir, dragged down here with no more regard for legal process than if we lived in the old days in Nazi Germany."

Cherie looks elegant today in a dark green pantsuit and gold shirt.

The sheriff sits down behind his desk. He stares glumly at her, as if he has seen the future and found it ugly.

"I do not like to think about Nazi Germany," my father offers.

After a minute the sheriff reaches into a desk drawer and extracts a brightly colored plastic and cardboard package, one of the kind that is sealed tight in the store to prevent pilfering. He tries to insert a fingernail under its plastic edge. He tries to tear the cardboard. He attempts to pry a corner loose. He gets a pair of scissors and jabs. He produces a knife and jabs more forcefully.

Cherie leans forward, watching. "What a shame, Sheriff," she says. "But if that there is a recording device, you are wasting your time. It was real forehanded of you to buy it at The Good Guys and be ready for our interview, but for recording, you need our permission and we aren't giving that. So you can stop fighting with that recalcitrant little mean whatzit."

She settles back in her chair, looking pleased. "Those packages are absolute hell, aren't they?"

I suspect Cherie is editing the truth in saying the sheriff needs our permission. My understanding is that he's the sheriff and can record if he informs us. But he, like me, isn't sure about this. He watches Cherie, who sits back, smiling placidly. Then he puts his equipment away and rests his hands flat on the desk.

"The date is April 25, 2006," he intones, staring at his west wall, "and the time is two-seventeen. I am about to start the interviewing of Edward Day." He seems to be aiming this speech at an imaginary TV camera.

"*Professor* Edward Day," I interject.

"I have been a professor since May 1966," my father says. "It was a unanimous decision of the tenure committee.

"I wasn't supposed to know," he adds, "but the department secretary told me."

The sheriff ignores this atypical bit of boasting. He clicks a mechanical pencil; he jiggles something else. He scowls at Daddy and speaks clearly and distinctly. "Where were you on the night of April 12, 2006?"

"Goodness," my father says. "That's much too long ago."

"When the young woman was shot."

My father stares pleasantly.

"You were there when Rita Claus was shot."

"Oh. Yes. That was her name, Rita. What a terrible shame."

"Did you shoot her?"

Cherie is on her feet, yelling. "You have no grounds for this question. In fact, sir, this whole sequence of interrogation is out of line. I have changed my mind, sir, I would love to have a recording of this procedure; let's get that play toy out of your drawer."

The sheriff seems unsure what to do. After a brief scrabble, the recorder package comes out again and he manages, with a single ferocious gesture, to rip it open. Once more he states the date and time, and questioning is resumed.

"Did you see who shot Rita Claus?" is what he asks Daddy this time.

My parent drums a finger on the table. He thinks. He says, "Seeing. That is difficult to determine sometimes. Seeing is not usually thought to be definitive. There is a passage, 'Shoreland will turn into water / Watercourse back into shoreland.' Lichtheim 1, 141. Many things are quite hard."

"Shit." The sheriff reaches a shaky hand to punch the machine's *off* button. "Now listen, old man"—shaping his lips as if my dad were stone deaf (which he's not)—"you can start stopping that right now. You aren't fooling me. You're trying to avoid answering."

"Sheriff Munro." Cherie is on her feet. "Cease. This."

"You're being obstructive," the sheriff shouts. "There will be consequences."

"I will remember every evil word." Cherie's intonation gets very Southern.

The sheriff gives the impression of dodging around her. "Did. You. See. Who shot her?"

"Yes," my dad says calmly. "I saw."

I stop breathing. So, I think, does Cherie.

The sheriff blurts, "What are you saying? You *did* see?"

He reaches toward the machine. "Hell." He jiggles and clicks. "Shit." Daddy's interesting answer didn't get recorded. More buttons get punched. "Now. Please repeat your answer."

My father stares.

"You saw? You saw someone shoot her?"

Daddy seems puzzled. "Ah. Do you think so?"

"Goddamn it to hell, answer."

"Sheriff Munro," Cherie says, "you've asked that question."

"There was a gun," my father says. "She may have been afraid of it."

"Who?"

"She may not have understood this."

"Not the one who was shot. Not Rita Claus." Sheriff Munro sounds desperate.

"She is a nice person," my father says. "Perhaps she was finishing. It is hard to be sure."

"Stop that!" the sheriff yells.

Cherie is half on her feet again, saying that *this is enough*, and *my client and I will be departing now*, but then Daddy says, "Rita was the victim. She wasn't the person with the gun," and Cherie subsides back into her chair.

She lets the sheriff replay the tape from *Please repeat your answer*. Daddy listens. He seems nervous and plucks at the knees of his pant legs.

"Now," the sheriff asks, "is that your testimony?"

"I have no idea. The man on the record is confused."

The sheriff says, "That is your voice," and my father says, "I wonder," and the sheriff says, "You can wonder all you like, but a fact is a fact," and my father says, "Very debatable."

Cherie sits back and lets all this happen.

Sheriff Munro gets up to walk around the room.

Cherie has relaxed into her chair back. She crosses her legs, which reveals purple and gold stockings. She looks interested and prepared for something even more interesting and in no way ready to close off the proceedings yet.

I would feel sorry for this sheriff if he weren't such an evil bastard.

He produces a pack of gum and pops several pieces in his mouth at once. He tours the room some more.

Then he returns to his chair. "I have another matter to discuss.

"That is the purloining of artifacts from the museum."

Daddy looks at him attentively. He has begun humming under his breath. It seems to be, " 'Put another log on the fire.' "

"What do you know," the sheriff asks, "about the disappearance of artifacts from the museum?"

Cherie again is halfway to her feet. Her voice gets harsh enough to saw glass. "I am reporting this behavior."

My father says, "The disappearance of artifacts? I am so sorry."

"Answer the question, please. What do you know?"

"Don't answer, Croc. You don't have to."

"Was there an ankh?" Daddy asks thoughtfully. "No, I think not."

"Edward Day—Professor Day—did you take any of the objects that are missing?"

"Crocodile, we're off. Outta here. Absolutely this minute. This is finished."

My father sighs. "I doubt it very much about those artifacts. None has a ritual significance."

Cherie says, "We are going, and all of this is on tape. All that last exchange, Sheriff, in the tape where you browbeat my client and try to entrap him. That tape better not disappear. It better be all ready to go on exhibit. Because I am going to use it in my case, big time."

"Lo, the private chamber is open, the books are stolen," my father recites, "the secrets in it are laid bare."

The sheriff sits for a minute staring broodingly at Cherie and my dad. Then he clicks off his machine and says, "Get the hell out of here."

Daddy objects that some questions haven't been answered. The sheriff tells him for God's sake, to go.

Out on the street, Cherie is protective. She puts her hand on Daddy's arm and calls him Ed. "Ed, darling, are you okay?" I'm glad to hear her dropping the Crocodile nickname. "Did all that hurt your feelings?"

"I am feeling all right." He gives her a solemn look. "I rise above being yelled at."

Cherie suggests, and he accepts, the idea of a chocolate sundae at Bettie's Diner.

*   *   *

"I sure don't like this stuff about the artifacts," Cherie tells me.

"I believe there is a jade statue of Apis involved." That's what my father offers.

"The creature"—Cherie jerks her head toward the sheriff's office—"is setting something up. I think he is getting ready to frame you, Ed dear. I am suspicious. My training has taught me to suspect the worst, and with this clown, I do."

Yes, I agree. I do, too. I suspect the worst of everybody, and that includes you, Cherie, my love.

⌐ Chapter 15

It is the day after our struggle with Sheriff Munro and I've decided to devote this morning to exploring the museum.

It has just reopened. I'm going to come in the front door like an ordinary person and look at some of the exhibits.

It's a bright California day. The air smells of sage. People are lined up in an orderly but wobbly line at Egypt Regained's main door. The line goes out to the parking lot, along the edge of it, and ends up against a flower bed.

Most of these customers are clutching white squares of paper. Apparently Egon put an ad in the *Chronicle* about the reopening. We were closed for a week and now we've been open for two days.

I ascertain by craning my neck toward a lady's newspaper and reading it upside down that Egon's ad doesn't say anything about murder or accident or any of that negative stuff. NEW ARCHAEOLOGY UNVEILED, it headlines.

There aren't any new exciting displays yet. That's for when Scott unveils his discoveries. For now, all we have are murders.

The public, of course, knows about the murders. Steve the boy reporter has done a good job of publicizing them. He has put Rita firmly into the picture, even though the sheriff calls her death "an event in a local nightclub," and refuses to link it to the museum.

"Is this where it happened?" a customer asks Bunny at the door.

Bunny enjoys this. "Not the lady murder, dear," she tells the client, who is pink-haired and wears glasses on a rhinestone-studded chain. "But the gentleman, he died right here."

Bunny is probably a pretty good guard. She makes the women relinquish their big pocketbooks and shopping bags. "It'll be teetotally safe at the check stand, I promise you."

"Good *good* morning," she tells me. "Came to help me out?"

Yes, I'll help her out. I have just learned that I am leaving Egon's elegant establishment. I will probably leave tomorrow. My Manor boss called this morning with a complaint: "Hey, I said a couple days. Come on. Get back here." It would be a nice gesture for me to do a spot of work before I depart. I've been a parasite, eating Egon's meals and sleeping in his excellent beds and feeling apprehensive and peculiar because I don't understand what's happening. It'll feel good to get back to work and back to a safe and boring Manor.

I really should take my dad with me, too. This place is weird.

I move into the left-hand side of the door and start grabbing tickets.

"Just punch it and give it back," Bunny instructs, handing me an instrument.

When I ask, "Why punch?" she shrugs. "Sump'n to do."

"Damndest thing," she says. "Couple more of those little object doohickeys disappeared last night. But that display case where they were was locked. It's not just me sayin' so. Mr. Rothskellar—I mean, Egon—he ast me to call him that—he said so, too. I got him to check it.

"So we're guessin' somebody has got a key."

"A former employee?"

"Has to be, doesn't it? . . . Now, ma'am, that's a real pretty pockey-book and I know you're proud of it, but you got to leave it with me.

"Meatheads," she tells me, aside.

She is a sturdy lady, and today, with the morning sun hitting her shoulders, she looks like a female cop sent by central casting. "Bunny," I ask, "is that a gun on your belt?"

"Nothin', babe; I mean, no sweat, it's just a toy gun, Buck Rogers, dear . . .

"Taser gun," she adds after a minute. "Won't do swat in a crisis. Good for killing flies."

I try to remember what I learned about Tasers in the lecture they gave at the Manor. Tasers hurt.

Bunny's khaki pants and shirt are crisply ironed; the gun, which is fat, rests on the protruding part of her gut.

"Bunny, do you like being a guard?" I wave a guy in a wheelchair on into the museum. A wheelchair would be an excellent place to hide a stolen artifact, but so what?

"Sure do, dear. I always had these little diddley-squat jobs before: make hamburgers, serve hamburgers; the best I ever had was ring up money for hamburgers, which ain't all that thrilling. Del Oro College offered a two-and-a-half-month course in being a guard and I took it and that was that. Got a job here right off. Nice uniform and pay and I felt good about what I did. Makes you know you're doin' somethin'."

She shifts her belt and plants her feet farther apart. "This job is real important to me. I like the work and it's got benefits. Fringe benefits I didn't know about. Besides the real good pay. I'm home now; I got every intention of staying. Get it?"

Yeah, I get it.

Although in some vague way I don't. Bunny seems threatened. Surely she doesn't think I'm competing for her job?

"And I guess the last couple of weeks didn't discourage you?" The tail end of the museum-viewer line is coming through the door.

"Nope, not-a-tall. That kinda thing don't bother me none."

"You were worried about Mr. Broussard."

"Like, when I asked at dinner? No, baby, not worried; I just wondered if anybody noticed anything special when he collapsed. That first time. But nobody did."

"What kind of something special?"

She shrugs. "Nothin'. I sure din notice anything. Come on, we get to sit down for a while now." She leads the way to the marble bench that curves along the wall of the entrance lobby.

She produces one of Egon's ads from her pocket, folds it several times, and waves it in her face for a fan. "Whoo-ee! My daughter says the only thing wrong with the job is the standing around. You sure get to do a lot of that. I forget, dear; you got kids?"

I'm momentarily struck silent. Some place in the last couple of weeks I have aged fifteen years, enough so that Bunny thinks I might have children stashed away, kids old enough to be living an independent life somewhere without me.

" 'Cause, dear, if you don't got kids, you wouldn' recognize the signs I see in your little dad. Like, he's been real excited lately? He runs around, sorta holding his breath, looks at a book, drops it, picks up a sandwich, eats a quarter, tries one damn thing after another. My kids' kindergarten teachers used to call that a wall-climbing kid, but what it is, is just plain overexcited. Know what I mean?"

Bunny looks at me; I'm not sure whether her scrutiny is solicitous or prying. "Y'know?" she pushes.

I say, "Sort of." Of course I know what she means; it's the manic phase of Alzheimer's and it comes with being overstimulated. Which is happening to my dad. Happening here. Talking to Egon, whatever that amounts to, gets him all excited, and so does fussing with a computer, whatever that involves. Bunny is watching me interestedly. I turn a bland expression her way. Somehow I don't really trust this lady.

"An', dear," she is saying, "then we got the little objects, you know? The artifacts? Like them getting snitched. And your dad . . . well, I don't like to tell you this, but he had one of those things—an unkh, is it?"

"Ankh," I say. "A symbol of the life force." I suspect Bunny knows the correct name just as well as I do. She works here; she deals with the material all the time.

"Yeah, ankh, right. Little blue thing." She makes the bowknot shape in the air. "Well, he had it in his pocket. And pulled it out and showed it to me, just as bold as brass."

"He has a couple of those of his own."

"Yeah, but this one was ours. It had a splash of orange paint on the bottom, and I remembered that. Knew it right away."

She pauses, looking at me, triumphant. "He told me he found it lying on a table, but we don't do that, lie them out in public. It was locked up, and he had to of got the key and taken it." She looks at me again, sideways, which comes out oddly on her, since she has a broad face and fat cheeks.

"Bunny," I say, "you want something from me. What?"

She and I are both sitting on the same entry-hall bench. She slides away a few inches. "Hey, baby. Want something? What could I possibly want?"

Well, damned if I know, Bunny my dear.

Bunny is a ridiculous name for a fat lady in a tan guard's uniform.

"I don't know," I say aloud. "Thank you for telling me. That was considerate."

But I know my dad well. He wouldn't take artifacts from the museum. If an object were carelessly left lying around, though, he certainly would pick it up.

"You bet it was nice of me to tell you," Bunny says belligerently.

So I've made an enemy. Seems as if I already had one anyway.

I tell Bunny I'm going into the museum to see some exhibits.

"You just help yourself, sweetcakes," she says. "I get fifteen minutes now. That's in my contract."

In the main hall the public has been organized into orderly lines. People are queued up to look at the stone head of Osiris, at the wooden head of Hathor, at the calcite carving of the Vizier Papy, at the canopic box containing four canopic jars. (Canopic jars are animal-headed jars containing the vital organs of the mummy.) One of the Harouns is serving as guard to marshall the crowd, and Egon is delivering a lecture.

"Here we see the goddess in her guise as a cow's head," he says. "We acquired this image from a dealer in Paris, but before that . . ."

People are staring, mouths open and eyes glazed. I'm not sure what holds their attention. Maybe it's that Egon looks so white-haired and learned, just the way a museum expert ought to look. Maybe they're hoping that if they hang in long enough, they'll understand something. But Egon doesn't deliver that sort of lecture. He doesn't tell his audience who Hathor was and why she was worshipped. He just talks about how this particular artifact he's pointing at got to come live in Egypt Regained. "Before 1910 the provenance is unclear," he announces.

Maybe all these people are thinking about the murders and trying to fit them into the setting.

I lurk on the outskirts, observing people, categorizing, feeling like an anthropologist watching the natives at their cultural recreations. I should be taking notes.

And also, I'm observing Egon. Everything makes me uncomfortable lately; I add Egon to the list. My main question about him is the one about my dad. Of course, Egon sees what everybody sees. My dad has Alzheimer's. Medium badly. Egon is faking when he says my father helps in the museum research. Daddy couldn't possibly help in anything; he costs money and gets in the way. And now the sheriff and Bunny both think he swipes the tchochkes.

I have to get my dad out of here. He'll be heartbroken; he'll protest and sulk, but it's got to be.

Suddenly, without any visible shift, Egon in his lecture begins saying something interesting.

"Now this collection"—he's talking about the canopic box—"was found in the exploration in 2001."

I turn off the note-taking anthropologist and start listening, since 2001 was the year when everybody was in Thebes. I'm interested in the expedition of 2001.

"The box was found by a group, a group of my friends, actually." Egon is constitutionally incapable of telling a story straight. "Found in the tomb of the merchant Intep but behind a wall, a wall that we all thought had been . . ." He rambles on before announcing, "I have a picture here, quite an interesting photo actually, a photo of us, actually, on the scene of the discovery, so to speak."

The photo, framed, is laid faceup on top of the glass case. I'm fast at getting to it; I circumvent a batch of pink-haired ladies and bend over the photo frame. I'm interested in any picture of the gang back in 2001, the year of Rita's Thebes stories. But especially I want to see what Danielle looks like in the picture. Also Marcus Broussard. I've thought about both of them a lot. And I've been making my usual mistake of forming an image beforehand. The images are blurred around the edges but include the following details: Marcus, whom I've only seen laid out flat and dead-appearing, is trim, suave, and foxy. Danielle looks like me, which is a stopper. She also looks like a man-killer. Another stopper. Come on, let's see that picture of these people and clear this stuff up, all the gang cheek by jowl at the entrance to the tomb.

So here we have it: a photo. It's a standard flashlit dark tomb setting: dust, rocks, hanging electric bulbs, a passageway off to the right, a crumbling plaster wall. Five people lined up in a matey row, mostly smiling that forced dead-on photographic smile you get when the cameraman says, look up, now smile, say rhubarb. Egon's on the end, white-haired and avuncular, holding the canopic box aloft. And I guess that's Marcus under the hard hat. A disappointment, the picture doesn't tell me much; one guy in a hard hat looks like any other guy in a hard hat. Sturdy, medium tall, well-muscled arms protruding from short sleeves, hat down too far.

Off to the side is something I recognize. That little shape back there is my darling father. The sweet thing. Standing in the passage so as not to grab the glory.

But wait. Don't leave yet. There she is, of course, Danielle: tall, and despite her khakis, curvy, and yes, as George said, with plenty of hair. Radiating a lot of something. Nervous orgones. Vivacity, brains. Staring straight at the camera, but you feel she'd stare straight at you just that way—assessing.

The perfect archaeological babe. I could put her in a movie today.

Does she look like me? Hey, I wish.

She's the kind that puts her arm around people. One arm encircles the neck of Marcus, dislodging his hard hat some; a hand plays with the corner of his shirt. And the other arm is around the neck of a perfectly recognizable Scott, smilingly handsome, manly, and silly. Egyptian archaeologist meets photo op. Next to him slouches Rita, black hair short and upstanding. The two younger guys are wearing hard hats, the rest of the gang not. Why? The rest of the crowd doesn't go into places where rocks get dropped on them?

I put my finger on Danielle's image and raise my voice. "Egon, who's this?"

Maybe I sound commanding or excited; Egon moves in

right away, squeezing people aside, excusing himself to the ladies. He peers. I think his faultless brow furrows. He says, "Hmm." He adds, "You know, I'm not absolutely sure."

Like hell you're not sure, Egon. "Listen, she's special. You'd remember."

Egon furrows his face; he does a spot of thinking with hand pressed against brow; finally he says, "Oh," and "Yes." He has made a discovery. "That lady was named Danielle. She was a friend of . . ." He pauses before deciding whose friend she was. "A friend of Scott's."

"Yes," I say. "She was a member of the dig."

Egon is judicious. "Well, not exactly."

"But she was there. Everyone talks about her. She gets into this picture."

Egon looks vague. "Yes."

After a minute he seems to have made a discovery. "She was on a neighboring dig?"

We are standing there, me with my forefinger on Danielle's nose, when further evidence is supplied by a guard. One of the Harouns, complete with label and turban.

He has squeezed his way through the crowd and now bends over the picture. His turban is on crooked, and pink scalp shows through his close-cropped blond hair.

"This lady here?" He points at the smiling face. "That lady's name is Danielle."

"Haroun," I ask, "how on earth did you know?"

"Your dad. I got interested because she looks so sort of— special—and I asked your dad and he said, 'That lady there? Why, that lady is Danielle.' Then he went on to tell about how interesting it had been, finding that box of stuff.

"He said the box held some of the insides of the

mummy," Haroun elucidates. "They take the guts out of the mummy and put them in separate boxes. I thought that was a real interesting fact."

I have moved from the museum into Egon's office. I am sitting there now.

I haven't been in Egon's office since we first moved in here. It spreads out around me, the usual luxurious Egon mix of oriental rugs, marble-topped furniture, Egyptian artifacts. There's an Egyptian lamp stand with a fake taper. A picture window with a picture of part of the garden.

Egon sits behind his slate desk, hands folded relaxedly on top of it. He smiles. "No need to thank me, my dear. We were glad to have you stay here with Edward. What a fine person he is."

He knows that I'm leaving him soon, going back to the Manor; he thinks I've come to say what a great visit this has been. Even though there was a murder or two while I was here.

"Egon, I want to ask you something."

He lets a slight frown appear on his forehead. "Truly, Carla. I do not know much about her. That Danielle."

Well, that wasn't what I was going to ask, but it's interesting that he thinks so. "I want to talk about my father."

"Oh. Yes. Wonderful, wonderful."

"I'm curious about what you've learned. From interviewing him."

"Interviewing? Oh, surely." Egon leans forward and frowns at his slate desktop as if an answer resides there. "Well, you know. It was to talk about archaeology."

My expression probably indicates doubt.

"He is, of course, you know—yes, surely you know very well—a truly well-informed man."

I let that sit for a while. Then I ask, "Yes, but what did he *say*?"

Egon seems to think I'm being rude. "Well, my dear, of course." He waves a hand. "Details, you know."

"He has trouble remembering. You know that."

Egon again does a hand-wave.

"I don't understand. Honestly, Egon, I really don't. What could you want him to talk about?" When he simply looks polite at this outburst, I decide to invent some facts. "He seemed troubled afterwards. Upset. Thinking about what he'd been telling you."

That gets results. Egon sits up straight and undoes his hands, which have reclasped themselves. He says, "Oh, my."

"It troubled me. I hate to see him upset."

He says, "Hmmm," and "Upset." He broods. "I wonder what . . ."

This is offered contemplatively, as if the rest of the sentence would be, "I wonder what exactly," or "I wonder which of the things he told me got him upset." He doesn't sound as if he were going to finish, "But none of that stuff was upsetting."

"I think I should know about it," I say, pushing my advantage. "It's troubling." I probably add something extraneous and stupid, like, "I'm his daughter."

I don't think I've ever seen Egon angry. But to my surprise, unexpectedly, I see it now. It's an impressive sight. Moses, confronted by unbelievers. He gets lines in his face. He half gets out of his chair. He raises an arm. "Carla. Professional archaeology. Things that matter. Part of what an archaeologist does.

"Much of it is *serious* work." He hits *serious* hard, to indicate that I am frivolous and wouldn't understand.

He leans on the desk. "And now I am quite busy. And I truly feel we've consulted enough."

No, Egon, we haven't consulted enough. But I don't want to arm-wrestle you on it. I'll just mill around and ask some other people some more questions.

Chapter 16

I come down Egon's steps two at a time, which is not a good idea, considering that they are marble and are slippery.

At the bottom of the steps is Scott Dillard, whose sleeve I grab on to. "Drill some sense into my head, will you?" I demand.

"Blues Enthusiast." He more or less straightens me up. "What in hell is the matter?"

"I don't know what's the matter. No one will speak a straight sentence."

"And you think I will? I'm flattered."

"I don't think you will. You were here and I grabbed."

"Okay, okay." We are on the gravel path that slants down the hill toward the prettied-up statue of Hatshepshut. "Let's walk."

"My dad is crazy," I say. "My boyfriend's in love with another woman. She spends half her time lording it over me about what great sex they have. The sheriff is trying to put my father in jail. Egon . . . what's Egon doing with my dad? Have you been watching?"

"Yep."

"And is it weird?"

"You could say that." Scott puts an arm around my shoulder. He squeezes. Maybe my grandmother, if I had one, would think he is squeezing too intimately, with too much of his left-hand body impinging on my right-hand body, but at the moment I don't think so. I regard all that as just fine. Scott is a handsome man and I'm lonely. Shut up, ancestral grand-maternal voice. "Egon is always somewhat weird, you understand . . . Listen"—Scott squeezes a bit harder—"I'm sorry you got mixed up in all this."

"I don't even know what *all this* is," I say. "First, the murders. Then a whole bunch of other stuff. Something about your discoveries. Your exhibits."

"Oh, *shit*." He puts a lot of energy into that *oh, shit*. "I wish you'd never even heard of it."

"Well, thanks."

"I wish *I* hadn't. Me. Wish I weren't involved. I wish I were running a gas station in Center City, Kansas."

I move away. "Cut it out. Your discoveries? All that stuff you turned up? Egon's New Archaeology Unveiled?"

"Fuck all that."

He's so fierce that I step back a foot and try some remark about new knowledge always being valuable.

"Oh, yeah? How about not new, not real?"

"Of course it's real. For God's sake, how real is anything? And you're in line for the Hartdale."

"Hartdale? A whole lot of talk and publicity and garbage. And the charm is way gone."

We've kept on walking. I try to sound consoling, or wise. "You'll feel different when it happens. When that committee arrives . . ." I stop, realizing that I picture the committee as the group of grinning, toothy people who race up to your doorstep with the giant magazine contest check in the TV ads.

Scott says, "Yeah, hell." We walk a bit farther, scuffing gravel. "Some things, at first, they seem worth anything. Any sacrifice, any concession. And then you wake up one night wondering if you've sold your soul to the devil."

"Egon's the devil?" Hey, I think, no way. Egon is laughable and ridiculous. The devil is handsome, dark, sinister, fast. Egon goes around saying, "Wonderful, wonderful."

"I know what he's been doing with your dad," Scott says.

I stop our parade along the graveled walk and grab him by his other arm. "I absolutely don't get it. Getting my father to talk about archaeology? He does okay if he remembers what century we're in. Half the time he doesn't know the difference between something he learned in archaeology and . . ." I stop here, stuck for an example. "And something he saw on *M*A*S*H*."

"And half the time he does know and comes up with a fact that might help someone that was trying to fill in gaps . . . Yes," Scott continues, peering into my probably distressed-looking face, "he doesn't know it consistently. But if Egon can find out, someone else can, too. I don't know what Egon's looking for. Maybe it's dangerous for your dad."

I'm silent for a minute. "My father has damaging knowledge?"

"Maybe.

"Listen," he continues. "I didn't know whether to tell you. I didn't want to scare you. But I guess . . . Oh, hell . . ."

Scott is holding on to me and he smells good—a combination of fresh, energetic human being and herbal something, a vaguely pine undertone, probably aftershave. I have a heavy impulse to snuggle in and hug. But the situation is unfortunate. Right now it would seem too much like coming to an imaginary daddy for comfort.

"And I saw something pretty bad," Scott continues. "Egon was hypnotizing him."

"Hypnotizing!"

"Well, anybody can do it. You know that."

Yes, I do know it; I know from working in the animal lab. We had a book on hypnotism; we all read it and we hypnotized the animals to get them relaxed. Bunny rabbits get hypnotized by a straight line on the floor and repetitive stroking. We also tried it on each other; human beings require more elaborate measures. Like, "Now think yourself into a calm, quiet place; now let your shoulders relax, now loosen up your arms, let go your fingers . . ."

Try that. You can almost do it to yourself.

Okay. But my dad. When the person is all relaxed, you suggest stuff like, "Go back into your past. Remember the time when . . ." Oh, hell and hell. My dad. His mind is frail anyway. A poor little wobbly, imprecise mind.

"His grasp on reality . . ." I say aloud.

"Yeah. It's not too definite."

"You saw Egon do this?"

"They were in his office and I was in the hall. Egon didn't know I was watching.

"And your dad was way under. It was bad. Flat on his back and Egon doing this flim-flam about *relax, undo your toes, the ends of your toenails, feel your feet unclench, feel your arches loosen, let your feet turn outward,* and so on and on. I came by Egon's office and heard a couple of sentences and wanted to bang on some pots to disrupt his routine. Except I thought it would scare your dad."

When I just stare at him, Scott says, "That's dangerous stuff. I don't know what it does to an older brain, but I've seen what happens with a younger and upset one . . ." We've been walking slowly down the gravel path from the residence and we've reached a marble bench with lion armrests; Scott strokes the lion's carved mane. "I had a friend my age once who . . ." He doesn't finish this sentence.

This scares me. "Of course it's dangerous, Scott. It's dangerous for him; I know that; he's got this old fluffy mind; who knows what's going to push it over or bury him completely or wreak some irreversible harm. Oh, damn, damn."

I sit down on the bench. "It's all my fault. I shouldn't have let him come here, knew it was a lousy idea, but he wanted it so much, and I just said, okay, okay . . ."

"Ed has different ideas at different times. About what he wants."

"Oh, come on. He wants to feel useful. That's his thing these days. Feeling useful."

"Well, I guess he was useful on this; Egon was hovering around, saying, 'Oh, yes, yes,' and making that hand wave he does, and Ed was talking in that funny monotone people get when the stage magician puts them under . . ."

"Talking about what?"

"Egyptian poetry; I couldn't exactly get it; he was chanting. Middle Kingdom stuff, I think. And then something or other that really bothered Egon; he yelled out, 'Wake up, Ed, wake up.' Real bad. You're supposed to wake the subject slowly."

"Did it upset Daddy?"

"Sure it upset him. He flailed around and almost fell off the couch. Egon got so involved in patting him and smoothing him—'Oh, my, oh, dear,' he was saying—that he didn't see me there and I sloped off. But I guess your dad was okay; he was at dinner later; he looked okay."

"Okay is not okay. Scott, you're supposed to be a friend. Why didn't you tell me?"

"Who says I'm a friend? Is it safe to have friends around here? Anyway, I am telling you now."

We walk a few feet before I say, "And you didn't hear what Daddy said? The thing that set Egon off?"

Scott's tone is guarded. He says no. Maybe it's because he keeps his face turned away that I think he's lying.

I wait a minute and then announce, surprised at how firm my voice sounds, because I'm feeling awful, "We're leaving. We're leaving tomorrow."

"A good idea."

He adds, "Yeah, a good idea. Sorry you got into this. Not really your affair.

"Oh, hell," he adds this with extra intensity, as if the coda is, *It's my affair and I'm stuck with it* . . . "I'll be sorry to have you leave. Can I come visit?"

"Sure." I say this automatically because I'm thinking about how to persuade Daddy to come with me, and knowing that it will be difficult. But when I think about Scott visiting me at the Manor, I find that yes, that would be okay. Good, in fact. "Sure, come anytime. The work I do there isn't that fascinating. I can always rip myself loose."

The trouble with having an agenda with my father—that is, something I want to discuss and am planning an approach to—the trouble with that is the way my preoccupation shows. My dad guesses something is up. He raises his guard.

He and I are walking in the museum garden. He's looking at me sideways. "Daughter, dear, I am guessing. Something troubles you."

Oh, nuts.

"Perhaps you should not let it trouble you."

Oh, yes, I should.

"I have found that the worker who worries while he is attempting a delicate job . . ."

"Daddy"—I can't stand any more of this—"it's time to leave here. To leave the museum. To go back to the Manor."

He is equable. "I will miss you."

"You have to come, too. You're needed back at the Manor."

"No, I'm not."

"They count on you, dear."

"No, they don't."

"They miss you at the Manor."

"Not much."

"They talk about you a lot."

Sometimes I think my dad's Alzheimer's is partly under his control. He can summon it up when he needs it. Now, for instance, he decides to have some short-term memory problems. "Manor? You are going back to a manor? What manor would that be?"

I don't waste time on this. "We've been here a long time."

"Yes. Very profitable."

"Both of us have had a nice holiday."

"I have not had a holiday. I've been working."

"Now it's time to return."

"You may come back here to visit."

We stop, side by side on the gravel path, with our faces turned toward each other. I say, "Oh, sweetheart."

"Yes," he agrees cheerfully. "I am your sweetheart."

"Let's walk down the hill," I say. And off we go, cheerful, synchronized.

My dad is a very good walker.

I must say, this stay at the Scholars' Institute has improved his physical condition.

The museum lands stretch out on both sides of the main building.

"Ah. We are going to look at the trains," my father says in a voice of discovery. "I was out here last night with that lady. The one with the belt."

Bunny. I wish Bunny wouldn't try to get chummy with my father.

"Trains appeal to the curious personality," he announces. "These are the only trains in these parts."

I say, "They have trains near the Manor, too." He pays no attention.

These trains are Southern Pacific, like most of the ones in California. They don't carry passengers anymore, but there are still beautiful long freights and engines with satisfying whistles. The freights seem to come by about twice a day, but I've never tried to clock them. Maybe I should; he's acting so interested.

I remind myself of our main topic. "Tomorrow," I say, in a tone of high conspiracy, "I'll help you pack your suitcase."

No answer to that. He looks at the trains. "I think I know a song about a lonesome whistle."

* * *

A string of freights is parked on the siding: several orange-painted, old-fashioned, wooden SP cars, the ones with the sliding doors, and a chain of flat cars piled with containers waiting to be transferred onto long-distance trucks. Plus, near the end, a couple of refrigerator cars, bright white and waterproof-looking.

Daddy gives a satisfied sigh and settles down on the bank. He rests his feet on a rock and links his arms around his knees. "I like to think about where they are going."

Sometimes he sounds perfectly okay at the start of a conversation and then veers off suddenly when your attention is deflected.

"This one would not be going into Constantinople. It is too late in the day. That is a very tiring journey. Sometimes you have to stand up the whole way."

Constantinople is the old name for Istanbul and is in Turkey, and my mother is supposed to be there. Is it good or bad that he perhaps thinks of her?

The grass makes prickles, which feel nice through my jeans, a sharp warm reminder about being alive. Susie says the museum is death-oriented, and sometimes recently I've felt she's right, what with the two (or one-and-a-half) murders. But I've never felt that way about the Egyptian burial cult. That's life-oriented—eternal life–oriented. How good that would be, the kind of eternal life they imagined, relaxing forever under a date-palm tree. I reach for my dad's hand.

We're facing a refrigerator car on which someone has been very busy with spray paint. A name, which may be Jay, or Fay or Tay or maybe it's a tag, JAY or whatever, has been done several times in that angular script they like. I wonder if the angles are to keep the spray paint from dripping too much.

There are some designs, too. Squiggles and lines and loops, in blue and black paint.

My father, also, is looking at the refrigerator car. He leans forward. Finally he says, "Aha."

He likes to say "Aha." People don't say that anymore.

"Someone has drawn me an ankh."

After he points and I apply myself, I can see that, yes, some of the squiggles and loops resolve themselves, perhaps, into an ankh, the two loops, the knot, the middle stem.

It's a pleasing design. Continuity, integrity, enclosure, fulfillment. I can understand it becoming a symbol for life.

Rita wrote a paper on the ankh-sandal theory, which I read when I went through her computer files. She thought the ankh was originally based on a sandal-strap design. A sandal is basic and close to the earth, but I don't really buy the idea that the sandal strap is the model. For one thing, sandals weren't that universal in ancient Egypt. Most people just went barefoot. Sandals were restricted to the upper classes, and the ancient Egyptians were too practical to think that eternal life belonged to the rich alone.

"How very nice," my father says, "of someone to imprint an ankh on this railroad car. It shows up well, doesn't it? And some of the other designs, which appear at first to be mostly writing, well, when you stare at them long enough, you can see that they also contain ankhs.

"It seems very fitting to have the ankh on a railroad car.

"The railroad gives one a wonderful feeling of freedom

and escape, don't you agree? And the ankh—eternal life—what is more emblematic of escape?

"The ankh is so important, daughter. But of course, it must be approached cautiously, like any universal symbol.

"I told that friend of mine. But he didn't listen. Not much. Not usually. Not very often. I am so very sorry."

"Daddy," I say, "are you talking about Mr. Broussard?"

"Who? What are you saying, dear?"

"Mr. Broussard, the trustee. He died with the ankh in his mouth."

"Ah."

"You told him something?"

"Ah."

"You told him he couldn't do something?"

"Many people talk to many people, dear."

"But you did talk to him."

"Talk to him, dear? Why, of course I talked to him. *A strange bird who bred in the Delta marsh / Having made its nest beside the people / what-will-be being hidden according as one says . . .*"

My father is quoting poetry now and that usually means he's gone off into a world of his own, one that I can't get him back from for ordinary conversation. When I ask what he told Mr. Broussard, he says he is tired and would like to go back to his hotel.

And when I mention the Manor, he says "What-will-be is hidden. But the freedom is there. The freedom to escape is there.

"O, freedom," he says, surprising me. That has got to be a refrain from a song.

ㄱ Chapter 17

The next morning I'm rehearsing arguments to get Daddy back to the Manor. *I need you. Belle is counting on you. You can help me with check-in at night. Mrs. La Salle will be visiting; she'll be heartbroken if . . .*

Et cetera, et cetera.

I'm still rehashing this when a low-voiced commotion outside gets me to the door. It's Rob. Oh, great. Rob, and also my dad. Rob, I do not need you right now.

Rob is holding my father by the arm. He looks at me defensively. "I came to see him. Ed is a good friend. Of long standing. Carla, I have every right to visit my good friend." He pushes his jaw forward.

Daddy smiles. He doesn't look defensive, but he looks peculiar. His hands and part of his suit and face are dusted with bright blue powder. He is extending what appears to be a pizza box. That, also, has blue powder on it.

"Carla," he says in a tone of discovery. "There you are. We couldn't find you."

His pizza box rattles.

"Someone has given me some attractive artifacts."

He marches into the room and plops the container down on my bed. He lifts the cover, emitting a spray of blue. The box does appear to have held pizza in its previous incarnation.

Inside some little doodads are kicking around. I bend over and stare and finally identify these. A string of Egyptian beads, a carved fish, a carved ibis, a smaller unidentifiable bird (very blocky), and a representation of a seated figure, probably a monkey or baboon, chopped out of some kind of vivid blue stone. The stone has started to deteriorate and that's what is making the blue dust storm. The clay beads have picked it up. The bead string ends in a clay cat; he is now an indigo cat.

"Your father needs more supervision," Rob says. "You should be watching him."

I'm struck with the awful thought that these are the items missing from the museum collection. Once again, here's my dad in the middle. Being set up. I indulge in an imaginary plot where he's accused of theft; the sheriff arrests him and he's off to Innocente, this time with no reprieve.

Daddy punctures this scenario by saying, "I wonder. I do not think I understand. Because, you know, I have looked at these objects. Carefully. And I do not think they are really ancient Egyptian. Except possibly some of the beads. It's hard to tell with beads. Reproductions have their place, of course, but these aren't even very good ones. I wonder what someone was trying to say?"

He turns over the cat pendant in a gingerly fashion. "This cat, now, might be a real Egyptian artifact. Of course he's very small. He is hard to see because he is covered with the blue dust.

"And, well, I find it hard to believe." He looks at his finger and thumb, which are now bright blue.

"You see," Rob says. "He needs supervision. That"—Rob seems to be pointing at the cat, but apparently it's the blue dust he's targeting—"that substance, Carla, is poison. This is serious."

My father speaks here. "Carla, I really think that this baboon, which is very badly carved, by the way—I really think . . . Well, there was a case where a Roman courtier . . . no, it was a papal emissary . . . there was a case, a famous case of poisoning that involved something. Something sent in a letter. This substance. Which is so beautiful. A striking and emphatic blue. But very bad for carving. And so prone to disintegration." He wiggles his thumb and forefinger together and stares at them.

"I do not understand," he says. "The figure seems to be carved from a lump of copper sulfate. That is a very strong poison. Already, from touching these things my fingers have started to hurt . . .

"There was a case once, sometime," he finishes solemnly, looking down into the pizza box and then up at me.

Rob, who has been jeeping around beside him, gets into action. "Ed, we must wash your hands, very carefully; come along now; careful, don't touch anything else . . ." After that I hear his voice from my bathroom above the running water, "Did you touch your eyes? Your mouth? Did you lean over the box and inhale?"

"In*hale*?" My father's little voice makes this sound like a questionable activity.

"Did you breathe in?"

"Of course I breathed in."

Rob turns off the water. His voice rises. "Did you breathe in hard?"

"Yes, I did. That's what you do when you're surprised. I was surprised."

Now Rob's voice sounds clipped. "Ed, did you touch your hands to your mouth?"

"Yes."

"You did?"

"Yes." By this time I am in the bathroom, staring at my father. He looks—I think I'm interpreting his expression accurately—pleased with himself. "I touched the baboon to my mouth. It is, you know, associated with Thoth, the scribe. But I didn't taste it. Even though that's what it said to do. It said, 'O, taste, O, see!' But I didn't taste it. I started to, and then I didn't."

Rob says, "Damn."

I ask, "*What* said, 'O, taste'?" No one answers me.

"Of course I knew it was poison," Daddy says. "And poison shouldn't count if it is knowledge or understanding. Because those are paramount. I understood that.

"But still I decided not to. I just touched it to my lips, lightly. I felt that should do."

Rob says to me, "We're going to the hospital. Get your billfold, or whatever. Goddamn it, Carly, what the hell; you're supposed to be *watching* him."

I don't waste any time protesting the unfairness of this. I find my billfold. I go down the hall and locate one of Daddy's tweed jackets. And I'm the one who remembers to bring the pizza box along, wrapped in a plastic bag so as not to get more blue on anything.

In the car I'm also the person who thinks to ask again about the message, "O, taste."

"Oh, that," says my father. He sounds pleased. "It was on one of those strips. The kind you get in a cookie?

"Printed," he adds.

A printed something like a Chinese cookie fortune. "Let me have it, dear."

He sounds amazed. "Why, I threw it away. It was completely blue. No use to anyone. I could read it that one time, but after that it was no use; it was too blue.

"I threw it down the toilet," he adds, squelching any ideas I have about reclaiming the slip and maybe learning something.

Rob says, "Shit," but under his breath. He smashes some numbers into his cell phone and talks for a while to someone named Tallulah. "She's there; she's waiting," he says as he hangs up. "It may not be too bad."

North Coast Hospital is on the outskirts of the town of Conestoga, if you can talk about outskirts for a town that's a block and a half long.

The hospital sits at the end of a cornfield in back of the far end of Main Street, on the opposite side of the street from the Best Western. There's a nice stand of eucalyptus trees in front of the hospital.

Rob lives in a building owned by the hospital, one of the old Conestoga houses divided into apartments. I spent time in Rob's apartment when he and I were together. He's close enough to the hospital to be able to walk across the cornfield to work. This used to strike me as cheating; it should be harder than that to get to work; most hospital employees live in Half Moon Bay.

Of course, I don't care about any of this now.

North Coast is a medium-big hospital. It's large enough to serve all of Del Oro County with its wide spread of artichoke and lettuce and garlic farms; it serves the guys that work on these farms, the folks that own the farms, the ambitious people who sometimes live in the county and commute to San Francisco. "Sure," Rob says, "they got a poison control center, with all the pesticides we're using? You betcha."

He steers us past the hospital reception desk, where he is greeted with, "Hey, Rob, can't stay away, huh?" And down halls where people call out, "Rob, listen, I forgot to ask you . . ."

He has my dad by the arm and tells him, "We're on our way to see a real nice lady. She'll talk to you about that poison."

"Copper sulfate," my father says, "I knew not to eat it."

"Right. She'll maybe take your picture. Maybe take a blood sample."

"I like having my picture taken."

Tallulah's parents must have been romantics, to give her a name like that. But they produced a straightforward, cheerful woman with short brown hair. A lot of women doctors are the straightforward type. "Well, hi, Dr. Day," she greets Daddy, "we got into some blue powder, did we?"

"Copper sulfate," Daddy clarifies.

"Yep, not such a great idea. Now listen . . ." And she tells him that she's going to be doing a lot of things, but none of it will hurt, and the idea is to find out how much damage the blue powder did. "We hope it hasn't made you sick, Dr. Day."

"It could have," Daddy tells her solemnly.

I like Tallulah, who treats my father respectfully. Obviously Rob has cued her in about the Alzheimer's. While she is poking and photographing, Rob and I sit in the observers' seats.

"Well, I don't get it," I say.

Rob's still acting as if I ought to have prevented this.

"Why anybody should want to . . ." I'm silent for a minute. "Scare him, I guess."

Rob says, "Uh."

"Hurt him, d'you think?"

"Yes, I do."

"But so far everybody at the museum has been hearts and flowers. Egon, Scott, the guard. They all act as if they love him. The sheriff's the only one who doesn't."

Rob says, "Uh," again. *"Somebody really* dislikes him. You ought to have noticed something."

"Quit blaming me, Rob. You're doing it because you feel guilty."

"Guilty? Why should I feel guilty?"

Good question. Guilty about Cherie, of course. Because as long as I'm sort of available, you're not supposed to look at anybody else, didn't I tell you?

"Damned if I know," I say. I debate telling him the hypnotism story and decide against it.

He says, "Christ. What is going on at that place? It's super weird. Whatever possessed you? I just don't get it. And for now you've got to . . . absolutely got to . . . get him out of there. Yourself, too. Both of you. What in hell were you thinking?"

I save for later my lecture on how Rob is interfering and bossy and has no rights over either me or my dad.

Tallulah is helping Daddy sit upright. She pats him on the shoulder. "Don't get upset, guys; I think it'll be okay."

"Just get him the hell out of there," Rob tells me, between his teeth, under his breath.

Tallulah kicks us out with instructions to bring Daddy in again next week; she wants to watch his liver; she thinks he got hardly any of the copper sulfate and it will be okay. "I'll try him on calcium. There's an innovative treatment; we had good luck, believe it or not, using it on sheep. Shots of calcium. I just gave him one."

Then she has to tell us the story of how the sheep got into the copper sulfate. And were cured.

Out in the car I say to my father, "Daddy, we have to move back to the Manor. They need us there. Tomorrow."

My parent fusses with his seat belt. "I can't go back to the Manor."

He's in the front seat; I'm in the back. I lean forward and Rob, also in the front seat, leans across; we pile on him with, *Of course you can. It's what you need to do. It's time for everyone to go back. That's what happens at the end of a visit. I, Carla, have to go back, too.*

"No," he says, not angry at all.

He looks at me blandly. He doesn't get shrill or excited; he is quietly flinty. No.

Rob and I confer after we get my father to his apartment. It's not a good conference. Both of us are cross. Rob is blaming me. I'm blaming myself. "I can't just kidnap him."

"You've got to lure him back."

"He wants to feel needed."

"Think of some problem. Some duty. Something to offer."

I'm completely stymied. There are no problems or duties at the Manor. There are three meals a day and television and bedtime. "Get him to start on his memoirs," Rob suggests.

"Oh, ha ha."

We get wilder in our suggestions. "Someone there has a translation problem." "A message from the gods."

"My mother," I say. I look at Rob and say, "Something or other about my mother." Then, pretty quickly, I'm glad to say, I counteract that. "Hell and hell. What's the matter with me?" I get up and start marching around. We're in the Resident Scholars' Lounge. I pull down a couple of books and slam them back into their slots. "I know better." After a minute I sit down again.

Rob is pitched forward in a lounge chair, not lounging. He's watching me moderately calmly. I guess he looks sympathetic. "Sure you know better."

"The only way is honesty."

"Uh-huh."

I start mapping a campaign. *Daddy, this is really important. I don't ask for much, here's something you can do for me. I do a lot for you.*

"Lay it on, right?" I ask.

"Well, it's true."

"He loves me."

"Sure, he loves you . . . Say it's just for a while," Rob adds.

Even that's sort of a lie, but yes, I'll try it for now. "Sure, just for a while.

"Something you can do for me," I improvise. "Just for a while."

* * *

You should be honest with your Alzheimer's parent, but only moderately honest.

"Rob, thank you." I look at him, and he looks good. Reliable, helpful Rob. Handsome, too. He looks almost good enough for me to feel friendly toward him again and to decide that his fling with an elderly blonde is okay. Just human nature.

"Cherie will be really worried," he announces. "And concerned. She loves Ed."

Which ends my friendly feelings. I hustle him out of there fast and go down the hall to see if Scott is still up and would like a drink.

We sit in Egon's kitchen, all stainless steel and marble, and share a bottle of Egon's vodka. I tell Scott the story about the copper sulfate and he gets at first incredulous—"Jesus! *Un*believable!"—and then really mad. "My God," sloshing vodka and pacing around between the reflecting surfaces. "Carla, this has got to stop."

I agree that it has to stop but Scott says, "No, it *has* to stop," with a force that makes me feel he can arrange it. "Damn it, kid, you've had too much. Ed's had too much."

He leans forward to kiss me and does it with a lot of energy and precision. I stand up and we kiss some more. Then I sit down on one of Egon's marble surfaces with my back against one of his reflecting surfaces and we continue kissing. Except that I wouldn't call it kissing exactly. It keeps on and becomes more of an all-out experience.

"Let's go upstairs," Scott says. And I say, "No."

And he says, "Let's." And I say, "No."

He's forceful and clean and handsome and he smells good. The idea is totally attractive.

We get upstairs and I'm ready for something more to happen, and while it almost does, it doesn't.

That's my fault. But I'm surprised that Scott pays that much attention to what I say.

The next morning at breakfast Bunny says, "You're leavin'? You didn't ask me was that okay . . . Well," she adds, "I'll just have to come and see you, won't I? I mean"—she's been staring at me; is it possible that even Bunny, whom I think of as excessively dim, can read my expression?—"I got to come over and see Pop. That is some real sweet guy. I will miss him."

Rob telephones. "I have to come by sometimes to pick up Ed for his calcium injection," he reminds me. He is sufficiently defensive to add the sentence about how he is one of Daddy's oldest friends.

Oh, shut up, Rob.

And Cherie telephones, "Darling, you're clearing out of there? Pretty wise, I guess. They'll find out; that place will be a morgue without you. And I'll be by the other place, the Manor, is it? I think I got great news, prob'ly real heavy news, can't wait to see you, we'll have a grand old gossip, can't wait."

And when I get upstairs I find that Scott has slipped a note under my door: "Tomorrow night, eight o'clock, rescue mission? I'm glad for your sake you're going, not for mine. I like your hair when you just let it hang."

Was that what my coiffure was doing last night? I may have had it scrunched up in a ponytail that came undone. It had plenty of encouragement.

⚱ Chapter 18

My father and I are back at the Manor, and he is enormously apologetic. "My dear. I had no idea it mattered so much to you. Of course I am glad to be here. As long as that is what you want. Glad to be back here with you."

He looks around his room with its bay window and shelf full of Egyptian figures. "I had forgotten. My Egyptian collection. Here, a very nice shabti, ready to watch over me." He holds up the little figure, its arms folded, a row of hieroglyphs down its front.

"Somehow I forgot." He frowns at the rest of his room. "It seems smaller. It's not as nice a room as that other one. In the other hotel. I think I miss that other hotel."

I protest, "But you have so many wonderful things here." And I get into a listing of what is wonderful at the Manor, all of his books and artifacts and care and love. He looks troubled and uses the word *needed*. "Truly needed, I think I was truly needed."

"These books here were written by you," I say, pointing to the ones in the blue jackets. He examines me as if I am speaking ancient Urdu. He suggests that maybe I was the one who wrote them.

And finally he climbs into his window alcove and announces that now he will take a nap. This traveling around has been tiring. Good night, Carla.

He's depressed already. I'm depressed, too.

That night I try to make a list, but fail. I'm not good at lists. I tend to fixate on one aspect and get unable to move beyond it.

This is supposed to be a list of subjects to investigate. Anything to chase in connection with the murder or murders, because I haven't left those events behind by moving back to the Manor. The deaths are still present at the bottom of my psyche; if I can solve them, I can solve all my other life problems, including where to go with my career and how to keep my father content. But (I've said this before) I'm not good with lists. They start out well and end in one- and two-word cries. Marcus . . . The sheriff . . . Rita . . . Hypnotism . . . Copper sulfate . . . When I get depressed or frantic, my handwriting changes.

"Hello, darlin'."

It is the next day, and my fan calls have started. This is guess who, my principal bane, the lady of my bad dreams.

I wish I could decide definitively how I feel about Cherie. If I didn't really hate her, I might really like her. Maybe someplace in another galaxy we'd be best friends.

"Darlin', I am coming over to see you. Dynamite news. Real electrifying. Some good, some bad. I am dying to share."

She sounds too good, her dynamite news can't be that she has broken up with Rob. She wouldn't be panting to spread that around.

"Come for lunch, Cherie."

"Absolutely, beautiful girl. Can't wait. You're gonna be blown away."

Well, as Cherie has said, dynamite. That is, Cherie herself, ensconced in triumph at a Manor luncheon table, is dynamite. She sparkles and doesn't patronize. She calls everybody darling as if she means it. She asks sympathetic, insightful questions. Her airy bubble of a voice floats above the clink of silverware; it says all the right things. "Oh, my God," she declares, "I just adore this place. Look at this wonderful meal," (a choice between fish or steak). "Imagine you-all, living here. Right here in this terrific decor." Her gesture encompasses carvings and plaster, high ceiling. "And the gorgeous view." A lawn, bright green, splashed intermittently by a rotating sprinkler.

Maybe it's Cherie's voice, I decide, squinting at her. That Southern warble indicates big-time joy and commitment. She gets believed where others get questioned. The dining room ladies love her. They nudge each other and eat their ice cream and look happy.

I have a hard time tearing her away and off to Daddy's apartment, where we can shut the door and share her dynamite news. My father, of course, wants to come, too. But I've forestalled that with a schedule in the library of two hours of country and western DVDs. He's transfixed by country and western.

"You will never guess," Cherie starts as we get the door shut. "No, no tea. Vodka? Oh, my. Well, I guess I could. Just a teensy glass.

"Now then, listen"—she takes a healthy slug—"listen up, this is so totally amazing. I knew all along something was wrong, didn't you?"

"Where?" I ask. Sure I knew something was wrong. I think about it. "Who with? With whom?"

"Dear heart, of course. With Slimeball. Our sheriff."

I say yes and wait. Cherie is set to continue.

"Well, dear, turns out he has a record. Back in 1980. Car theft. He was a naughty young man in his last year of high school and he didn't actually steal this car, his friends did, but he was along and, well, real boring story but not to the governor's office when I went up there and showed them the records."

"Wow," I say.

Then I realize that this is a very partial tale. "I guess I don't get it, Cherie. Somebody had to check his record before he got to be sheriff. They don't just pull a name for that out of a hat."

"You bet they don't. Like, usually the sheriff's elected. This time it was an appointment, because your previous guy resigned and went off to Alaska. The governor's office gets to appoint somebody. Some friend of a friend. And sure, they check the records, but I guess this time a little arranger managed to lose those records."

"And you found them."

"Oh, darling, I did. I am real good at finding things." Cherie takes a self-satisfied slurp of vodka and settles back into Daddy's easy chair with one foot under her. Today is one of her pink days; she is wearing her pink pantsuit with the rhinestone buttons, her size-four feet sparkle in matching sling sandals. Her hair glistens glossy and bright. I wish I could make my hair sit close to my head like that.

"You didn't ask," she says, "what's gonna happen now. Well, this governor we have now is a prize horse's ass and just about his only program is war-on-crime. He thinks he's gonna eliminate crime from California. Especially teenage crime. He had a fit when he heard about this. He fired our friend, like yesterday. So now we don't have any sheriff at all."

I'm silent, trying to imagine either of the sheriff's deputies as interim officiants. One is tall and one is short and both are blocky. Both look as if they've been stuffed with horsehair.

"Do not fret, darling," Cherie says. She sets her glass down and dusts off her knee in a proprietary way. "Although I do not like this here governor one tiny particle, there are some people in the lower offices that got left over from previous administrations, you understand? And these people are friends? If you follow me?"

"And they've been telling you that . . ." I peruse Cherie's face. She looks too satisfied for her news to be the simple fact that she knows who the next sheriff will be. "Cherie!"

"Yes, love?"

"You wouldn't!" I say.

She smirks.

"You don't even live here."

Is that a smirk? Maybe more a triumphant smile.

Both of us understand that I am saying, *You wouldn't accept the appointment as Sheriff of Del Oro County*, and she is saying, *Oh, yeah? Why not?*

"You don't even live here," I repeat.

"I do now."

I gawp. There's something wrong with this idea. It takes me a minute to catch on to the flaw. She lives here now. Are the domestic rules like the international ones, and can Cherie become a resident of the county by marrying—well, by marrying a resident, namely Rob?

Oh, Jesus.

"I'm buying a house here," she says.

"Ah," I say. "Wow." This takes a minute to percolate, then suddenly I become appreciative. "Hey. How great.

"I mean," I stumble around for a minute, "you're gonna be the sheriff?"

"Looks like it. I mean, for them it's just this minor appointment in a real small county. Something a lower office can handle. The governor doesn't even need to see it."

"Wow," I say again. That's an inconclusive comment, but I am trying to get all the angles straight. Cherie will be sheriff, which is a lot better for me in many ways. But she will be living here, full time, next door to Rob, so to speak. And that is not good. So is the situation a washout for me?

I waste a full half-minute speculating on the aspects of Cherie and Rob. Like, how badly suited are they? She is an accomplished, handsome older woman. He is a young doctor. In some ways he seems younger even than he is. She is nervous and intelligent and ambitious. She bounces around. He is solid and reliable. Maybe a little on the stolid side.

When she is seventy he'll be forty-nine, which sounds better than now, when she is fifty and he's twenty-nine.

"The other thing I have to tell you," Cherie interrupts all this. "Sweetcakes, how about just another teeny bit of that stuff? Life is on the tense side these days."

I divide the rest of the bottle between us.

"Well, darlin', one part of this news isn't a shock exactly, more just what everbody thought all along. But the other part is a surprise and a bit of a tummy-grabber. Anyway, here goes."

She takes a meditative swallow. "He was murdered. Marcus Broussard, that is, victim numero uno. That's what everybody thought, right? So that's not a surprise; that's the part we assumed, just from the surrounding circumstances. The one that's a surprise is the *way* he was murdered."

"And?" I say. Actually Cherie is waiting with her mouth half-open to tell me the rest of it. I don't have to do any prompting.

"Darlin', he was stabbed."

I think, but just for a minute, because almost right away I can respond to that. "Oh, no, he wasn't."

"Oh, yes, he was."

"Cherie, I saw him. He was laid out, on his back, his arms stretched out . . . There wasn't any place to hide a stab wound. There was no blood."

"Darlin', there was. But in a place where you don't exactly look."

I say, "Well, maybe," still trying to summon up my memory of Marcus Broussard spread-eagled across Egon's garden plantings of lavender and oleander.

"Baby, this is the part that is kinda gross: he was stabbed in the ear."

That rattles past my own ears. I stare at her and say, "Huh?"

"Yeah. Weird. I mean it. Exactly like in Shakespeare. Bang, right on through the eardrum and into the brain."

"Cherie, I saw him close up. I held his hands in my hands."

"And did you see his ears?"

No, I didn't. Not really. Ohmigod. An ear. Why is that so awful? "Hamlet's father wasn't stabbed; he was poisoned."

"Well, darlin', I know all that, into the porches of his ear, okay? So it's not exactly the same, but it was the first thing I thought of and I'll bet the first thing you thought of, too, if I hadn't said it first."

"You have to be still for someone to stick something in your ear," I say. "Not running around. Sort of knocked out, like Hamlet's dad."

"I know, I know. But this is what forensics up in Sacramento says. They did a big fat report and I'll be glad to let you look at it. Which I prob'ly shouldn't, but I will. Incidentally, he had three wives."

"Marcus Broussard had three wives?"

"Not exactly all at once, I guess, but that part's unclear. The reason I raise it is that one of them—I don't know yet which one—is the person that ought to see the forensics report. But since I am almost the new sheriff now, I will do what I want and you may see it, too."

"My goodness," I tell her. It's a time when no comment is adequate, so I use a proven inadequate one. "Hey. . . . Stabbed in the ear," I say after a minute. "What with?"

"Somethin' sharp."

"A stick?"

"Maybe. But more likely something metal. Some long skinny piece of metal with a sharp end."

"And they searched the grounds for a weapon that looked like that."

"Of course not. In the first place, Slimeball didn't have the brains to search for anything; I guess he was absent from crime class the day they did that page. And, secondly, no-body knew until now they should look for that kind of a weapon. So, no."

"It's late now, to look."

"A'course it is, but we'll still try. I got my two Klingons down there right now poking around."

I survey her; she's perky, very handsome, and fast. "God, are you going to be a new order around here."

And Cherie, who is unfolding her legs, nods compla-cently. "New order, I guess you got it. Totally different or-der, different species, right?"

"No, Daddy's not okay," I tell Rob, who calls about five o'clock. "He says he misses the museum, he wants to go back there; he thinks of it as the Promised Land that he got excluded from. I guess he'll get over it. He'll forget."

I let this slide into an uncomfortable minute. My father does a lot of forgetting.

"Thank God he's out of there," Rob says. "You, too."

I say, "Yeah, yeah," because Rob has put some possessive emotion into that *you, too*. Unspoken message: I, Rob, con-tinue to help; I am Old Reliable; I got you to leave that place. In a minute he's going to tell me that my father is his oldest friend.

I tell him that I had a nice session this afternoon with Cherie.

He says, "Oh. Fine," in a suppressed voice.

"She didn't say anything about you."

Rob says, "Uh-huh."

"How's that relationship doing?" I persist. There's a pause.

What answer do I want? Do I wait for him to say, Terrible, or Wonderful, or We're made for each other, or We're breaking up?

"Fine," Rob says.

You can't accuse him of being verbose.

"Maybe I could come over to see Ed this evening," he says.

I advise, "Don't."

I don't want Rob this evening because Scott is coming this evening.

Also because I don't want him.

He says, "Well, I have to come tomorrow anyway to take him for his calcium shot," and hangs up, quick, before I can beat him to it.

♟ Chapter 19

Scott shows up at eight o'clock in his rented convertible.

"I think we should head south," he says.

"Okay. What's south?"

He pulls out a map and we cluster over it. A BMW, even a rented one, has a good dashboard light.

South is Santa Cruz, Monterey, Carmel. I tell him that I went to school in Santa Cruz and I don't want Santa Cruz and he says, *Well, then, maybe Monterey?* and I say, *Okay.*

"There are a hundred and fifty restaurants in Monterey," he announces. "Some have a fish theme and some have a Mexican theme and some have a rob-the-tourist theme. There is one farther along, in Carmel in somebody's garden that I went to last month and kind of liked. I went there with Rita, but I guess I'm okay to do it again."

We decide, yes, we'll go south and to Carmel.

We start off down the coast road, which is too dark to see

the scenery, but you can kind of feel it: bushes and hill on one side, cliff-edge and ocean on the other.

"This road will be real quiet until Santa Cruz, when it turns into a mob scene," he says. "Maybe I can circumvent that." He drives with one hand, capably.

"Reet and I," he ventures. I haven't asked, but maybe he wants to fill in the silences. Maybe he wants to talk. "We were sort of lovers, maybe I told you, and then we were sort of friends. I miss her. I miss her a lot."

I say, "I'm sorry."

"Yeah, right.

"Hey," he adds quickly, as if he thinks I found *Yeah, right* off-putting, "I know you're sorry."

Well, I did get off-put, but he pushes along with, "You really helped, did I say that? I'm not good with saying how I feel. Even with *knowing* how I feel."

Quit it, chum, you're getting at my unarmored places. Any guy that admits to vulnerability and then admits that . . . Oh, phooey.

"Sorry," he says. "Difficult stuff. Too personal."

We have a half-mile of darkness with ocean noises off to the right. "When I first met you," I finally essay, "I thought you were a horse's ass."

"I probably was."

"You were snotty. Mean to Rita."

"Damn right. She could get to me. To see somebody go under like that. And kind of on purpose, know what I mean?"

"Yeah. I saw."

"I identified. I do those things, too."

"You!" I fling the word out across the darkness. I'm amazed. "You're the least . . ." I can't think of the right word-cluster. "You're in control."

"It's a pose . . . I used to think I was. I talked myself into that."

We're approaching some lights. A big red sign announces SARTORI'S ITALIAN. Laughter and a few bars of music make the road feel even emptier.

"Jesus," he says. "It got me down about her. But lately everything gets me down. Like, I've been thinking back and brooding about death. I don't get it."

"Oh, come on."

"First somebody is. And they're here and they're part of it. And then bang, all of a sudden, out. And what's left?" He gestures off to the side, where the bank and the bushes are. "Nothing? Memories? We're supposed to console ourselves with that? 'The person lives on in our memories'? Phooey."

I start out on the speech about how as long as you are alive and remembering the person and grieving for them and recalling the good things they did and all that. It does sound kind of thin. And underneath I'm thinking that Scott has really taken off about Rita's death. It's the kind of response you get from somebody who's had other experiences with death and feels these previous experiences reviving each time a new one happens.

"Did you lose somebody else earlier?" I ask. "Somebody important who died on you?"

He jerks the car slightly. We are passing the intersections leading into Half Moon Bay. "No." He sounds cross.

We have quite a bit of silence as he negotiates some lighted crossings.

"Tell me about your dad," he says abruptly after we start again onto the dark part of the highway. "Doing better? Settling in okay?"

I get the idea: this recent subject is dropped. We spend

the whole twenty-five miles between Half Moon Bay and the Santa Cruz approaches talking about Daddy. I give the latest on him and accept Scott's sympathy. I decide Scott keeps starting subjects and then dropping them. I'll return to some of this stuff later. I want more about Rita, death, the Hartdale. And Danielle. I really want to hear from him on Danielle. She keeps sounding important to me.

I don't understand you, Scott, I think. *It's always intriguing not to understand someone when you think there's a complicated second person below the top one. If you follow me.*

He manages to drive skillfully and not say anything much all the way into Carmel.

I'm debating whether or not to share the news about how Marcus Broussard died. And about how Cherie will be our new sheriff. I decide on silence. Scott is withholding stuff from me. He'll learn all these info bites pretty soon.

Meanwhile I can feel superior.

"Superiority is evanescent," I tell Scott as we climb the hill into Carmel, which brightens up beside us, all lights and gas stations and even one Carmel-type cottage left out beside the road.

Scott says, "Huh?"

I like Carmel, in spite of its phoniness. My great-grandmother should have bought a cutie-pie house here instead of the one she bought in Venice.

I tell Scott that when Rob and I lived in Santa Cruz, we hardly ever came down to Carmel. We were too poor. The town is quaint and charming, and quaint costs money.

Scott's restaurant in the garden has heat lamps and colored lights and a quaint, charming main building to retire to

when the fog is in. Tonight there is no fog. The waitresses
wear Laura Ashley prints, which Rob once described as the local equivalent of peasant dress. The menu is extensive. Both
Scott and I opt for crab salad and chardonnay. I think (a) that
I know some important things Scott doesn't yet know, and
(b) that I really don't miss Rob at all.

"Do you miss him—what's his name, Rob?" Scott asks.

Oh, cut it out.

Over dinner we talk first about my dad and about research
into Alzheimer's, which Scott says is getting more daring
and maybe looking hopeful. I keep forgetting that he has
had a year of med training.

We sip industriously at the chardonnay. And he finally
lets me broach the subject of the Hartdale, which I've been
poking at for several minutes.

"Hartdale?" he inquires. "What's that?"

I give him a hooded look.

"Hart-dale." He fools with his napkin, twisting and un-
twisting it, doing a pretty good Gollum handwringing imitation. "Hates the horrid Hartdale."

"Cut it out."

"What? My liver? Cut out my liver?"

"Scott, stop it. Why do you think you hate the Hartdale?"

"Sweetheart, I don't just think I hate it, you try yearning
and scheming and leching for something and waking up at
night in a cold sweat because you're never going to get that
or anything else and you'll go off to the next world and no
one will have the faintest idea you were ever here. And
then . . ."

"Yes?"

"And then you learn all you have to do is kiss Egon's ass."

"Bullshit. Egon's not that important."

"He's an example. Maybe he is important. How the hell do I know. One day I'm working away the best I know how, a little brainwork here, a little cheating there, just like everybody, no particular results. And all of a sudden there's an explosion and a shift in the time-space continuum and . . ."

"And you're famous?"

"No. Prospectively famous. It's guaranteed. Certified . . . platinum card."

He doesn't spill his glass, although he looks as if he's going to. He tilts it and then sets it down fairly carefully and puts his head in his hands.

"What you want," he says, not very clearly, "is supposed to be the best and you think you're the best and you've got to have it. And then something happens—a couple of things happen . . . The sort of events that . . . Oh, *shit*.

"Nothing specific. Just life," he mutters into his cupped hands.

Bro, I think, you aren't getting away with that, *Just life*. It was something big and specific. Nobody is ready to shop the Hartdale because of free-floating world-weariness.

I reach out and touch his wrist. After a minute he grabs on to me with the other hand. He says, "I'm ordering another bottle."

Chardonnay is okay, I think, if it's not too sweet. This one is dry.

After a while and a spot of bottle-opening, he himself reverts to the topic. "So suddenly it seems completely phony and you think you're chasing the—what is it?"

"The bluebird of happiness?"

He shakes his head. "Something that turns into something else."

"A pot of gold."

He's gloomy. "That just disappeared?"

"Well, it was at the foot of the rainbow and you know about rainbows."

"N'yaa." He refills our glasses. "What I want is the metaphor where it doesn't exactly disappear; it's still there but you suddenly think, *What is this anyway, what the hell is it worth, look at it, how crumby and grubby it is, why was I chasing it?*"

I don't tell Scott, "But the Hartdale? How can you, even after a bad night, think that about the Hartdale?" I know that I, as the noncompetitor listening to Scott's story, am supposed be above it all. But let's face it: I'm a child of our society. I grew up right here, in our crumby, grubby culture. There's not a chance in the world of it happening, but I'd give my eye teeth to be on the short list for the Hartdale.

By the time we depart Carmel, both of us are pretty far into the chardonnay. Perhaps Scott should not be driving, but then, neither should I. I let him go ahead and rev up and we strap ourselves in, both of us wobbly. The moon is out in its crescent guise, some stars are arrayed. And I have my agenda planned. I am going to wait until we are moderately well along the way, say eight or ten miles, and then I am going to broach the subject of Danielle.

" 'I went down to Saint James Infirmary,' " I begin, filling in time, but also touching on my topic, yesterday's love.

Scott says I have a nice voice but it would be terrific if I could keep a tune. I try another lament. " 'Give me one for my baby and one more for . . .' "

"For God's sake, cool it," Scott instructs.

So okay, maybe I touched a nerve. I let five minutes go by until we're beyond most of the lights and distractions. We're on the four-lane highway that will eventually hit State One. The wind whips, but the night is friendly; it's not cold. "Tell me about Danielle," I say.

"Good God. Why?"

"I'm curious. How old was she? How did you meet her?"

"Cut it out. What's Danielle to you or you to Danielle?"

"Don't quote."

"Danielle was a pretty girl I was in college with. Why do you care?"

"You talked about her; Rita did, too; so does my dad; so does Egon. Everybody mentions her, but nobody actually says anything."

"So, forget it. She was just somebody."

"Somebody important."

"Just somebody."

"And I saw a picture of her."

"A picture? What picture?"

"A shot of all the gang on a dig. She was in it."

"Oh. That picture."

"She was nice-looking."

"Uh-huh."

"Long blond hair. Good shape."

"Listen, what the hell are you doing?"

"And," I pursue my advantage, "Rita's boyfriend had a picture of her."

"Rita's boyfriend? Who the fuck is Rita's boyfriend?"

"Rita's boyfriend is this fairly neutral jerk named George Marziano and he had a studio picture of Danielle."

Scott tries to drive the car into the divider. He corrects

and pulls it back, not doing too well. We wobble for a while. He says, "What in hell are you into? All of a sudden you talk about Rita's boyfriend. And I knew Rita really well and never heard anything about a boyfriend and now you say it's a boyfriend who has a picture of Danielle?"

"He does. Or he used to. A studio picture. A big, glossy, nine-by-twelve shot."

"Of Danielle? What's she doing?"

"I don't know. I didn't see the picture. Rita got rid of it. Danielle was nude, though; that's what George says."

Scott tries now to drive the car into the right-hand lane of traffic. He says, "Christ crucified. Cut this out right now. Quit talking about Danielle."

"You'd better pull over," I instruct.

"I won't pull over. I have no intention of doing so."

The car is wobbling irritatedly. The highway has almost reached the side road that leads to State Highway 101, which we don't want, but where there is a traffic island with a gas station and a sign that reads, COFFEE — SNAX.

"Pull over," I say, "we'll get coffee. I could sure use some."

"No."

"Yes," I say. "Please."

To my total amazement this works. Maybe I sound sufficiently humble and nice. Maybe he really does want to talk about Danielle. Or to find out what I know about her. He negotiates the lane traversal with only a couple of close calls and we skid, tires protesting, into Mack's Crossing—Gas.

Nobody's around who looks like Mack. Gas is dispensed by machine and so is the coffee, which I can see inside in a shiny blue-and-red machine. A Latina lady in a red muumuu sits beside a large sign that says, CLERK HAS ONLY TEN DOLLARS IN CASH.

Scott parks on the side and trails on into the snack cubicle, where I can see him negotiating with the coffee machine. Eventually he comes out with two plastic cups. He gives me one and slumps against the steering wheel, holding his cup carefully upright, sipping slowly.

Finally he says, "Danielle was my girlfriend in college. She went to med school and I followed. So why do you care?"

"And she got to be an archaeologist?"

"Sure. So did I. She was really smart."

"What kind of smart?"

"Any kind you like. Fast. Intuitive. Intellectual. Photographic memory. Restless. Why in *hell* do you care?"

"And she was pretty."

"She was beautiful."

"She had a lot of boyfriends."

"Lovers. She had a ton of lovers. She had me, she had Marcus, she had somebody named Nizham, she had a couple of curators. They weren't exactly lovers; they were in love with *her*; she didn't care spit for them."

"Did she love you?"

"She kept coming back to me."

"Rita liked her."

"Rita hated her. Reet was jealous of her—lots of people were."

"You always talk about her in the past tense."

"Yeah, I do. I talk about a lot of stuff in the past tense. I talk about being here and finding or not finding something on that dig and maybe getting the Hartdale and all that other stupid crap in the past tense. Danielle is past to me. She and I are over. Will you for God's sake get the hell off my case?" He grabs my coffee, which I have only half finished, and, managing to hold two cups in one hand, lurches out of the car and toward the trash can.

And we depart Mack's with screeching tires. We have a couple of near misses getting back into the intersection.

Scott is driving so tensely that I decide I'd better be quiet. So I am quiet and he is quiet and this keeps up for miles and miles. He's driving as if he is still really angry. Furious, you could say. Snapping the steering wheel back and forth. There's almost no other traffic, but after we leave the towns behind us, the road gets very narrow and there is always that invisible drop down to where the ocean must be.

"Cool it already," I say once and get no reaction.

He grunts when a fox darts in front of us.

That's the only sound all the way back to the Manor. He skids up to the entry and leaves me to open the car door for myself.

Which of course I always try to do. But Scott usually has those antediluvean good manners that go with what I suspect is his landed-gentleman background.

"Listen," he says when I'm out of the car and on my feet, "this is somebody I was real close to once and not anymore. I had strong feelings about it once and not anymore. I don't like to talk about it. And it's my business. Are we clear?"

"Clear as a bell." Which is a lie. I don't believe for a minute that statement about him having strong feelings once and not anymore. I can really recognize strong feelings right here in the present when I sit beside them.

⌐ Chapter 20

"Well, I don't understand," Susie says.

I agree that it is all kind of peculiar.

"I have tried to understand. I think Cherie is an absolutely wonderful human being. But Cherie and Rob? Carla, *you* belong with Rob."

Susie is in Berkeley and I am at the Manor. I'm not sure whether that makes her easier to talk to or harder.

"You and Rob are the perfect couple."

I decide not to deal with that. It's totally untrue; Rob and I were not very well matched. We were barely a couple at all. We disagreed and had power struggles. We had known each other much too long.

"I don't know how I would feel about Cherie and Rob if it were not for you and Rob. But Cherie has a friend here in Berkeley."

"Is that Susie? There on the telephone?" my father asks. "What is she saying?"

I tell him in an aside that she is coming down to the Manor and I tell Susie that I'm not interested in Cherie's boyfriends. What happens between her and Rob is their business.

"I called you because my dad misses you," I say.

"Oh, and I miss him. And I miss you. Yes, of course I will come, and I will talk reasonably and understandingly to Rob."

"Susie, please, don't do any such thing. Come down and don't stay with Rob, stay here. I'm inviting you . . . And another thing I wanted to ask, this is special: I want you to try to get something for me. A peculiar, hard-to-get movie. Only about four years old, but limited edition."

"Oh, I have that friend, Chippy, who has the wonderful video store. I love getting rare movies."

"This one is dirty."

"Carla, what do you mean 'dirty'? If you're saying that it deals with sex, why, sex is a natural aspect of the life cycle; nothing natural can possibly be dirty; of course I will be happy to ask Chippy for it."

I am probably imagining that Susie sounds extra-enthusiastic about the dirty aspect of Marcus Broussard's film. I give her some details while I'm brooding about Cherie's Berkeley boyfriend.

"Susie will have lots of things for you to do," I tell my dad after I've hung up.

He says that she will take him to the museum because she likes the museum and will be distressed to see that he is not still there.

*   *   *

Here at the Manor my dad's best friend is Mrs. La Salle, a handsome old lady with close-clipped silver hair. She lives here only half the time; the rest of her life occurs in San Francisco, where she does work that I conjecture to be glamorous. She used to write a San Francisco society column; I suspect her now of doing the anonymous gossip page for the *Nob Hill Gazette*. She won't talk about it, possibly to save being exclaimed over by the other Manor residents, who are too admiring. As well as uncomfortably jealous.

She says, "Something stupid is what I do. I'll tell you sometime."

Susie is thrilled to find Mrs. La Salle in residence. "My favorite person. Except, of course, for you and Ed, who don't count, being relatives. Daphne is wonderful. So alive! So stimulating! . . . Daphne, my dear"—she zooms in on Mrs. La Salle—"Carla wants me to believe some ridiculous story about you writing for a society paper."

"Indeed." Mrs. La Salle smiles, catlike. She and Susie are diametric opposites who liked each other the minute they met. They unite today around my dad, who sits between them, looking sullen.

Susie wears nile green and wraps herself in both a red cashmere shawl and a green-striped Chinese shawl. Mrs. La Salle has a trim oyster-beige suit. One lady sits on one side of Daddy, one on the other, like an innovative fashion ad. "I would be perfectly happy," he says, "if the three of us were together at my museum."

"But there is so much to do here," Mrs. La Salle says quickly.

"We'll go outside and look at the mermaid," Susie offers. (Our mermaid is a copy of the Copenhagen harbor one.)

"And do Tutankhamen on the computer." That's Mrs. La Salle.

"The library has a new archaeology video," Susie adds.

There is a pause while everyone thinks. "Furthermore," Susie bubbles, "I have brought along an interesting movie. It is an art movie that I got in Berkeley."

I've been so immersed in my father's objections that I forgot about the pornographic video. I say, "Susie, darling, not right now."

"And why on earth not?"

"What kind of a movie?" Mrs. La Salle wants to know.

"Let's leave it 'til later," I say.

My father is suddenly interested. He likes the fact that I'm opposing the idea. "What's this all about?"

"It is a pornographic movie," Susie says brightly. "Some of them are quite good; this one is just interesting."

"The object of pornography is to alert the senses." That's my father.

We are in the Manor's library, a mahogany-paneled, over-furnished retreat walled with bookcases. Most of the books have green and gold bindings. There is a mahogany-housed big-screen TV, a blue-flowered Versailles-type rug, and a lot of gilt-framed paintings of misty women.

"It would make a change," Mrs. La Salle approves.

I try, "I really think . . ." Making faces at Susie has no effect.

My father says that he is quite interested. "I would like to see Susie's movie. The pornographic one. Of course, the union of Re and his sister in Egyptian mythic tradition—that is not pornography—oh, no; the ignorant Western observer fails to understand; that is the union of all the natural forces of . . ."

He trails off and looks around the library walls. "I would enjoy seeing your movie, Susie."

"And you shall. Of course you shall. It is stuffy in here; the environment is encapsulating. That movie is probably exactly what we need. I will go up this minute and get it."

I consider sticking my foot out to trip Susie and then sitting on her, but that doesn't seem like a workable plan.

"Are you comfortable?" I ask my father. "Is that chair all right for you?"

"What are you fussing about? Of course it's a good chair. I know how this arrangement works. She can make the movie appear on that TV screen.

"This will be interesting," he predicts, sitting back.

Marcus Broussard's movie is in color that has been treated to be mostly blue.

The opening shots, playing behind the title, "Crashes," are of mountains, gullies, snow, and a white bird bleeding and dripping. There's a list of characters (Fineas, Harpy One, Harpy Two, Harpy Three) and a note, "The actors playing these parts are your enemies." The opening scene shows Fineas, an anonymous blond youth, banging on a splintering doorway. He pushes his way into somewhere. There are dark passageways. And candles. Quite a bit of dark blue film. He stumbles, grunts, curses. A voiceover says, "She was gone; this was the worst." We arrive in a tomb.

Or better, a crypt.

"Oh," I say.

The crypt is Egon's crypt.

My father announces in a pleased tone that he recognizes

this place. "You could say that I have been there. It was better lit. And there were no beetles."

This time there are six-inch black beetles and also some rats. Plus three women who wear hoods or masks and black outfits with holes over the bosoms and pubes. One woman in gloves and executioner's hood approaches Fineas. Her long silver fingernails protrude from the ends of her gloves. She puts her face next to his.

"Oh, dear," says my father.

I say I think we should stop. He says we shouldn't. Mrs. La Salle makes snide comments about the originality of the material. Susie says it is all natural, if somewhat extreme.

Fineas gets engulfed in black fabric and laid out on the floor.

I put up with this for several scenes of wrestling and disrobing until the appearance of a Laborador retriever. Then I get up to turn off the video player. I don't like dirty movies with animals.

"No, don't," says my father. "I am noticing something interesting."

I stop, because he really does sound interested rather than disturbed.

"Can you do that bit again? Just before they roll over and the rat runs over his foot?"

I turn to Mrs. La Salle, who does the mechanical tricks; again we see Fineas engulfed and surrounded, draperies in heaps, the flickering background of the marble crypt.

"It's very badly lit, of course," my dad says. "But there's something wrong. On the top layer of the sarcophagus. Something scratched. The light had it just right for a minute. Oh, dear. Can you run it again?"

We do. We run it three times. By the third time I can see that there are some scratched-on hieroglyphic marks along the lip of the top coffin. The one that Egon says he is saving for himself. The marks flicker up for a minute and then they're gone.

"I had it for a minute," my father says. "Part of what it said. I understood it. And now I'm forgetting. I am forgetful these days. Oh, dear."

He looks down at his knees. "I am going to my room. My museum needs my assistance."

"What will we do with him?" Mrs. La Salle asks, watching the door through which he has just exited. "I could follow to his room and try to read poetry, but he won't be receptive."

"Edward is so intelligent. So complicated," Susie says thoughtfully.

"He's likely to do anything." Mrs. La Salle is brisk. "Last year he simply left us. Took off."

Susie looks sad and says ah, yes.

"But how would he get there?" Mrs. La Salle asks.

And now three things happen in rapid sequence.

First Cherie visits. Then Rob calls. And then my father receives a photograph.

Cherie arrives at my office sounding bubbly, Southern, and distracted. "Darlin'. How are you, sweet one? You can't imagine, the extent to which—well, dear, I have been thinking of you. Every single minute. Things have been so upset. That place, that museum place. And the goings on there. And things maybe startin' to come to a head. And dear, I have been talking to Rob. Of course I have been talking to Rob."

She is still more or less at the door of my cubicle, where I have been grubbing my way through a stack of bills. Now she comes in and sits in an overstuffed chair. She is a symphony in pink. Her pink stockings have clocks. "Darlin' Rob and I have talked and talked and talked. And you maybe remember, talkin' is not Rob's best thing? That isn't his primary skill? But, sweetheart, I was determined, and we kept at it, and it was hard; I'd be the last one in the world to deny it, it was hard, because, you know, Rob and I—well, what was so wonderful with us was that we were so different—you've experienced that?"

Cherie is uncomfortable. She crosses her pink-clocked legs and squints at the fake Renoir that Management has supplied for my office wall. "Well, dear one, you know, Rob finds it hard to express his true feelings? That was something with us from the start."

There's a reverent pause while Cherie lets the impact of this statement sink in. And I think, *Yes, Cherie, I am beginning to get this. It is more or less going where I always thought that relationship would more or less go.* I find that I don't feel the least bit triumphant and only moderately interested.

". . . So Rob an' I talked and talked," Cherie continues, "and I jus' made him stick at it, and it finally came out that our values are a whole lot different, know what I mean? And our life views, and the way we think about world events and how we react to people—especially the latter. Carla, isn't it amazing how much difference that can make?"

I think the English translation of this is that Rob found out about Cherie's Berkeley boyfriend and had a fit. Maybe she told him about the boyfriend.

"So," Cherie is saying, "it has been a good encounter, that little thing between me and Rob, and I do not think we hurt anybody, and the main thing I am worried about is that you maybe are mad at Rob. Are you?"

I stare at her and don't answer.

"Because darlin'," she continues, "if you are, you should know that the whole time—absolutely the whole time—we were together he was lonely for you and was talking about you. And that was one of the things. Well, dear, there were several things. But it was a wonderful relationship. And, Carla, oh, really . . ." She leans forward and essays a kiss on my cheek, not the kind of kiss that the recipient has to return. "Oh, darlin', us women have to stick together."

Cherie, who has an excellent sense of timing, is now rising. She announces in departing that she has remodeled the sheriff's office and installed a two-person jail, that she is way worried about those murders at the museum but is collecting meaningful evidence and the crimes are going to be solved, and that she loves my darling dad. And that she thinks about me all the time.

She doesn't tell me Rob is all mine again, but I guess that's the spirit of the encounter.

After she is gone, leaving behind her a waft of very good perfume, I stare at the spot where she has exited and find that I'm not feeling much. I don't seem to be really mad at her. Nor at Rob. A line of one my dad's songs warbles through my head: "Where it all goes, the dear Lord only knows . . ."

A couple of hours later Rob calls. He sounds emotionally disheveled. He doesn't say anything about Cherie.

"What are you doing about your father?" he accosts.

"What am I doing? What should I be doing?"

"Carla, I say it in all friendship . . ."

"No, you don't."

Rob is cross and I am cross. "You have not been taking adequate care of him."

"And who are exactly are *you*? To tell me what to do?"

Rob says he is one of Ed's oldest friends and I say no, he isn't; Daddy has lots of friends older than him . . . than he . . . and furthermore he has no rights in this situation anymore.

To which he says if not, why not, and are you watching him.

And I hang up.

I tell my father, who is listening, that it was the Avon lady on the phone and he, to my surprise, seems to remember an Avon lady from somewhere, and says for her to bring him a hairbrush.

"I have been getting some interesting phone calls," he says after a few minutes.

"What kind? Who from?"

He says he isn't sure; they are the kind of phone calls that fade out when you think you're just starting to hear. "Something about a chlorine shot? Do you think I have that right?

"I was worried by the idea of a chlorine shot," he continues. "It made me feel insecure. Shots are dangerous. Should I be concerned about the shot that hospital lady is giving me?"

And finally there is the photograph.

This starts with Sunshine—our part-time worker, who has a bolt through her eyebrow—coming to my office and saying, "Hey, Mrs. Day?"

Sunshine is sixteen and I am twenty-six. The difference in age is so vast that she calls me *Mrs.* "Yes, Sunshine?"

"Your dad—Dr. Day—I think something's the matter."

It's 10 A.M. I haven't seen my father today, which is my fault; I didn't go in to breakfast, just grabbed a piece of toast on my way by the kitchen. I push aside the pile of bills I've been shuffling through and follow Sunshine out.

Sunshine is underage, of course, and is supposed to work less than full-time. My boss, Belle, likes to save money.

Daddy is lying in his alcove in that fetal posture he adopts when things are bad. Knees against chest, hands clenched under chin. When I say, "Daddy, what's the matter?" he doesn't respond.

He is squeezing a hunk of paper in his clenched hands.

"He just lays like that," Sunshine says appraisingly. "Kinda weird."

I approach him and try to undo his bent arms. They are very stiff.

"I mean," Sunshine offers, "sometimes I feel like that, but I don't ever go ahead and do it for a long time, know what I mean?"

When I get my father's arms undone, I discover that the paper is an envelope. I pull it loose and open it. There's a photograph inside. A photograph of a person covered with drapery and with arms spread-eagled, but standing as if being supported from the back. At first I think it's a picture from the famous Abu Ghraib torture scenes and then I look at the face, which is exposed enough to be recognizable. The face is that of my mother.

The figure in the picture has a rope around its neck and another around each wrist. There's a long metal instrument on the floor.

I drop the picture. For a minute I'm shaking too much to pick it up.

"Hey, Mrs. Day," Sunshine intrudes, "what is it? What happened?"

What happened is that this picture here shows my mother being tortured.

Almost right away, on top of my reactions of horror, I understand that this is a fake photo. Somebody got a picture of my mother's face and pasted it onto another picture. The other picture really is an Abu Ghraib one.

My mother is perfectly recognizable. It's her from my childhood. She was—I guess I've said this before—a beautiful woman. She had blond hair, which she kept short. She had straight classic features. She never wore makeup.

If I rack my brain long enough, I can figure out which picture this shot of her was cut from.

Right now I want to comfort my dad. I tell Sunshine thank you, good work, great of you to be so observant, and send her off to her next client. Then I sit down on the bed beside my dad and start talking. "That was a fake picture, Daddy. Someone made it to be mean. The picture is a lie. Constancia isn't really there. Constancia is not being hurt."

He twitches at my mother's name, but otherwise doesn't react.

"Do you understand, honey? She's all right. Constancia isn't there, she's not the person in that picture. They took a photo of somebody being hurt and they pasted my mother's face on it. Nobody is doing those things to her."

Again, the only part of this speech Daddy reacts to is the name of his ex-wife. I think for a minute and decide that he always called her "Constancia," not "Connie." I sit stroking his arm and saying, "She's all right, really; Constancia is all right."

After a while I start singing it. This feels very foolish but I do it anyway. The tune I choose is "The Wheels on the Bus." "Constancia / is all right, is all right / Constancia is all right."

It's a long time before I get a reaction, which happens suddenly: "You seem very sure of that."

And in a minute he is sitting up and asking reasonable questions.

"What is that a picture of, then? Who could have done such a thing? Where did they get a photo of your mother?"

He moves to sit straight and rubs his eyes. "Do you know, Carla, I don't think about her very much. I would have said I don't remember what she looked like. Is that possible?"

I say, yes, it's possible.

"But I believe I dream about her . . . Dreaming is a problem. Sometimes I'm not sure whether I have dreamed an experience or actually done it.

"I think I must have loved her," he adds after a minute. "Is that possible, too?"

I say, yes, possible. I advance the opinion that people's emotions are unchartable. My father is upset and I am upset, which makes me sound like his Sunday school teacher.

We try to probe the question of how he got the picture— did he find it? Did someone hand it to him?

He thinks it may have been slipped under his door, but he's not sure. "I seem to have forgotten everything this morning until now. Is that possible, too, Carla?"

Oh, my, yes. Bad show.

I take the rest of the day off and settle down to watching

television, side by side with my dad. We watch *Antiques Roadshow* and *Spongebob Squarepants* and the children's show where they teach you the alphabet. In between times I canvass the hall to see if anyone has noticed a stranger who might have put an envelope under Daddy's door. But nobody has.

"Someone who would do that would do anything," Mrs. La Salle says. "I don't want to scare you, Carla. But be real."

🐦 Chapter 21

And now my father is missing.

I am in pursuit, driving much too fast down the bends and jerks of ocean-hugging Highway One. And I am very upset and very scared.

"Well, naturally; we knew he would take off." This is Mrs. La Salle's comment this morning when I show her his empty bed. The bed is sketchily, inadequately remade, the way it would be if he himself had pulled the covers up after getting out of it. Sunshine says, Uh-uh, she doesn't think he had breakfast this morning, though maybe he grabbed a popover, y'know? She didn't see him. Susie says, "Oh, the dear man, the pull of freedom was too strong."

How would the pull of freedom get him from the Manor to the museum, where I'm sure he is?

A telephone call to the museum produces an automated

voice describing Egypt Regained's celebration today of *Dr. Scott Dillard's Amazing Discoveries*. Tickets are hawked. I can't get through to a human being.

Of course my father is there. In the middle of it all.

He doesn't drive and has no money but he's a bear with transportation problems. Remarkably inventive. My aged parent can station himself out in the middle of any road and look sad. And get a ride. Or he can borrow busfare from an indulgent stranger. And even figure out the schedule. Or there are taxis. There are even people like Egon who might come and get him, if Daddy could remember Egon's cell phone number. Oh, hell.

On the other hand, maybe he went to the hospital to get his calcium shot.

Once last year he called an ambulance. If you announce in a quavery voice that you are eighty-six years old and feel bad, they will come for you.

I drive somewhat faster.

In Conestoga I decide against a detour to the hospital. Yes, I am worried about his copper sulfate level and his need for a calcium shot, but I'm more worried about the note I found in his inexpertly made bed:

Hi Ed—and thinking of you here at the museum. Have you been practicing your answers to get into that boat to the Other Shore? I am waiting for you, old chum; remember that talk we had about not prolonging things? You and I both think eighty-six is too damn old. Copper sulfate is a messy

avenue to the new life; there are better ones. Try the sample
attached. I send it with love. Marcus.

There are indentations in the paper. Something has been
attached with a paper clip.

A flying visit to the hospital to consult about poison
wouldn't help; I have no idea what Marcus sent him from
the other world.

I don't even want to think about this; I just want to act
fast. I'm glad neither Susie nor Mrs. La Salle could come with
me. I need to work unimpeded.

There are exactly two people who know enough about
my dad's situation to have written that note, which is computer printed in an imitation script. Scott Dillard is one
such person and Egon Rothskellar is the other. I get a moment's clutch in the belly remembering how good it was to
kiss Scott Dillard. Leaning against the shiny stainless steel
machinery in Egon's kitchen.

Scott has the brains and knowledge and drive for anything. He wanted to get my dad and me out of the museum. He probably knew about my dad's marriage to
Constancia. He probably knew her. He's involved to his chin
in plots and schemes.

And he's smart.

Another thing. Oh my God. I haven't wanted to think
about this, because I kind of liked him. But Rita's death?
Scott was at our table in the Best Western. I walked away, out
to the ladies' room with Rita. She had her back to him, the
perfect target.

I told myself I could see him the whole time, out of the
corner of my eye. Well, could I?

And Egon wasn't even there at the Best Western. Bunny

says he was at the museum. They were both at the museum, prowling around, trying to figure out who was stealing the doodads.

Egon's been doing some evil things to my dad, and he's not long on brains. But people don't get jailed for stupidity.

Egon is stupid; Scott is smart. Somebody at the museum has been killing people. Two people: Marcus, Rita. And now somebody has it in for my father.

Somebody smart. What was the matter with me, necking in the kitchen with a guy that I knew in my heart might, just might . . .

If I drive any faster on this road, I will project myself off the cliff and into the blue Pacific, which lurks there to my right, utterly beautiful, utterly dispassionate.

Let's plan ahead. What I am going to do now? I will enter the museum through the main door. Right away, I'll start looking for my father in all the museum nooks and crannies: his own Edward Day Room, upstairs in the pottery and artifact rooms, restrooms, closets. I will also watch out for Scott. When I see him, I'll . . . I'll figure that out later.

I'll look downstairs in the crypt.

I have to slow down; there's more traffic now, all headed toward the museum.

Finally I'm at the gas station and church in Homeland and turn inland on the gravel road that leads to Egypt Regained. And right away I'm part of a small traffic jam. One of a line of vehicles waiting to see *Dr. Scott Dillard's Amazing Discoveries.*

Ten minutes into a slow creep, I drive my car up onto the verge and abandon it, nose pointing into the weeds. Then I start toward the museum on foot.

People in the cars that I pass wave at me. They don't seem to mind waiting; they're in a holiday mood. Amazing Discoveries probably involves Mummies. And Treasure. Maybe something about Eternal Life. These are the wonders people come to Egypt Regained in search of. Certainly they're worth waiting for.

I want to push these people out of my way. Stupid moon-faced dopes, lounging in their big cars, getting in my way when my dad is settled in some corner, curled up in agony, coughing his guts out.

It takes me fifteen minutes to reach the end of the gravel driveway. There's a big pileup of traffic there with a youth in a red visibility vest signaling *stop*, *go*, and *proceed* at the SUVs, Chryslers, Cadillacs. Under his red vest he wears his long white Arab outfit.

I circumvent him and his traffic and quick-step for the entrance. Daddy was okay last week about the copper sulfate and didn't eat it even though he was instructed to do so. But will he be sensible this time? I send him a mental message: *Darling, Marcus didn't really write that note. You know he didn't.*

Now I'm at the entrance door. Please, goddess, don't make me stop and make chit-chat with Bunny. The folksy exchange about me, about my dad, referred to as Pop, about that place where we're staying—what do we call it—some manor or something?—and how are things there?

I think I'm going to throw up.

Thank God no Bunny guards this entrance. Just one of the Harouns, who recognizes me and lets me in ahead of the line.

And inside is a battle area. Some of it is organized, some of it not. The organization happens in haphazard queues,

one group waits for a lecture, one has lapel buttons for a
tour, banners overhead advertise, AMAZING DISCOVERIES.
CELEBRATION AT 2 P.M. People shove and drop things and
buy books.

There is no sweet old white-haired gentleman.

People are sitting on benches, fidgeting, gossiping. They
think things are funny. Maybe they're waiting for the Celebration, maybe for lunch. A smaller sign, pointing up the
stairs, announces, BUFFET UPSTAIRS. 12 NOON.

I circle and elbow, poke into corners, squeeze around
sturdy ladies in lavender pantsuits, invade the book sales alcove. I get called down, "Sweetheart, take it easy, we're all in
here together, right?" I wriggle into the Edward Day Room.

I go upstairs, disregarding people who yell at me that the
buffet isn't until noon.

Back downstairs I try Egon's office. It's sturdily locked.

I scan each face. Anybody halfway sensible-looking gets
asked, "Have you seen . . . ?" I'm looking for a small, erect,
white-haired man. He wears a tweed suit and, probably, a
vest. He is very gentle-appearing.

Do you know that sixth sense that tells you when your hunch
may be right? Well, I don't have it. But finally I stand still
and review the places in the museum to search, and there's
only one I haven't hit. The crypt. And that's kept locked.

Daddy liked that crypt.

"Hey," I address a Haroun who looks familiar, "do you
know my dad? Dr. Edward Day?"

"Hey, yeah, sure." The Haroun seems grateful to be ad-
dressed by a fellow human being. "Sure I know your dad."

The Haroun surveys me, friendly. "You're his daughter, right, Dr. Day's? Didn't you go to Santa Cruz?"

I am definitely going to throw up.

The Haroun also went to Santa Cruz, but he was four years behind me. In spite of the clot in my throat, I talk to him. Maybe my father isn't here at all. Maybe he's not full of poison. The minute I tell myself that, my stomach clenches, bruises my ribs, starts to invade my throat.

I should have checked with Tallullah at the hospital. Don't they have a universal poison antidote? One that works on anything?

I should have shipped my pride and called Rob. He's a doctor.

I should have slept on my dad's window seat this whole last week. What's wrong with me, pretending the Manor's safe? Anybody can get in there. There are side doors, back doors, basement doors. It's a leaky Victorian mansion. There are French floor-to-ceiling doors. Oh, Christ.

"Hey," says the Haroun, surveying me closely, "you all right?"

No, I'm not all right. I examine him. "What's your real name?" He brightens up. Probably he thinks, poor guy, that I'm making get-acquainted gestures.

He's not one of the blond crew of Arab attendants; he has dark hair and dark eyes and a lively expression and he looks more Berkeley than Central Valley. He says his name is Walt. "You gonna pass out?"

"Listen," I say to Walt, "I'm looking for my dad. You remember him? I've looked everywhere. I need to get down in the crypt."

We do some jockeying where Walt says, "Oh, the crypt,"

and I say, "My dad forgets. Suppose he was locked in down there?" And the minute I say that, my stomach clenches again so I have to turn my head away.

Walt says, "Locked in. Oh, Jesus." And pretty soon he has gotten the electronic keys from their secret stashaway and we have fought our way through the crowds in the main room and the lobby and we're at the closet with its access to the downstairs staircase. "Now watch it on the way down," Walt cautions. "I gotta get back. You can get out at the other end."

It's dark on the staircase, but he turns a switch that produces a halogen glow that bleaches everything white. Then he slams the door. It closes behind me and right away the air gets eerily silent, a complete TV mute-button effect. All gone, the clamor from upstairs. We have stillness and stone and glare, plus the scuffle of my feet. And that intrusive medieval church cold rock smell, with something extra—incense, maybe.

A scary combination. I remind myself: I'm looking for my father. Later I can think about being scared.

I'm scared about him.

Also about who else is down here.

An enemy? Sure. Maybe.

Somebody sent him poison. Somebody sent him my mother's picture.

Somebody means ill.

I grab the metal handrail and take the steps slowly and listen to my own footsteps and try to stay alert for other sounds. The scrunch of a little, scared person in the dark.

The steps are stone.

Maybe he's not here at all. Maybe, if he's here, he can't . . .

I won't go there.

At the bottom of the stairs is the passageway with the recessed cubbyholes and the skulls. Ceramic skulls, that's what Egon assured our tour group. The recessed places are painted blue. There's no light in this passageway and none ahead in the black crypt-space, but the glow from the stairs shines down the passage for a while.

I take a minute to wonder about building something that imitates the Paris charnel house. Skulls and femurs, ribs. A claustrophobic avenue of skeleton pieces poked into a wall. Was it Egon or his grandmother that wanted this art piece?

If it was his grandmother, she was a pretty weird old lady.

I do not have a flashlight. I remember that Rita brought a flashlight when she came down here. I wish you were here, Rita. I wish your flashlight was here. The dark is marching closer, tighter; I have to feel ahead for each step.

I don't see another light switch.

Daddy, dear. Maybe I do have that sixth hunch sense. I think I'm having it now. I know you're in here, parent mine. You're frightened. When people are scared, they freeze and don't make noise. They lie clenched on themselves, waiting for someone to find them. Hey, old trooper, I'm coming. Hang in.

Thinking stuff like that is something to do besides freaking. I almost don't feel like throwing up.

A pause, holding on to the wall, which is too slick to hold on to. The passage has gotten so dark my feet are lost. Blue jeans on my legs, then nothing. Ahead another nothing; the world just stops. Maybe a bend in the passage. Midnight. Then maybe the crypt.

There's got to be a light switch. What did Egon do when he took us down here? Did he make a magic gesture with a remote?

I keep going, feeling ahead with each footstep. The ground isn't level; maybe it was carved from the same rock as the walls, uneven, slippery. I stretch my right hand out, grasp rounded as if for an imaginary flashlight.

At the bend in the passageway I've reached it. The point of no return. Around the corner it's totally dark. If he's in the crypt, I won't be able to see him.

How did Egon turn on the lights? I scour my memory.

And what's the floor plan of the crypt? Memory does better here. The crypt is circular. Or maybe octagonal, with columns marking the eight sections. In the middle is the sarcophagus, in two parts like a giant double wedding cake, one layer below, one above. There's carving, and columns, and a separate lid for each bit. Egon's grandmother lies below and Egon himself will rest above.

Cherie and I shared a joke about "grandmother below."

Probably I should have told Cherie what I'm doing today. It's time to get over my Cherie reservations.

I think I hear something, maybe a tiny scrape, maybe something moving. You don't get building-settling noises in a carved underground tomb, do you? Not unless you're having an earthquake. And I won't go there, either. The sound could be rats. Or my imagination. Or my dad, lying damaged, curled, moving his legs a little.

Or it could be somebody creeping quietly.

With or without a light, I've got to march on into that dark space.

But first, I'll search my backpack. I don't know for what. I've been wearing it over my shoulder and I'll give it the old police run-through, maybe hoping for a matchbook because there was a time, way back then, when I would have had plenty of matchbooks. Once upon a time restaurants gave matchbooks.

I slide the pack down with an appalling crash and start throwing stuff out on the floor. But then I can't see what I'm doing, so I scrape it all together again and maneuver back up toward the better light. And squat. Once more I upend the pack and right away get a mound of anonymous paper: bills, receipts, ads, mail, a mashed photograph of me and Rob. After that the hard stuff: lipstick, phone—oh, good grief, *phone*, but then I punch the button and it doesn't work down here—credit card case, wallet.

At the bottom of everything are crumbs, Kleenex, a ginger candy. And another lipstick. I haul that out and examine it and it isn't a lipstick. My heart goes plop. It's Rita's cigarette lighter. "Hang on to this in memory of me," was what she said that time in my room.

Rita, honey, ohmigawd, thank you. Today I do remember you.

A cigarette lighter is a whole lot better than nothing in a crypt, but it still isn't ideal. This kind, which has a flint, wants to die out after each energetic wheel-spin. Scratch, flame, subside, scratch again. Still, it lets me proceed down the passageway, foot by foot.

Feeling along and being apprehensive. Listening for my dad. Yes, I do hear that slight noise again. Now I decide, definitely, yes; it's the one someone makes lying down and scraping their leg on an uneven surface.

I am almost at the crypt now.

The lighter has a transparent chamber to hold the fluid. And I can see that it's getting low. Hell and hell. I leave longer spaces between crunches. But each flare doesn't show me much. A wavering vista of carved rock, flickering side-wall. Skulls grinning, like skulls.

Me stumbling, foot, by foot. Crunch, flare.

I'm in the crypt now. More shadows, more rock floor, a shadowy shape that could be the tomb. And at the foot of it something. A shape. A huddled human shape. I start to move as fast as I can, still being careful, saying to myself, *oh, thank God*, and *oh, be all right* and, *honey, I'm coming*. I'm almost there.

A protrusion that could be a foot. A mound like a person, folded into a heap. Two more lighter-tries and I've almost reached it. And it's not my imagination. There is somebody. A body. Somebody folded into a U.

My dad, my father. My brave old crazy parent. Down here and scared. Sick. Just as I thought.

But I do another lighter-flash and another view of the figure and I know something's the matter. Everything. The leg appears, wearing battered dark fabric. Dark blue fabric. Jeans. And the foot's too big and is wearing a sports shoe. I kneel beside it, frantically pushing the lighter-wheel.

I move the light farther along.

The person on the floor isn't my father.

It's Scott Dillard.

My lighter is down to zilch. A tiny fire-bubble at the end of a cotton string. Scott Dillard is unmoving. He's sprawled out across this rock floor. His head's half thrown back. His arms are outspread. His hands rest, palms up.

My light is about to go. I know Scott is the enemy, a murderer; I should be wary of him, but my response is autonomic. Not in my control. I reach out and seize one of his outflung hands and try to hold it.

My cigarette lighter dies.

But Scott, whom I had thought to be dead, isn't. He grabs me by the wrist. He holds me, very tightly and painfully. He says, "Get offa me, you goddamn bitch, before I knock all your teeth straight down your throat."

Chapter 22

It's so dark in the crypt that the air has texture. Souplike, as if you could drink it. I squat on the carved stone floor and Scott Dillard seems to be beside me. I can't see him but I can feel him, all right; he's holding me viciously by the wrist. He has just offered to push my teeth down my throat.

"Shit," I say.

I don't know why that one word identifies me, but I guess it does. I can hear him stirring. He says, "Carla? Oh, God, Carla? I thought you were Bunny. But you're not Bunny."

I tell him no, I'm not, and he says, Jesus Christ. I can hear him trying to sit up. He says, "She tried to kill me."

"My father," I say. "Have you seen my father?"

"Zapped me," he says. "With that electric thing."

"My dad," I ask. "Is he here?"

"Why in hell," he asks, "don't you turn on the light?" We are not having a very meaningful conversation.

I ask him again about my dad and he says, "What are you talking about? Do the lights." Then he explains that the light box is up ahead someplace and that once I get the box open, I will see the numbers; they glow in the dark; it's 662 to turn on the lights. "She tried to kill me. I think I'm having a heart attack."

It takes the two of us at least twenty minutes to find those lights, and in total-deprivation dark, twenty minutes equals four hours in the real world while I crawl, bump into sharp obstacles, claw my way up walls, every so often asking about my father, with Scott saying, "No, your voice is in the wrong place. You've got yourself turned around. More to the left. Oh, Jesus Christ, all right, I'm coming myself." Followed by scraping and groaning and a crash and scream.

Until finally I find the right wall and scratch my way to the light box and push the numbers.

Ka-zowie. Electricity. I'm blind for a whole minute.

"My dad," I say, as soon as I can keep my eyes open.

And Scott says, "She hit me with something."

"Bunny hit you?" I'm disbelieving. I'm ready to think the worst of Bunny, but this has come on me suddenly. "How? What were you doing? Where's my father?"

Scott is sitting up, bent over, caressing his third lumbar area. "Oh, my God in heaven."

"I think my father is down here," I say.

"Yeah, I think so, too."

"My dad? You think so? You've seen him?"

"She zapped my memory."

"You can't remember? This is about my dad! And you can't remember?" I grab him by the shoulders. He says, "Oh, God." I tell him not to be such a baby; he looks all right.

"I'll remember. It's coming back. In pieces." He's still caressing his back; he pulls something out of there, a small spear-shaped tag. "What the hell?"

"It's a Taser tag. Think about my father."

But then I have to explain. I recognize the tag from a security lecture at the Manor. "From a Taser gun. It shoots these things." I take the little red metal object. It's about the size of a fingernail.

A Taser gun shoots an electric charge that's supposed to stun you. Apparently it hurts a lot. And sometimes it's fatal.

Scott puts his head on his knees. "I give up. I resign from the whole mess. I'm sick of it, sick to my eyeballs. I'm out. I resign, withdraw; I'm not here anymore; they can find somebody else to be their golden boy. I'll go to San Quentin and they can finish me with their lethal injections and you can come witness. How about it, will you be a witness for my execution? Because they're going to. And I don't care."

"Where's my dad?"

"I don't know."

"And what do you mean about being executed?"

"Executed. Terminated."

"Come on," I say, standing up. I'm dizzy, I guess from the kaleidoscope of sensory inputs. "We should get upstairs and get you some help."

"No." He almost shouts this. "That's how it started. I told them. Said I was going upstairs. Going up and making a speech."

"Well, sure. They're expecting you. The place is full of people from Kansas; Middle America's waiting. Egon's going to unveil your amazing stuff. 'Scott Dillard's Amazing Discoveries.' Of course you make a speech."

"Not that speech. Another speech. A speech about how I

won't do it, about how he's a filthy fraud, all the stuff was fake, Marcus invented it and Egon went along. I'm out of it; I give up; I'm not doing it."

"I haven't the faintest notion what you're talking about," I tell him.

"Your dad caught on." It takes him a minute to say this. His eyes wobble unfocusedly. "You know? He noticed the hieroglyphs."

"Scott, listen." I grab him again by the shoulders and again he screams and I have to let go. "Think now. Think hard. You're not making sense. What happened? With my father? Is he hurt? Where is he?"

Scott looks at me as if he were seeing six people.

I'm probably taking a big chance. I don't know the result of combining alcohol with shock. And anybody can see that Scott's in shock. This guy may be dangerous. Also, in dangerous condition. The hand that grabbed me by the wrist is vibrating. His eye-pupils, when they stop revolving, are tiny. His breathing jerks; he's cold.

I feel around him to his back pants pocket.

If he were his usual self, he'd decide I'm getting personal.

I find his silver flask and pull it out and shake it to be sure there's something inside. Then I unscrew the cap and hold the flask to his lips.

He drinks. For a minute he seems moderately grateful. After that he subsides back into his rocky cradle, muttering religious remarks.

So I grab him by the ankles and get rough. "Scott. Come on. Get it together, shape up, focus. WAKE UP." I don't ask, Are you a man or a mouse; our Manor lecture implied that Taser is pretty vicious.

"Where is my dad?" I ask.

"Why, here I am," a voice announces. It's my father's voice, and it indeed belongs to my father, who is walking down the passageway from the blue skull alcoves. He does this almost silently; he's had years of investigating passageways where if you coughed you could destroy priceless evidence or bring the roof down on you. He emerges, pad, pad, delicate as an old cat, and looking pretty alert and catlike, come to think of it. There are a few flakes of plaster on his jacket. I start rushing at him and he pauses. "My dear, have you been looking for me?"

I stumble and half fall and pick myself up and stumble further to embrace him. "Where were you? How are you? Are you hurt? . . . Oh, good lord, let me look at you . . .

"Why couldn't I find you?" I ask after a minute.

"Quite amazing, the construction here," he says, brushing off his shoulder. "Scott, are you better? I think you were feeling poorly."

"Listen, Daddy. Concentrate. What's happening? Did you eat anything? You didn't, did you? Where were you?"

"You know," he says contemplatively, "I don't know what he was thinking about. But there are passageways behind some of those places. The blue chambers where the relicts are."

"The alcoves with the skulls," I interpret. "Sure. Oh, right. I should have thought . . ." I'm pretty incoherent. "One of them has an aperture behind it."

"A passageway. Small. But I climbed down it. Of course, it was very tight. But I don't mind that."

I remember, from experiences at the Manor, that Daddy really enjoys exploring small confined areas. Back to basic archaeology, discovery, the thrill of the birth channel.

Scott is sitting up now. "That was really smooth of you,

Ed. You figured it out and got out. And I got really zapped
here. That bitch Bunny. He told her to; she's a genuine min-
ion of his. I feel godawful."

Daddy is solemn. "You were hurt."

"And you noticed them," Scott says. "The hieroglyphs.
What an idiot I was. What an idiot all along. Stupid, stupid, jerk, jerk. Carla, it's all been a fraud."

I'm trying to juggle six subjects at once. Scott is probably the enemy, but it's hard to think that of someone who's
calling himself a jerk. "Hieroglyphs?" I ask. I want to get
back to the subject of my dad, and why he was hiding, and
whether he's in danger now. But both he and Scott are fixed
on this hieroglyph idea.

I look around. There are hieroglyphs on the wall painting, but those aren't the ones Scott's aiming at. He's watching the upper layer of the sarcophagus. At first I want to
object that there's no writing there, and then I see that there
is. Scratches, really. Just the way Daddy said when he saw
Marcus move. Scratches around the lip of the top container.
They don't look at all as if they were part of the design.
They look like amateur defacement. Like graffiti. The kind
of defacement kids do. The kind that somebody inscribes in
wet cement. "KM loves MK." And so imperfectly done that
I can see it only from certain angles.

I bend my head and squint and finally see a whole row.
Yes, hieroglyphs, and yes, I can make out one word.

"Adore," I say. The figure for *adore* is easy for a nonscholar
to remember. It looks like a wine bottle with a TV aerial
sticking out of it. It's usually for describing one's feelings
about a god, as in, "Oh, great one whom I adore."

It says, "The woman whom I adore," my dad announces.

"Jesus, I meant it. I really loved her," Scott says. "I loved her; I was crazy about her; I put her in that sarcophagus. And then I wrote that inscription about it. And what a fool I am. I went along with this whole fraud and then I killed her. An accident, I guess. I thought it was. An accident, sure. What an idiot."

"Idiot?" says a voice from somewhere underground. "No, Scott, no. *Idiot,* no, no. Turncoat? Yes. Or traitor? Yes, yes. Traitor to the ideals. The ideals of Egypt. To the spirit of Re and Horis and Amun and Anubis and the renewal at Thebes and . . ."

These sounds come from inside the rock; the person doing them must be marching down the passage toward us. The person—it's a he, that's a man's voice—the person doesn't move silently, like my dad. He sounds out, loud and muddled and bass-echoing, from deep inside somewhere, a booming bray of voice with a stony crunch of feet, rock bouncing and tinkling, everything reverberating. For a minute I think I know the voice, and then I think I don't, and after that I'm lost. A ringing, declamatory tone belting out from some distant loudspeaker system.

And finally a figure emerges. Tall, ungainly, maybe a revelation from Marcus's movie or a god detached from the fake Egyptian wall-mural. It teeters as if it's on stilts. White garments flow around it. "Betrayal!" it says. "Betrayal, treason, infamy." It wears a teetering gold crown.

Finally I recognize it. It's Egon.

I've never seen Egon look like that.

I've never heard him sound like that, either.

How long has he been in the passage?

He marches forward, spacing his rocking steps. What you'd call measured. His garment is voluminous, white-pleated; he sports a five-tiered gold and turquoise jeweled collar. Both the collar and the robe look regally Egyptian although the robe is a woman's costume. A queen's probably. I think it came from a display upstairs.

Underneath everything I can see Egon's usual suit and shirt.

He's balancing a tray. There's something on the tray that skids around but doesn't slide off. Maybe a small silver bottle.

"Scott!" he booms, as if he's just discovered him. He balances forward. "I've brought you a drink. A suitable drink. Designed for a traitor. A dispatch toward ignominy. For someone who deserts his cause. Not Roman, though, no, no, not noble Roman, not in any way, more African than Egyptian. But perfect for you. I've brought a friend with me; she's right behind me; here she is . . . ."

He turns to aim himself and his crown toward the passageway. And Bunny appears there, framed by the arched exit, shuffling out, looking sturdy and ordinary in her usual guard's uniform. Her face is stolid; she fixes her small squinty eyes on Egon.

"Well, sh-oot," she says.

"My friend here," Egon says, gesturing at Bunny, "will disable you. She has the appropriate measures. And then we will administer. Probably pour it down your throat. A corrosive substance . . . ."

I've been surprised by all this, the kind of surprise that zaps you speechless for a while, but now I'm beginning to come to.

My dad stands off to the side, holding on to one of the peripheral pillars. Scott is still disabled in his rock cradle, his back against the sarcophagus pillar. I am standing in front of the sarcophagus, probably with my mouth ajar.

The scene is ridiculous, insane, unreal. Maybe if I shake my head, the entire outrageous prospect will disappear. I say, "Egon, what in hell is happening; what's the matter; why are you dressed like that; it's dramatic but really, really weird . . ."

As I'm talking, I can see I'm not having any effect. Egon's face is unmoving. Not to mention strange. It's decorated with makeup, a heavy line around each eye, lipstick, an orange bar down the forehead and across the nose. He blinks as if there's too much light. He clears his throat.

"Scott"—still in his loudspeaker voice—"we will complete it. Your work of corruption. Your very own work of self-corruption. My drink will demolish your guts, bleed you out through your eyes, through your eyes and ears, your bowels will deliquesce into stinking red decay, you'll writhe in agony on this floor. This floor which you have so desecrated. Because you are a turncoat, an apostate, a renegade . . ." Egon stops to draw a deep breath. He stands with his head back, his crown wobbling and his tray held aloft. He's going to start talking again in a minute.

Bunny slouches against the wall of the passageway. Is it possible that she's chewing gum?

"My friend"—Egon gestures at Bunny—"will disable you. She has an effective tool. And I . . ." He sets the tray down on the roof of the sarcophagus. Yes, the tray has been balanced on top of a gun, he's holding that; it's clutched in his right hand. A big gun, shiny, black, and effective-looking. "I have a weapon. There are so many of you."

He aims the gun at my father. His voice moves into a combination of stentorian and whiny. "I truly did not count on so many. These duties. They pile up. They mount so tediously . . . Stop that!" This is to Scott, who has started to move. "I will have her hit you. Or I will hit you. Hers will paralyze, mine will kill." He sighs loudly. "I will have to shoot you."

Scott is trying to get away from him. But Scott still can't stand up. He moves himself over the rocky floor, but doesn't travel far. He says—his voice sounds okay, wobbly but also somewhat stentorian, like Egon's—"You're stark raving crazy. Totally nuts. I've known it for a while."

Scott is eight million percent right, but I have the feeling this isn't the best approach. "Egon." My own voice squeaks out from some far-distant place. "Are you going to do a ceremony?"

I swallow and breathe and try again. "A cleansing ceremony? A repositioning ceremony?" I've never heard of a repositioning ceremony, but it's a good idea. Especially if Egon will need to think about it.

"And you," Egon says, still stentorian, still to Scott, "are a murderer." His body is pointed at Scott, although the gun in his hand travels back and forth across all of us. Egon handles the gun easily, as if he's familiar with it. "A murderer. A cowardly one. Killer. Killer of the woman you loved. But you didn't have the courage to do the act and then be proud. Not a liberator. But that is what I am. I am a liberator . . ."

Then, "A ceremony?" he says, jolting slightly. He acts as if my words have just reached him on a delayed mail delivery. "No, I didn't think of a ceremony. Not until now. A ceremony is always good. Always helpful. Elevating. I think she would approve.

"My sainted grandmother, Kirsten." He supplies this like a footnote.

"She is always with me, of course." He's addressing me now. I've been promoted to being his audience. "She's with me, at my side, guiding me. She directs my hand. She stands behind when I decide. The decision is mine. But it's also hers. Her ba flew in my window. It is blue and striped and entirely beautiful and I knew totally that everything that has happened was right. She told me so. She said, 'The judgment of Osiris has arrived. Villainy and treason surround you; the air is thick with them, but you have the duty of liberating . . .'" He pauses for a minute. "Were we talking about a ceremony?"

I just say, "Yes." I don't make a speech. I'm beginning to be anxious about this ceremony.

My father speaks. "A ceremony, Egon? Surely purification is needed. Before performing it. It seems so confused and hot down here."

Egon aims his gun at him. He says, "This old man needs an ankh in his mouth. He knows too many things."

"Truly," Daddy says. "I am so sorry to say it. My memory is bad these days. But you know, I don't think you can perform a ceremony. When it's so confused. It won't come out right."

"You are blathering." Egon's face is bright red. His gun hand wobbles.

"It is really too bad," Daddy says, shaking his head.

"This old man—this evil old man—has been watching from his corner. He is an extraneous force." Egon hawks loudly; he has something caught in his throat.

"You evil old force"—he points himself at my dad again—"I contained you. Took care of you. Reined you in, made you helpless for a while. And the sheriff helped. He helped a lot—he contained you, too. And I surrounded you. And magicked you. And the ba of my sainted grandmother—she intervened. Why are you still here? You aren't supposed to be on this side. Not on this side of the river."

He turns toward Bunny at the passageway. His crown slides down, half over one eyebrow. "Bunny, yes. The time, I think, yes. The time is now. The time for action. Perhaps both of us together. You can aim and I can aim. Both at the same time. It is necessary to counteract him. He's an evil force . . . All together, you and I, yes . . ."

He moves his head in Bunny's direction. He doesn't even look at her. He wants her to shoot and he will shoot, too.

Several things suddenly happen simultaneously. Scott wrenches and scrambles himself to his feet. I, who used to practice aikido moves with Rob, fling myself at Egon bodily, aiming my right shoulder at the arm holding the gun.

I unbalance Egon. He staggers backward into the middle of the room.

Bunny produces, from somewhere in the back of her clothing, a very large Buck Rogers–type weapon. She says, "Well, crud."

She shoots Egon. Her gun makes a kind of muffled pop. She has to do it twice, probably because his robes interfere with the Taser tag.

"So," she says. "Not a good bet. This guy is nutty as a fruitcake. God, what a bunch of feebs . . . Now, Miss Society Pants"—it takes me a minute to realize she's addressing me—"what about you get your butt up those stairs and call your little Southern girlfriend sheriff and get her over here to get summa these dopes arrested. Jesus. Whatta mess."

But I have more or less put it together that Bunny was Egon's little helpmeet and has now gotten scared of that role. I'm not in the mood to be ordered around by Bunny. I reach down and grab the gun out of Egon's hand.

I tell Bunny that if she shoots me, she will stun me all right, but if I shoot her at the same time, I'll kill her. "And," I say, "I *will* do it. I know how to shoot this thing. I took a course."

Which is an arrant lie. But "taking a course" makes it sound good.

She stares down at her Taser. "Told me it was just for crowd control. Wow. Some crowd control."

I take Bunny up with me while I make the phone call to Cherie.

My cell phone works from just outside the door, and two minutes later we are back and I am sitting with my spine against a pillar. I survey my scene.

I have the Taser in my hand and Egon's gun between my feet.

Egon is still out of it. I'm not sure if another stunner blast would kill him, should he begin coming to. But I'm willing to try.

My father and Scott are sitting on the gravel. Daddy has found a packet of peppermint Jelly Bellies in his pocket and has passed them around. Now he is eating one.

Bunny, looking sullen, is camped against the far wall with her arms folded.

"So," I say to Scott. "Explain."

"Why don't you just let me die?"

"That's Danielle up in the top sarcophagus."

"Sure. Yes. Did you just catch on to that?"

"No, I didn't just catch on. I've thought it for a while now."

"I put her there."

"I thought that, too."

Actually, I decide, I could hardly not think it. Scott was advertising the fact. Guilt will make you do things like that.

"I put her there," he repeats.

We both look up at the top sarcophagus with its hieroglyphic scratches. "She doesn't smell," I say. I hate to get circumstantial about this, but the idea has been bothering me.

"Oh, God. Herbs, essences. The whole mummification bit. Oh, Jesus." He puts his head in his hands. "She looked lovely."

"And you killed her."

"I did."

Give Scott credit, he really doesn't want to excuse himself. I say, "It was an accident?"

"We fought. You know. She was furious about this plan Marcus had; she came at me. I pushed her. It was down here; she slammed her head."

There's a silence while we both think about this. It's perfectly possible, of course; this gravel is treacherous.

"And so Egon blackmailed you."

"Yeah. Absolutely. Blackmail. Report this and you go to jail. Go along with me and I'll put her in my tomb and cover for you. And after that I'll work for you. Build you up, you're the discoverer of the wonderful tablet. Make you famous."

"But you liked the idea. Fame, fortune, publicity. Yale."

"Sure. I loved it. For about ten minutes. The Hartdale; are you kidding?"

"Egon thought it would make the museum famous."

"Well, it would."

"And especially you. He took you up on the mountain and pointed and said, 'All this can be yours . . .'"

"Damn fucking right."

"Would anyone like a peppermint Jelly Belly?" my father asks. "They're a bit sticky."

I tell him to just enjoy them, sweetheart, we'll all have lunch in a while. Egon stirs and groans and I aim the gun thoughtfully at him. But then he subsides.

"So how did it all start?" I ask.

Scott pulls out his flask, looks at it, and then squeezes it back into his pocket. "Marcus. Marcus and his damn play-acting. The jokester of the Western world. Thought he was so bleeding cute."

Marcus, Scott says, was trying to prove something. He would show up the group he called *The Archaeological Establishment*; he'd propagate a hoax and get a lot of publicity and have all the stuffed shirts dancing around in joy (that's how he put it), then reveal it.

"He was an artist, remember? He carved this tablet that proved Nefertiti is Smenkhare. Smenkhare's the next pharaoh down the line. And there's this theory kicking around that Nefertiti lived on after her husband died and that she is really Smenkhare. A queen ruling as a man. Which is popularly appealing because Nefertiti is so glamorous-looking. Nobody respectable believes it, though. It's one of those Tutankhamen-curse kind of popular theories.

"Marcus was thrilled shitless about his plan. It would show how gullible everybody is. He produced this gorgeous tablet and he was going to release all these rubbings and photographs. Advertise them, publicize them. And then lose the evidence. Or say it was stolen."

I say, "Oh."

Scott looks at me and says, "Yeah?"

I say, "That's why the artifacts here were disappearing. Egon was losing them on purpose. He was building up a case for the stuff to vanish at the last minute."

Scott says, "Yeah. Egon loved Marcus's plan. It would make Egon's museum famous. And rich. And Egon enlarged it and hyped it and suddenly Marcus realized he'd invented a monster. It was out of his control; Egon had grabbed it."

Scott subsides back against the gravel. "And Egon got nuttier and nuttier. And Marcus, who wasn't nutty at all, just full of pranks and stunts, tried to back out. Publicly. Which Egon didn't like. So Marcus got dead. And then, Christ almighty, Rita got dead.

"I didn't want to believe it," he says. "I told myself maybe Marcus just died of heart failure. But then came Rita. And Rita was *shot*."

He leans back against the base of the sarcophagus and closes his eyes. "Why don't you get your cute Dolly Parton cop down here? This scene is getting stale."

🐦 Chapter 23

Cherie is not interested in hearing about my ordeal in the crypt. She wants to move forward into the future. "So, tell me, lover-girl, what do I do with these idiots you have shoved off in my direction. How many of them are guilty?"

"They're all guilty."

Cherie has Scott and Bunny in her new jail cells, which are really just back bedrooms for the building she took over from Sheriff Munro. A deputy sheriff sits in the hall by the bedrooms cradling a rifle and reading a comic book. Egon has been dispatched to Innocente, where they can test and measure him and decide how crazy he is.

Cherie isn't really asking what to do with everybody. She was systematic and by-the-book in getting them arraigned. Now she's making conversation. "That Egon is a piece of work."

"You can say that again."

"Did you know about him? I mean, of course you didn't know, but did you kinda guess?"

"I knew he was weird and I thought he was untrustworthy and I knew he'd been mistreating my dad."

"Mistreating your dad? Darlin'! How did he mistreat your dad? That's terrible. I will get him for that."

I describe the hypnotism sessions and Cherie is horrified. "Sweetheart. That is but-awful! Maybe I can dredge up a shrink for your daddy. My God! I mean, a shrink to test my darlin' and see if he's okay and that he doesn't carry away any deleterious effects from all this. Oh, my God, I should have gotten into things sooner and intervened and unmasked that evil bastard."

Cherie and I are talking in the mahogany-paneled Manor library with the surrounding shelves of green-bound books. Cherie, as usual, looks lovely. Her hair gleams. So does her lipstick. Today is one of her pink days. I waste a minute thinking of the future surprises for Del Oro County miscreants when they meet their new sheriff.

"Well," she says, "now we know why that evil sheriff was pursuing and tormenting your sweet dad. He had been bribed to do it, did you guess? By that Egon creature?"

Egon, it seems, has been talking, to Cherie and then to the Innocente people, nonstop. "Jeez, morning, noon, and night. Can't shut him up. My stupid deputy was too stupid to take it all down. Had to hire an extra secretary.

"So Egon bribed the sheriff to go after your dad so he'd be the suspect for the stealing. The one they'd nail for taking the little whoosies missing from the museum. You know. . . ."

"But that Scott cat is the one I feel sorry for," Cherie finishes, as Susie and Mrs. La Salle and my dad come into the room. We are having lunch together. "That Scott is one very cute stud," she confides, while being enveloped in Susie's swathes of handwoven shawl.

"Who is?" Susie inquires. "I love attractive people. Human beings are meant to be attractive. So many of them do not fulfill their potential."

Mrs. La Salle is her usual erect and elegant grand duchess self in a pale lavender suit. She wears one amethyst earring and holds hands with my father.

For a long time I thought Mrs. La Salle had designs on my dad. Now I do not think that exactly. I know that she understands about his Alzheimer's and associates it with her brother, whom she feels guilty about. But there's still some sort of electricity between her and Daddy.

He smiles at us and says that the menu for lunch is chicken à la king and that he is not really looking forward to it, since it is just chicken with cream sauce. "And I am puzzled by the name. How did it get to be *la* king? A king is a male being."

"Popular corruption in terminology," Mrs. La Salle instructs as we turn toward the dining room. "How are you, Carla?"

I don't get a chance to return to the subject of Scott until after lunch, which is filled with discussion of the menu, the weather, of how Cherie is dressed, of whether Egyptology is a science or an art, and on Susie's part, with how great it is that Rob and I can get together again.

"Not that I would ever criticize dear Cherie," Susie says. "Cherie was following her star. Of course. And her energy cycle briefly intersected with Rob's. But we agree now that that wasn't the definitive, true answer."

My father suggests the stars are interesting, and sometimes there is an intervention by Ra. Or Horus.

Mrs. La Salle wants to know what will happen to the museum and my father says, "Oh, I need to go there, to my museum," and Cherie says, "Well, now, they are having a trustees' meeting and Elena Broussard has been chosen trustee head."

Yes, she says, Elena Broussard is Marcus Broussard's wife, his latest one; she is interesting and forceful and—"Well, I don't know, darling Carla, maybe a bit too forceful? But maybe you'll like her. You should go to see her. Maybe you can work with her. I worry about you, you know."

Back in the library, after everyone else has scattered to take naps or write letters, Cherie and I sit together with a bottle of Irish Mist. "This stuff will give you the mother of all headaches. Go easy." And she takes a healthy slug, but from a small glass.

"So what will happen to him?" I ask. "Scott."

"Darlin', I wish I knew."

"He's guilty."

"So he keeps saying. All the time. And you might think he'd get Brownie points off for saying it, but I'm afraid not."

"It really could have been an accident. She slipped on the gravel in the crypt."

"Sure it could. The dude needs a good lawyer. If I were in the business, I'd love defending him. Darling client. Cute. Verbal. Does a super penitent act."

I'm silent, thinking of Scott's penitent act. I tell Cherie that I think he has a rich family; they ought to be able to spring for a hotshot lawyer. The arrests were only the night before last. But surely he's had time to get in touch with his family?

"Refused to try. Adamant. He's settled down in my new cell like a kitty-cat in a closet." Cherie pats her blond head. "Depressed, I guess. But I doubt he's going to off himself."

This upsets me. "Make him get to that family."

"Baby, it's tops on my to-do list." Cherie shrugs and takes another nip of Irish Mist. "But the other one that bothers me is that lying fat liar Bunny. Because I think Egon is telling the truth about her. He says she zapped Marcus."

"And killed him?"

"No, Egon killed him, later that day. But then down in the crypt she zapped Scott. And I can't convict her on either one. Egon is a nothing witness and Scott's no good, either. Confessed killer, right?"

I agree. It's pretty depressing to think that Bunny can waltz off, free as a flea, to be a guard some other place, maybe in a prison, and have another weapon to shoot at some more people.

"If she sticks around this county, I will emphatically keep an eye on her," Cherie says.

And she adds that she doesn't know what narrow sharp object Egon used on Marcus's ear, Egon goes all weird about this and talks about the vengeance of Horus. But she thinks it was probably an arrow shaft.

"There's a bucketful of those things upstairs in the museum in a glass case. Skinny and flexible. One of them without its arrowhead would be perfect for jabbing into somebody's brain."

I glance sidewise at Cherie. Her crisp bright hair and smooth pink suit identify her: elegant, innocent. Not like a sheriff or a murder expert. Or a ghoul. She catches my eye and winks.

Later that day, after tea, we are all in the meadow and heading down to look at the trains.

Cherie has organized the expedition. I've told her that my dad will probably be disappointed since the trains he really, truly loved were the ones near the museum. "He liked them because they had those graffiti that he thought were the ankh. You know, that symbol of life."

"Yes, dear, I know."

"He's going to be disappointed. These won't be as good. They don't have that."

Cherie squeezes my arm. "Just you wait, dear one. These trains are every bit as good."

It is a bright coastal day, the fog cleared, the air a translucent mixture of blue and white in pointillist dots, the ocean crashing off to our left, the Manor garden at its best with its surreal mix of palm trees, moss, and succulents bright, dew-spangled. We walk in a ragged parade, Cherie with an arm looped around my neck, Susie and Mrs. La Salle volleying a discussion about Susie's store. (Mrs. L. S. says books would be a good addition to Susie's stock; organic health books are small in size and sell well.) My father alternates being first or last in our parade. He negotiates among us now, faster than anybody, like a puppy, waving a small bulbous object. "An Engleman's prickly pear, I think. Carla, do you agree? Oh, I had to be careful in picking it. But I don't think it's ripe."

"Darlin'," Cherie says in a half-whisper in my ear, "what do you want to do now?"

"Now?" I ask, alarmed. No, Cherie doesn't mean in the next ten minutes; she means, as I had feared, with the rest of my life. What business is it of yours, Miss Busybody; why are you asking? "I haven't a frigging clue."

"Because"—she puts out a hand to stop me from saying

no before she's finished—"because, darlin', I am going to have to get rid of my two Klingons; I mean those two idiot deputies I inherited from Slimeball, and I am scouting around for replacements, and, well, I look at you and you are so smart and you did so well with all that weird mess at that museum, and . . . You get my drift."

It takes me a minute to recover. "Cherie, if you're propositioning me, I have no experience and no training and no skills, I was totally vague at the museum, and I don't know spit about the law, I'm one hundred percent unsuited; I've got the wrong personality, for God's sake . . ."

"And"—Cherie's arm, looped around my neck, squeezes my windpipe and makes me choke—"you are still mad at me for that Rob thing, for which I don't blame you, but believe me, that will pass, and . . . yes, darling Crocodile"—to my father—"I been noticing that flower, it is a gorgeous shade of yellow; how very percipient of you to choose it."

One of the things that I have to appreciate about Cherie is that she doesn't talk down to my dad.

"And," she finishes by squeezing me again, "I am not asking for an answer now, jus' run it up on your flagpole and see if anybody has an erection, or whatever. Think about it . . .

"Darling Croc, come and walk with me now." She finishes our conversation by holding out a hand to him.

The terrain is all downhill toward the trains. I resist the thought that, like so many things in life, the route will be uphill coming back. This is the same railroad line that goes by the museum, but twenty miles farther north; these tracks are cuddled into a depression that skirts the edge of the ocean. They are weedy but not unused; there is a line of cars parked on a second track, a couple of red ones, some yellow cars, a brown boxcar that announces its affiliation with CANADA, LAND OF CONTRASTS.

We stop to admire. Railroads always remind me of old movies.

"Oh," says my father, "a railroad, though not as nice as the museum one. I miss my museum. Do you think this line goes all the way in to Alexandria? That would be a good thing. I am glad to see a line which goes that far, although it isn't as nice as the railroad near the museum, which was my favorite and which I want to get back to; it had . . ." He has started walking along the track. And in a minute he calls from down in the hollow, "Oh, yes. Oh, here at the end. Yes, oh, I am so glad. Yes, there is one."

And at the end of the chain of cars, slightly separated by grass and a hand car, is a white refrigerator container with some blue scribbles on its side. There isn't as much graffiti as on the museum cars, not as complex nor as intertwined. But there are indeed several very clear ankhs.

"Thank God they didn't take it away since this morning," Cherie murmurs in my ear. "I was so afraid they would. That's the kind of thing that always happens."

By which she advertises, at least to me, that she was out here earlier today using blue spray paint.

"You see, darling Croc," she calls down to him, "this railroad near your Manor is just as good as the museum one."

My father doesn't answer. He is too busy casing out the car and making approving noises.

Cherie reminds me, again *sotto voce* in my ear, that I should think seriously about her proposition and that, in addition, things are pretty good for me now; I have my choice of two very attractive boyfriends. "Or men friends. I just hate that term *boyfriend*."

"If you mean Scott for one of them, he's not eligible."

"Darling, one of my very best men friends was in jail. That gives a lady a sense of security. And as for Rob. Well. He is real sorry he was . . . well, he's sorry he flirted with me. It was just for a while. After all."

I'm silent because I'm watching my father scope the refrigerator car. He has taken Mrs. La Salle's hand and is giving a lecture on the ankh. "This is a very clear example," he says. "In some ways it is a better ankh than the one on the museum cars. As you know, it is a symbol of the life-giving powers of air and water; it exists in"—he sweeps his arm in a semicircle to indicate something copious and diffuse— "everything, the grass, foliage, earth, ocean, atmosphere around us—in all of it . . . Daughter," he calls up after a minute, "what am I trying to say?"

"It's life on earth, Daddy," I shout down.

And he picks up, after a minute, "Yes, of course it is. Yes, life on earth.

"*Life*, as I said. Life in this world. What could be better?"